Legend of the Five Javean

Barbara Spencer

Matador
9 Priory Business Park
Kibworth Beauchamp
Leicestershire LE8 0RX, UK
Tel: (+44) 116 279 2299
Fax: (+44) 116 279 2277
Email: books@troubador.co.uk
Web: www.troubador.co.uk/matador

ISBN 978 1780884 271

British Library Cataloguing in Publication Data.
A catalogue record for this book is available from the British Library.

Cover design: Alex Morgan

Typeset in Sabon MT by Troubador Publishing Ltd
Printed and bound in the UK by TJ International, Padstow, Cornwall

Matador is an imprint of Troubador Publishing Ltd

A011269316

Ellesmere Port
Library
0151 337 4684/5
Monday
Thursday &
Friday 9-7
Tuesday & &
Wednesday 9-5
Saturday 9-1

S/T 12/18

Book No. Y

This book is due for return by the last date above. It may be renewed
if not in demand. You may renew by contacting the library.
Users of computerised libraries may call our 24-hour renewal line on
0845 1480148 or go online at **https://cheslive-koha-ptfs.co.uk**. Please
have your membership number to hand, and your PIN for online renewals.

Cheshire West
and Chester

Cheshire
Libraries

Cheshire East
Council

1947

The young warrior, his sword still flashing in a figure of eight, stared impassively at the carnage below, a trail of bodies marking his retreat to the cliff face. In front of him, stretched out in a valley covered by gentle darkness, lay the ruins of a village. Shutters wrenched from the flimsy walled houses as if by a giant hand, fluted roof tiles tumbling like a meteor shower and coming to rest beside the black-garmented figures on the ground – as still as dolls thrown away by an angry child.

The warrior's black jacket of coarse peasant cotton was torn and stained, its scarlet symbol mirroring the colour of the blood dripping from wounds on his chest and arms.

Nearby, huddled in a crevice torn out by an ancient earthquake, cowered a young woman. She clutched a large bundle to her chest, as if physically shielding it from the sword swirling through the air close by.

'Go through the waterfall. *Hurry*! I will hold them, never fear.'

Still at a respectful distance, the heavy cloud of squirming shapes drew nearer.

'But ...'

'Don't argue ... they can do nothing to help.' He pointed with his sword at the bodies. 'Save yourself – nothing else matters.'

'You can't do it alone,' she pleaded.

'Then the last of us will die too,' he roared. 'But not before I take these with me.'

The black-garmented figure swirled and, pulling a stick of dynamite from his sash, aimed it at the sea of dark-shapes, hissing and yelping in their eagerness to attack.

Bowing her head, the young woman, still clutching her heavy burden, headed for a narrow flight of steps cut in the side of the cliff. Seeing their quarry escaping, the menacing shapes flooded towards them. The young woman screamed as claws ripped into her head. Swinging round on his heel, the warrior raised his left hand. A shaft of light erupted and the attacking beast dissolved into a shower of harmless fragments, floating down onto the steps like confetti.

'Go!' he roared and tearing a chain from his neck tossed it through the air, a flash of green illuminating the darkness. Catching it, the young women gasped in horror.

'But you are now defenceless,' she protested and made to give the ornament back.

'It will keep you safe.' Bending low, he lit the fuse. 'This will keep me safe. Remember – don't return. I will find you.'

Stumbling slightly on the jagged edges of the steps, she began to climb.

ONE

Alison stood on the brightly lit hospital steps taking in some deep breaths of fresh air. After a day spent in theatre, operating on children in need of curative surgery, the night felt cool and clean. She glanced behind her where, safely tucked up in bed, the children were now recovering, their parents camped on the floor beside their beds for the night.

The streets below the hospital were dark and silent and, Alison shivered slightly, if she was truthful also a little menacing. Which was stupid, she shook her head firmly, because there was no crime in the little town – none whatsoever.

'Dr Shaw … Dr Shaw.' The porter tumbled through the door after her. 'You want me call rickshaw?'

Alison shook her head. 'I'll walk, it's not far.'

'But everyone sleeping,' protested the porter glancing down the steps at the silent rows of houses.

The young Englishwoman had arrived in the little town of Bantu only two weeks previously. She didn't feel particularly at home although the town's people had been so very welcoming, hastening through the open doorway of their thatch-roofed huts to shake her hand as she passed. And so very generous, despite their obvious poverty. She couldn't take a walk without being offered a gift of some sort; a banana or breadfruit, a dish of newly-prepared food neatly presented on a leaf, which she was expected to eat there and then. Not being able to speak the language she could only bow, offering a smile by way of a thank you, unable to detect from the spicy food which of the local delicacies she was trying that day – frog, snake or armadillo.

At home it might rain a lot but at least she could recognise what she was eating, she didn't have rats trying to gnaw their way into her bedroom at night, and the ground was flat. Here the streets were almost vertical, the small town surrounded by looming mountains. Beyond them, to the north and west, the great plateau belonging to Tibet.

A small plane had brought her as far as Kuto, the provincial capital, where the landing strip doubled as a field for sheep and goats. Low cloud had prevented the flight two days running. When eventually they did get going, the sight of solid rock, popping its head through clouds like mushrooms out of the ground, Alison had found somewhat nerve-wracking. Although not half as scary as the bus journey over the mountains. While the ancient vehicle might have an adequate number of wheels, it certainly didn't possess any brakes. The driver had careered across narrow mountain roads, with drops so fierce, they made Alison's eyes water just thinking about them. By the time they arrived in Bantu, six hours later, she felt both giddy and sick, and the only thing keeping her there was the horrendous thought of climbing back on the bus to return to the airport.

Her letter from the United Nations had spoken of an important agricultural region, the lives of many hundreds of thousands dependent on the rice and wheat it grew. That might well have been true if they had been talking about Kuto. There Alison had noticed both flat land and agriculture taking place. But Bantu? Someone in the newly created world-organisation had obviously taken a map of the Far East and stuck a pin in it. Beyond the plateau and crags that dominated the skyline, lay an inhospitable land, where nothing grew and no one ventured. Besides, except for club foot, hare lip and hernia which she had come to fix, the little population seemed

2

remarkably healthy and hardly ever needed a doctor – never mind a hospital.

Nodding goodnight to the porter, Alison trotted down the silent steps and headed for the river. In daytime, this formed a pleasant walk although it was now quite deserted. As the porter had told her, the townspeople slept with the moon and rose with the sun. The only buildings lucky enough to be supplied with electricity from the town's solitary generator, were the hospital, hotel, cinema, and the mayor's house, the rest making do with oil lamps and candles.

Her route lit by the moon ran alongside a tall buttress of rock, carved out by glacial ice perhaps a million years before, a tumultuously noisy river scurrying past on the far side. Her feet, in their soft-soled shoes, echoed dully on the path as if someone was beating a drum with muffled drum sticks. Nervously, her heart sped up and joined in – thump, thump, thump.

She glanced back over her shoulder, the lights of the hospital still visible. She could easily go back and ask the porter to get her a rickshaw. There were bound to be some round the back of the building, their owners fast asleep. That decided it. Tilting her chin high, Alison quickened her pace – the sound of her feet swallowed up in a roar like thunder as she passed the waterfall. Unleashed, the water hurtled down from the mountain edge like a chain-mail curtain, crashing loudly onto the rocks below.

The river flooded every spring and once the flood had subsided, squares of land, no bigger than a pocket-handkerchief, were planted with wheat, rice and vegetables. Although sufficient to keep the town fed, there was rarely any surplus to sell.

Surprisingly, people that lived near the river failed to notice the noise; it was only strangers that commented. Although, tonight, Alison had never heard it so loud. The rocks above the waterfall vibrated under the power of the flood, exactly like the snarl of a great cat. Remembering that leopards had been known to leave their forest habitat, to seek out chickens and pigs living on the edge of the town, she quickened her feet to a fast walk, catching her breath with difficulty in the thin air. Suddenly, she heard footsteps behind her – coming up fast.

Convinced she was about to be attacked, Alison backed up against the rock wall and turned to face her assailant. The moon surged from behind a cloud, like a runner out of the starting blocks. Its rays lifted the darkness and glinted on the metal clasp of her shoulder bag, which she was swinging purposefully, its long strap clasped in her right hand. There was little point in shouting for help, no one could possibly hear above the roar of water hitting the rocks. She craned her head towards the end of the walkway, catching a glimpse of the wrought-iron archway leading up to the hotel. She'd never reach it, the footsteps almost upon her.

A figure came into view panting harshly. And what Alison had taken for running became a sort of lurching from side to side, heavy and fast, from step to step. The figure, dressed in black from head to toe, stopped as if surprised to see her. It was badly injured, blood dripping onto a large bundle clasped against its chest.

Alison gazed at the figure, its mop of black hair sticky with blood, the doctor element in her no longer scared. A gouge, exactly like something a bulldozer might rip out of the earth, ran right across the side of its head, blood coursing down, mimicking the urgency and speed of the waterfall she had passed a minute or so ago. She stretched out her hand. To her astonishment the person clasped it tightly, its grip fierce. Then breaking away, it shoved the bundle at her, all the time muttering words that registered but which only Alison could hear. With a last repeated sentence, the figure vanished into the night.

'*Stop!*' Alison found her voice. 'Come back, you need help. Your head!'

Nothing answered, not even the moon, which faded away behind another cloud as speedily as it appeared.

Totally stunned, Alison stood there trembling. The relief

at finding herself uninjured was so great tears dripped onto her cheeks. Pulling herself together, she peered at the bundle. It was heavy and wrapped in a length of dark material like jute sacking. She tucked her finger under the edge and lifted it, flinching with shock when the bundle moved as if alive.

This was so stupid. Alison stared round at the dark pathway. First, she told herself firmly, lights – people – and safety. Hurrying now, she headed for the friendly outline of the archway, the thunderous noise from the waterfall fading as she distanced herself from it. Facing her was the wooded driveway leading up to the hotel. In the heat of the noon sun, this created a pleasing area of shade. In the menacing darkness, it instantly became a hiding place for wild beasts. At a gallop, Alison tore along the path and burst into the foyer as if all the hounds of hell were after her.

'Dr Shaw?'

The night-receptionist at the hotel gazed with horror at the young woman, her slacks smeared with blood, her blond hair escaping from its normally neat ponytail.

She happened to be the only foreign visitor staying at the Imperial Palace, Bantu's newly created hotel. As a result the staff had a deep, if somewhat suspicious, interest in her. For most of them, she was the first westerner they had come across – not counting the construction team that had built the hospital. She was also *very* young and, in the receptionist's opinion, far too young to be a doctor. Everyone knew that doctors were middle-aged men with greying hair and big bellies, who looked as if they knew what they were doing. Not a lady – *and definitely not a pretty, young lady*. That was before the hotel manager had peeked into her passport, which had been left at reception, proudly informing his staff that the lady *was* a doctor, and her age was twenty-six – quite old after all. She had been sent by the United Nations to help poor children, especially those with deformed legs that couldn't walk and those that had a split in their lip and couldn't talk. Now the hotel staff regarded her with overwhelming pride.

'Are you hurt?' He eyed the bundle. 'What is that?'

Back in the safety of the light, Alison found herself able to focus exactly on what she was carrying.

She shook her head, her legs still a bit wobbly. 'Not sure, Chang. But whatever it is, it's alive. Come and see.'

Chang hesitated. He eyed the switchboard nervously, its rows of plugs and wires silent, and shuffled his feet.

'Please don't bother to change into your uniform.' Alison smiled, well aware that the receptionist, in his white shirt and loose black trousers, was breaking hotel policy; the manager insisting that his reception staff wore uniform, a western-style green jacket and tight green trousers. Arriving back late the previous night, she had found the reception desk deserted while Chang changed in a cupboard, before running upstairs to discover what a guest wanted so late at night. She pointed to the shelf by the switchboard where he kept his neatly folded jacket and trousers. 'I'm with you.' She nodded down at her slacks. 'I like to be comfortable.'

The lobby was furnished with easy chairs imported from England. Not many, for the hotel was quite small with room for only a dozen guests. Carefully, and very timidly, Alison laid the parcel down and began to unravel the fabric. She gasped, the sound echoed more loudly by Chang, hastily peeling away the remaining layers. Two pairs of eyes, blinking slightly in the light, gazed solemnly up at her. Large ovals of crystal-clear darkness surrounded by a pool of glistening white; a baby and a slightly older child tightly bound together.

Speechless, Alison could only stare.

'Where did you find them, Dr Shaw?' Chang said, once the initial shock had worn off.

Alison shook her brains back into order. 'I didn't, someone gave them to me.'

'Who?'

'I don't know.' Again, the doctor in Alison's make-up took over. 'What an astonishing thing. Well, it's too late to do anything tonight. I'll have to take care of them.' Aware that

6

nothing happened in the provincial town unless the mayor knew about it first, she added, 'Perhaps you will ask the manager to inform the mayor first thing tomorrow morning.' She smiled down at the children still silently regarding her. 'They must be hungry and the baby's soaked, poor thing. Can you get me some milk and a change of clothing?'

Chang nodded and made to return to his desk. 'You want I call manager now?' he said half-heartedly.

'Don't bother. Tomorrow will do.' Gathering the silent bundle together, Alison trotted wearily up the stairs to her room on the first floor.

It was a pleasant room with views over steeply sloping gardens. The manager had assured her it was their *very best* room, with the *best* view, and how fortunate Dr Shaw had chosen the *best* month – October – to visit them. He was right, although Alison had so far only managed a brief inspection while eating breakfast, the forested slopes of the mountain peppered with dots of brilliant orange-red, like sparklers on fireworks' night. She had asked the name of the tree and been shown the flamboyant Gulmohar growing among the vegetation on the driveway, its golden branches and feathery emerald leaves covered with bright flowers.

Dropping her bag onto a chair, Alison quickly unravelled the lengths of cloth. At first she thought the children to be stuck together, as if they were conjoined twins. But once the wrapping had been removed, they rolled apart like segments of an orange, the older child still clutching the baby's hand firmly. The child sat up and stared at her. So did the baby from its position on its back, the expression in their eyes identical, wary and cautious as if Alison might be a wild animal.

Used to dealing with children that didn't understand English, she picked up the baby and, keeping her voice calm and comfortable, skilfully removed its long gown. Then, hearing Chang's feet on the stairs, quickly slipped off the older child's outer garment, hiding them both under the bedcover. It was only later that she asked herself, why? After all, it was only Chang and he wasn't even from the town. As far as she knew he originated from China, somehow finding his way across the border during the long war. Having decided to stay, he had won his job because he both spoke and understood English.

Chang was clutching a baby's bottle, several long cotton gowns, some cotton nappies and a tray of food.

'Chang, you're a genius. How did you do it – it's past ten o'clock.'

Chang's pale cheeks darkened slightly under the praise.

'Laundry-worker, she bring baby with her,' he explained. 'I brought rice for boy and food for you, doctor. Hospital porter tell me, you no time to eat today.'

Alison shook her head in bewilderment, astonished that her every move was common knowledge. '*Boy!* How did you know that, you've not been closer than six feet?'

Chang's face broke into a triumphant half-smile. 'My youngest son is same age. Look at his hair.'

Except for the mayor, who was rather large, everyone in the small town seemed pretty similar to everyone else. The men were only of medium height, compactly built, with neatly-trimmed black hair, while the women were both willowy and graceful when young, quickly becoming stringy after some years of marriage, like an old fowl. Alison had thought Chang to be no more than a teenager himself – well, twenty at the very most. Except the hotel manager would never have awarded such a responsible job to a mere boy. Chang obviously appeared much younger than his real age.

She turned her attention to the little boy sitting on the bed beside her. So far he'd not made a sound, his hand still outstretched and touching his sister. She noticed that his hair, already long, had been caught back with a cotton thread.

'Well, you're quite wonderful.' She smiled at the receptionist and expertly tilted the bottle into the baby's mouth. It gurgled noisily and started to feed. 'Whatever would I have done without you?'

TWO

Alison glared across the large desk at the mayor, a prosperous-looking gentleman wearing a tightly-fitting embroidered silk jacket over spotlessly white trousers. She gave an impatient sigh. Either the mayor was being extraordinarily difficult or he was extraordinarily stupid. There he was, calmly sipping coffee as if happy for the meeting to last several hours. Didn't he realise she had work to do? She hadn't time for comfortable chats, not with ten sick children waiting to be operated on that day. And while two abandoned infants might be important, they were at least healthy and well fed.

This was their third meeting and so far they had got nowhere, the two children remaining in her room at the hotel.

Early the following morning, the mayor had arrived in his chauffeur-driven car interrupting her breakfast. Admittedly, this was an hour later than usual because she had overslept, having got up several times in the night to check on the children. But not eating a good breakfast always left Alison feeling irritable and the mayor's visit had left her feeling even more irritable. The man had inspected the children, saying nothing except: *wait I come back*. Aware it was probably sensible to do what he asked – otherwise arrangements for working at the hospital might suddenly become unarranged – she had waited. And wasted an entire morning, since the man has not reappeared until after lunch, this time accompanied by his deputy.

The deputy was both a younger and slimmer version of the chief functionary, although not as nattily dressed. The white trousers worn by the mayor were a truly startling shade of white, something Alison considered a miracle, after watching women wash clothes in the river, beating the dirt out with stones. The hotel manager had discovered a wooden-sided cot in their store-room and had expressed his deep honour when Alison chose to use it. The deputy had stared closely at the children, shaking his head all the while, and the two children, now awake, had stared back. Then, again without a word, the two men had left.

It was now the following afternoon. Up until that point Alison had told no one about discovering the jade stone, carved into the shape of a bird, hidden among the wrappings. Nor had she mentioned that their little hands were so tightly gripped together, when she eventually loosed them, on each of their palms was printed an identical image. Fortunately, the mark had faded by morning. She hadn't mentioned the clothes either. Instead, she had rinsed them out in the basin in her room, leaving them to dry overnight, before carefully hiding them in her suitcase.

'Mr Mayor,' Alison tried to keep her tone patient. 'Has anyone come forward to claim the children?'

'No.' The man took a sip of his coffee, smacking his lips with pleasure.

'Have you searched the town for their mother?' Alison said, her tone rising slightly.

The mayor nodded. 'Yes. Search everywhere.'

'So what are you going to do? I can't possibly waste yet another day looking after them. I have so many operations to get through.'

'It is good, Doctor Shaw, you help. Children given you, you keep now.'

'Nice idea but quite impossible,' Alison chortled.

She gazed at the impassive expression on the mayor's face, suddenly aware he'd not been joking. For an instant she felt alarm, immediately replaced by a sensation of extreme annoyance. She might be in a foreign country but this was the town's problem – nothing to do with her at all. There was no way the mayor was going to off-load it. She spoke slowly, despite knowing that the mayor understood much more English than he let on.

'I'm here to treat your sick children,' she reminded him, smiling slightly. 'I can't possibly be responsible for them any longer; all today's operations have had to be rescheduled as it is. If there isn't an orphanage in Kuto, perhaps they could stay at the hospital until you find a family to take them. And may I suggest you widen the search,' she continued. 'Somewhere they have a mother.'

The mayor put down his cup. 'Today, mother's body found by side of river. She bled to death.' He shrugged. 'There is nothing more to be done. The children were passed on to you. Now they belong to you.'

Alison reeled back in astonishment at the rapid and very sudden improvement in the mayor's English. In all her other meetings with him, he had been careful to give the impression that his sole knowledge of the language was limited to about fifty words – most of them nouns. Now, he was adding verbs. This was definitely serious.

'*Belong*?' she repeated thinking she'd heard wrong. 'How can they belong to me?'

'I ask you, Doctor Shaw, did they have the outline of a bird on their hand when you found them?'

'I don't think so,' Alison lied and hoped she wasn't blushing.

The mayor sighed. 'My deputy suspects they are Javean. Now we have found the mother, I agree.'

'Javean? What does that mean?'

'It is what we call the tribe of people that live beyond the waterfall,' said the mayor, dishing all attempts to keep up his Pidgin English. 'The mark is present only on those that carry the magic of their tribe.'

'Magic! That's ridiculous,' Alison said firmly. 'Magic doesn't exist.'

The major picked up the coffee pot indicating to Alison if she wanted another cup. She shook her head.

'The people here believe in magic. Even if they did not, we could not send the children back to the plateau. Monsters live there. People that trespass beyond the waterfall do not return.'

Alison shivered suddenly cold. Outside the sun shone brightly, the office on the ground floor of the mayoral house opening into a pleasant garden made up of shady palms and mango trees, the new fruits already showing green among the leaves.

'I don't believe in monsters,' she said, trying not to sound as if she was arguing. Chang, before going off duty that morning, had warned her that since the mayor owned both the hotel *and* the cinema, no one ever argued with him. She smiled graciously. 'And I don't believe you do, Your Honour. You, like me, know they don't exist. The only monsters that did exist were the Japanese soldiers who ventured into your country in the past few years.'

'Doctor Shaw, you are a good woman. But you are still only a woman, and a woman's place is in the home caring for children. If you do not take them, they will be put in an orphanage where they will surely die. None will want them to live, once it is known they are Javean. You believe I have done nothing in the last two days?'

Alison did blush this time.

The mayor pointed down at his desk. Surprised, she saw her passport which she had surrendered to the hotel on arrival, two weeks before.

'I have already contacted the English authorities. By the time you have finished your work here, adoption papers will have been drawn up.'

'*That's quite ridiculous!*' Forgetting Chang's warning, Alison leaned forward and planted both hands firmly on the desk. 'The English authorities will never agree to ... just ...

allowing me to bring in two children. Besides, they don't have names or passports,' she argued.

The mayor bowed. 'I suggest choosing their names ...' He climbed leisurely to his feet. A big man, carrying signs of good food and prosperity in front of him, he gestured towards the garden. 'While we take the air in the garden. It is a peaceful place and I am sure you will choose beneficial names that will bring them prosperity. I have already thought of Elizabeth and Philip, after your princess and her new husband.'

Alison leapt to her feet in protest. 'Mr Mayor, I will walk with you in the garden. I agree it certainly has got very warm in here.' Agitated, she wafted a book in front of her face like a fan. 'I know you have the best interests of the children at heart, but I am *not* about to burden myself with them. I was sent here to help your country.'

The mayor nodded. 'Very good. This way you help my country.'

Alison ignored the interruption. 'When I return to England, I must search for a new job in surgery. Once working, I won't have time for myself let alone children. Please understand. *This is not going to happen*. Besides, I detest those names.'

THREE

1959

The house, to which two children were running, was the last in a little row of five. Built in the reign of Queen Victoria, a plaque, high up on the middle one, announced its year of construction as 1890. Liz tore up the hill from the main road, her feet barely skimming its surface, her brother running flat out a good five paces behind.

The house boasted a green front door and, since green was well-known to resist fading, quite half the properties in the long street were painted the same colour. Number 57, besides possessing an imposing lion's head knocker and a brass letter box, was protected from the weather by a glass porch. This had a fringe of garnet-red diamond-shaped panes around the top edge, the glass still fresh and bright even after seventy years, with matching tiles on the floor.

To a casual observer they might have been twins. Almost identical in height, they possessed fine features with widely spaced almond-shaped eyes and an identical shock of blue-black hair, which never looked messy and, most annoyingly for their school mates, stayed glossy and healthy looking even when they had chicken pox. They weren't twins. Phil was the older by a year although Liz, despite knowing her brother's date of birth from his passport, continued to argue the twins scenario. Reaching the garden path, she slowed to a cautious jog and grabbed her side. If her brother had any faults at all, it was a dislike of being beaten, always sulking for ages, and cramp was a good way of making sure he reached the door first. Phil panted up behind her and, with a triumphant smile, cannoned into the front door thumping against it heavily.

'There. Told you I could beat you,' he said, fiercely slamming down the brass knocker.

Viveca Paluski was in the kitchen cooking tea. Despite knowing her two charges couldn't possibly get home from school any earlier, she had been watching the clock for at least ten minutes. Recognising Phil's special touch on the door knocker, she smiled and, wiping her hands on her pinafore, hurried through the hall to open it.

She was a long, stringy woman and her hair, the colour of salt and pepper, was pulled back into a tight bun – any stray wisps firmly gripped into place. She had escaped from Poland with her two children at the beginning of the war. With her husband away fighting in the British army, she had found work cleaning floors in a munitions factory, leaving her children with a kindly neighbour. After her husband was killed, she had continued at the factory, even after they began manufacturing cars again at the end of the war, and had been thrilled when the neighbour told her that young Dr Shaw required a housekeeper. Even more thrilled, when she learned that being a housekeeper meant she no longer had to clean floors. Instead, her duties involved caring for two small children and cooking, both of which she loved especially with her own two now teenagers.

Unfortunately, at her interview Dr Shaw had misheard her surname – Paluski – hearing only Luski. Since her English was not yet good enough to correct her prospective employer, Mrs Luski she had remained. Liz, on becoming a toddler, had abbreviated it still further to *Lucy*. Ten years on, Mrs Paluski refused to answer to anything else – unless she felt cross and out of sorts. Only then did she demand the full version of her name. 'Mrs Paluski went back to Poland straight after the war,' she'd frown when the children forgot.

'So school?' She took Liz's coat, tenderly hanging it on a peg in the hall. 'Phil – coat on a hook please, not the floor. Homework?' the housekeeper continued, whipping the blazer from Phil's outstretched hand and hanging it up herself.

'We always have homework,' Phil groaned. 'It's like our teacher's got a gramophone record for brains. All he can say is: *don't forget your homework, they'll be a test on Monday.*'

Mrs Lucy's washed-out blue eyes lingered on his face. 'You all right, Phil, you look a bit peaky to me?'

'He's not sleeping, Mrs Lucy. He's having these bad dreams again, so he comes in with me.'

Phil frowned furiously at his sister.

'We can't have that,' Mrs Lucy fussed. 'You've got a perfectly good room of your own, Philip. What does your mother say about it?'

Phil pulled a face and shrugged.

'That means, she doesn't know.' Liz smiled sweetly.

Phil glowered. 'Only because I don't want to worry her when she's so busy.'

'Learning to drive,' Mrs Lucy sniffed.

'But if Mother learns to drive,' Liz said eagerly, 'she's promised to buy a car, which will be ...'

'Fantastic.' Phil finished the sentence. 'Besides it's not the driving that's bothering her, it's this conference next Friday. Doctors from all over the world will be attending.'

Phil and Liz were quite aware that Mrs Lucy found their habit of finishing each other sentences bewildering, sometimes replying to the wrong person – and, as often as not, mixing up their names.

Liz had tried explaining that twins were always telepathic, to which Mrs Lucy had retorted gruffly, 'I don't know where you get such strange ideas. Those library books, I'll be bound. I keep telling your mother, too much reading's bad for you.'

'Meanwhile, who looks after you children?' she grumbled.

'Darling Lucy.' Liz flung her arms round the housekeeper's waist. 'You know you do. If it was left to Mother, we wouldn't even have clean clothes. Remember when you had the influenza, and she forgot to pick us up from school?'

The grim expression on the housekeeper's face faded.

'And she never remembers when term ends,' Liz added, aware of the calendar on the kitchen wall, religiously marked with every school date, so Mrs Lucy could remind her employer in time.

'And you're the most super cook. If you left it to Mum we'd live on Heinz Baked Beans.'

'But you love baked beans.'

'I know I do, Liz. I was trying to make a point.'

'Well, your tea is ready.' Mrs Lucy smiled fondly. 'I've done baked potatoes and a lamb stew. Go and change first.'

The layout of all five houses was identical, with Mrs Reid, their neighbour, having the mirror image of their own. A long hallway, with a staircase running along its inner wall, led directly into a large and sunny kitchen, where a coal range provided both hot water and heat. Unlike its neighbours, number 57 had a wide glass veranda at the back. Here, the housekeeper dried washing on wet days and sheltered pot-plants through the winter. She liked gardening but her own two-bedroom prefab possessed only a square of lawn at the front, with two large peony bushes growing under the window. Although the dark-red flowers were very beautiful, they lasted such a short time they were hardly worth bothering with. The back garden was not much bigger, with only enough room for a clothes line, a few rows of potatoes, some long red stalks of rhubarb – which Mrs Lucy religiously manured every spring – growing through the rusted-out bottom of an upturned bucket, and a large clump of parsley. Any overspill of plants found its way into Dr Shaw's garden.

'Why did you say that?' Phil rounded on his sister the moment they reached her bedroom. 'I told you not to tell.'

'To force you into telling Mother.'

'Lucy won't blab.'

Liz began to giggle. 'No, but you can bet your life she'll insist you're a bit under the weather and suggest a dose of Syrup of

Figs to set you right.' She unpacked her satchel, neatly arranging the books she needed for that night's homework on top of her desk. She swung round, her gaze wide-eyed and innocent looking. 'And you know how much you love Syrup of Figs.'

Phil groaned. 'It was still a rotten trick.' He wandered across to the window. Dusk was falling, its giant paint brush softening the sharp outlines and blurring them into shades of navy blue. 'I like this room.'

'So do I. So don't bother asking me to swap.'

Besides being the smallest, Liz's bedroom lay directly over the kitchen, which made it both the warmest and the only one without net curtains – its window fortunate enough to overlook gardens and allotments. Their mother's room, at the front might have two big windows but it still felt like being in prison, the heavy white nets, designed to stop nosy neighbours from peering in, blocking both light and sunshine.

Quickly slipping off her navy gymslip, Liz hung it back in the wardrobe with her blouse and tie. She took down her red house-skirt and jumper from its wooden hanger. 'This morning before school, I had a go at drawing that thing.' She rummaged among the papers on her small desk. 'It's …'

Phil snatched the paper out of her hand. 'You couldn't have. I never told you what it was like.'

'You didn't need to.' Still cold, she pulled open a drawer in her chest and took out a cardigan. 'You know I can always tell what you're thinking.'

Liz busied herself buttoning up her cardigan. They could both read one another's expressions and finish sentences, although she was way better at it than Phil. Even so, that was child's play compared to what she'd recently discovered. Ever since Phil's nightmares, it was as if his thoughts had become so troubled, they were reaching out for someone to confide in – and had chosen her. Except Phil stubbornly refused to admit they were nightmares and, *very scary*.

The drawing resembled an elongated cat that had been run over by a car, although her HB pencil and rubber had left so many dark smudges, the exact species of animal remained unidentifiable. Liz peered over her brother's shoulder aware how truly awful it was. But then she'd never said she could draw except for flowers, and she was pretty good at those. Phil was the artist. He was the one with imagination. She flinched at the sight of its legs and paws projecting straight out on each side like propeller blades. They were terrible. Phil's thoughts had shown her an animal similar to a hyena, with long pointed canines and wings like a bird. Hers were like balloons covered in leaves.

Phil screwed up his face and quickly handed it back. 'It looks like a squashed cat.'

Liz replaced the paper on her desk, grateful not to have been questioned further. 'Hurry up and get changed. You know Lucy hates us being late for meals.'

Phil nodded. Halfway to the door he stopped and flopped back down on the bed. 'I'm not all that hungry,' he muttered.

Liz sighed. *Honestly, boys.* It was all very well pretending not to be scared. But a little stupid when your sister could read your face like a book. She yanked him to his feet.

'Yes, you are,' she insisted. 'I agree with Mrs Lucy, you look really rotten with those deep blue circles round your eyes, especially when your eyes are jet black – they don't match at all,' she tried to joke. Until a month ago, Phil had been the jokey one. Now he was frequently moody and bad tempered.

Relieved she had broken her promise and told the housekeeper, Liz ran her brother down the landing to his own room. Their mother would hear of it now and demand to know what was going on.

'If we get our homework done straight after, we can listen to The Goon Show later. And,' she added, 'if you get another dream tonight, you can always come in with me.'

*

The door gave out a gentle creaking as the knob was twisted and a crack of dark shadow entered the room. Liz's dreams were

19

mostly about dancing or taking part in an acrobatics display; performing cartwheels so straight that people watching gasped with delight and broke into cheers – except the cheers sounded more like frogs croaking. She stirred and, half-awake, recognised the noise as coming from her bedroom door. Reaching for the bedside light she flashed it on, its sudden brightness outlining the head and torso of her brother in the doorway.

'Switch it off,' he hissed. 'You'll wake Mum. Can I come in?'

Liz shifted across the bed allowing Phil to perch on the edge. He pulled the covers up to his chin.

'I'm cold,' he said, trying to stop his teeth chattering.

Liz glanced sideways at her brother noticing his pallor, sweaty tendrils of dark hair clinging to his forehead. She tucked the covers more closely round him.

'Bad dreams?'

'No, silly, I'm just cold,' he said, his tone defiant.

'Honestly, Phil, you really are a pain. You can't hide these things from me ... you never could.'

'So, if you already know, *stop asking*.'

Light flooded the landing and their mother appeared, wrapping her dressing gown round her. 'So what brings you into Liz's room in the middle of the night?' She peered short-sightedly at the two youngsters.

Liz made to leap out of bed. 'I'll fetch your glasses.'

'Really, Liz,' rebuked Alison. 'I remember perfectly well what you look like even if you are a blur.'

Phil's smile was lop-sided. 'Well, I'm not betting any money on you picking us out in a crowd if you're not wearing them,' he joked.

Alison flipped the back of her hand at him. 'So, what's the purpose of this late-night meeting?' she said, her tone sarcastic to show she wasn't serious.

Liz nudged her brother. 'Go on, you *have* to say.'

Phil nodded, his cheerful expression of a moment before banished. 'I know – or it's Syrup of Figs time.'

'*Syrup of what?*'

'Don't worry, Mother. It's a private joke.' Liz shifted sideways studying the expression on her brother's face. 'He's really scared.'

'*No, I'm not*! It's nothing, Mum, Liz is being stupid. Sometimes I get bad dreams – that's all. I expect it was something I ate for supper. You're always telling us you get nightmares after eating cheese.' Phil's smile was replaced by a shiver, his whole body flinching.

Liz nudged him. 'You can't go round shivering then say it's nothing. Either you tell or I will. And don't think …'

'For one minute you don't mean it,' Phil completed the sentence.

'Right.'

'Okay, then.' Phil swallowed nervously. 'I keep having these nightmares. They weren't too bad at first but they're getting worse. It's every night now. Sorry, Mum.'

'Nothing to be sorry about.' Alison perched on the end of Liz's bed, her tone changing to one of concern. 'So tell me about them?'

'I feel such a baby.'

'No need. Growing up's not easy at the best of time. Besides, we all get scared. And I don't mean spiders.' She screwed up her face at Phil.

'Liz doesn't.'

'Only because she lacks imagination.'

'*Mother*!'

Alison smiled at her. 'I meant it as a compliment, Liz. I've never met two children more dissimilar. While Phil has all the imaginative genes, you prefer science and maths. Besides, admitting you're scared, Phil, *that* takes a great deal of courage. You know the saying … a problem …'

'Shared is a problem halved.' Phil automatically finished the sentence, his voice as flat as a pancake. He heaved a sigh. 'But it sounds so silly when you say it out loud.'

'Try me,' Alison said, keeping her voice brisk.

'We're on a mountain, Liz and me, and there's someone with us – a tall figure in black. I know it's a man though I can't see his face. It's dark and we're gazing up at the sky. At first, I thought they were black clouds.' Phil described them, 'Like when we're going to have a thunderstorm.'

Alison nodded, pulling the collar of her dressing-gown more firmly round her neck.

'Well … the ground is covered in rock. At least, to begin with they're rocks. After a bit, they turn into bodies.' He shivered. Instantly, Liz, her eyes clouded with sympathy, slipped her hand into his gripping it tightly. 'The last few times, I'm standing there … *and I can't move*. It's like those dreams when you're running a race and your feet are like lead. There's clouds all around us. Only they're not clouds. They've alive. I can see wings … except they're not birds. They're … *animals*.'

Liz hopped out of bed and grabbed the drawing.

'I tried to draw them.' She showed Alison the sketch. 'It's not very good,' she apologised.

Alison grabbed Phil's hand. 'That must be so scary. Poor you.'

He nodded. 'It is, but there's more.'

Liz sat silently, her mind instantly picking up on her brother's thoughts. A flood of broken phrases and half-sentences poured through her head, as Phil sought the right words to describe what had so frightened him. At the far corner of her vision, she spotted a shadowy shape. At first it was rather sketchy, although still recognizable as human rather than animal. Long and narrow, its torso was strangely supple, bending in several directions at once, as if she was viewing it through one of those distorted mirrors you get in a funfair. It was clothed in a long black robe and wore a cap like an old-fashioned flying helmet on its head. The fingers stretched towards her as if trying to grab her.

She flinched back and the picture was gone.

'Tonight, I knew I was dreaming. I kept trying to wake up only I couldn't. It was ghastly. The monsters were attacking, swooping down from the air. But every time one of them did, there was this flash of light and it vanished.' Phil blinked banishing the pictures from his head. 'That's when I woke up. Even thinking about it now gives me the heebie-jeebies. That's why I come into Liz's room. I don't get the dreams in here.'

Alison got to her feet. 'You've done this before then? Good job we have a camp bed. I'll get some sheets. I do wish you'd said something earlier. Mrs Lucy says you're run down. She's insisting I take you to the doctor.'

Liz thumped her brother triumphantly on the back. '*Told you!* You should have reminded her that you are a doctor?' she teased her mother.

'I did. But according to Mrs Lucy, anyone that doesn't notice when their own child is poorly isn't much of a doctor.'

Phil gave a half-smile. 'I don't need a doctor, Mum. You were right. I do feel better for talking about it.'

'I was thinking ...' Alison paused in the doorway. 'I've got this conference in London on Friday ...'

'Yes, Mother. But Lucy will be here.'

'I know that, Liz.' Alison's reply sounded vague as if she had forgotten to listen.

Liz waited patiently, well used to her mother not hearing what was said to her. The astonishing thing was, at the hospital everyone said she was a most remarkable doctor and loads of children could walk again because of her. But at home, if lunch happened in the middle of her reading an article in a medical journal, it was always lunch that missed out.

'A couple of my friends, psychologists, will be at the conference,' Alison said, still looking puzzled, as if she was trying to remember their names (which Liz guessed she probably was). 'I suppose I could take you with me so we could run your dreams past them.'

'Like he's a nutter,' Liz said, hoping to force a real smile out of her brother.

Philip kicked her under the bedclothes.

'Sort-of, I suppose. We have to get rid of these dreams – or buy bunk beds,' Alison joked. 'It wouldn't harm to miss a couple of days of school. We can leave first-thing Friday morning, do my conference then stay on for a few days, if you like, sightseeing.'

'Yes – definitely.' Brother and sister spoke the words together.

'Okay, I'll get the sheets. We can talk about it more in the morning.'

Quickly making up the camp bed, Phil climbed into the sheets lovingly ironed by the housekeeper. 'Don't you just love clean sheets?' he murmured. Then, as if remembering something important, he sat up again. 'Mum?' he called. 'Could those dreams be something I remember from childhood?'

Besides being told they'd been adopted, their mother had said nothing about the circumstances leading up to that event. And while both brother and sister recognised she looked quite different from them, with her fair hair and blue eyes, they never gave it a second thought – too busy with their own lives.

Alison paused and her hand on the light switch trembled slightly.

'I don't see how they can be,' she said, her voice quite firm. 'After all, you were only about twenty-months old. Do children that young remember? I must ask one of my colleagues. He'll know. Besides, if they are memories, why didn't they start before now? It's much more likely to be some dreadful programme you've been listening to on the radio.'

'That's what I told him.' Liz eagerly volunteered the words, hoping they might convince her brother into sleeping at night. 'But you know Phil. He's glued to the set, even when it scares him to death. Last week I caught him with his hands over his ears.'

'But Paul Temple's brilliant and being scared is all part of the fun.'

Alison laughed. 'I have to admit, Liz, I quite like Paul Temple.'

'But you don't find it scary, Mother, he does.'

'I wonder who it was that said you lacked imagination?' Phil gazed dreamily at the ceiling. 'Oh, yes, it was Mum.' He grinned at his sister. 'You miss out on all the fun, if you can only imagine people reading from a script while a sound engineer makes the noises.'

'But that's exactly what does happen,' Liz insisted. 'How can you believe it's a horse galloping when it's actually someone clapping two coconuts together?'

'Surely not coconuts?' Alison murmured.

'It's not that at all,' Phil argued hotly. 'It's Paul Temple coming to the rescue of Steve, trapped in a burning building. That's when you get that fantastic music. Dun de dun de ...'

Liz blocked up her ears. 'Enough to make a cat howl, if we had one.'

Alison laughed and, coming back in, sat on her bed. 'You're obviously feeling better, Phil, which is good. But it would be nice if you could leave the arguments till morning.' She ruffled her daughter's hair. 'When I first saw you, you reminded me of a little owl. So serious.'

'*That didn't last long then,*' Phil said.

'NO! No pillows.' Alison shrieked and grabbed Liz's arm. 'It's the middle of the night and I need sleep even if you don't. I'm going to bed. Good night.' Phil opened his mouth. 'No. Not another word.'

As soon as they heard their mother's bedroom door close, Phil sat back up. 'Did you notice, she didn't actually say anything ... except that stuff about you looking like an owl. Pity it didn't last.'

'We had to have come from China.' Liz lay back down again, pointedly ignoring her brother's feeble attempt at a joke.

'Not necessarily. There are Chinese everywhere, if you think about it.'

'Does it matter?'

'Not about being Chinese, it doesn't,' Philip agreed. 'But if these are memories ...'

He left the sentence unfinished. Like a flash Liz sat up again. She stared at her brother, reading in his frightened eyes, the thought that if these dreams were real memories, then the place they came from had to be truly terrifying.

FOUR

The hotel in Ladbroke Square was a stately double-fronted house, with an imposing doorstep built entirely of white marble. An elaborate portico protected it from the weather, its columns strong enough to support a small roof garden on the second floor. At pavement level, gated railings fenced off a basement courtyard, containing a precipitous flight of steps and a row of dustbins. Once the domain of a cook and butler, it now provided a separate entrance for hotel staff plus a well-appointed guest suite, its windows barely visible at street level. With the exception of its immediate neighbour, which was identical except for the marble doorstep, the remaining houses flowed round three sides of the square in an unbroken chain. They were all tall, five storeys including the basement, and had two windows on each floor facing the square, white walls, a black front door and black railings. A communal garden, fashionable at the beginning of the twentieth century when fresh air was discovered to be beneficial for health, dominated the centre of the square. It provided children with somewhere safe to run around, while nannies pushed their infant charges down shady walks bordered by rhododendrons. With London growing at the speed of light, the demand for accommodation had reached an all-time high and quite half the buildings on the east side were covered in scaffolding, in the process of being transformed into flats for up-and-coming entrepreneurs.

Once upon a time, a commodious stable block had

separated the two buildings on the west side of the square. Stately enough to maintain at least one carriage and half-a-dozen horses, accommodation had been provided above the stables for a groom, his wife, and a stable boy. Recently, the old-fashioned rooms above the stables at Number 10 had undergone a transformation, and now boasted a bathroom with hot and cold running water, a small kitchen with a gas cooker, a dining-living room, and two small bedrooms. The stables had been made into a garage and housed a car, a single-decker bus, once the property of London Transport, and a work-shop, filled with tools and weirdly shaped objects, of which the majority were prosthetic limbs – with adult-sized arms and legs hanging casually off the wall.

For such an imposing and commodious building, its rear gardens were paltry, and hotel guests were granted access to the newly revitalised gardens in the centre of the square. Thanks to a committee of keen amateur gardeners, they now contained elegant flower beds set among tall trees of beech, elm and horse-chestnut. In one corner, an ancient and smiling statue of Pan peeked out from behind a thick arbour of honeysuckle; the spinster ladies on the committee considering its furry hindquarters and cloven hoofs quite unsuitable viewing for young families.

Although Number 10 had escaped bomb damage, it had lain empty for several years, before opening its doors as a hotel some eight years previously. It had been recommended by several of Alison's colleagues as 'absolutely marvellous', close to the hospital and not at all expensive, yet brilliantly clean. A couple of them did add a rider, saying that its owner possessed rather a strange hobby.

'But don't let that you put you off,' they said. 'He's an explorer or something, always off travelling somewhere. The hotel is full of extraordinary objects that he's brought back from his travels. Although, if you're lucky enough to find him in residence he'll be doing the cooking; then you are in for a treat.'

The owner had been absent when they had checked in on the Friday night, after spending the day at the conference. Apparently, he was expected back imminently and while the cooking was good, it wasn't any better than Mrs Lucy prepared for them at home. What was brilliant, though, were the sights. The weekend had been spent rushing about, wearing out feet and shoes, traipsing up and down the steps and corridors of the Underground, and Phil's new Kodak camera had actually run out of film in front of Buckingham Palace. But then, as Liz grumbled, he'd wasted quite half a roll on the guards.

'After all, Phil,' she moaned as they headed back to the corner of Bird Cage Walk, where Alison had noticed a wooden booth selling film, amongst its stock of confectionary and newspapers. 'Black bearskins are black bearskins. Once you've seen one, you've seen them all.'

'Rubbish! Mum, can I borrow your coat?'

Obligingly, Alison made a tent of her mackintosh to block out as much light as possible. Phil opened the back of the camera, carefully lifting out the used roll.

'I still need to get a shot of the sentry boxes at the gate,' he said, quickly fitting in the new reel and winding it onto the spool. He shut the back of the camera and stood up. 'I asked a policeman. They have to stand like that for hours and hours without moving.'

'They stamp their feet, I saw them,' Liz argued.

Alison put her mackintosh back on, buttoning it up, since the day, although bright and sunny, had a cold wind. 'You've only got twelve exposures this time, Phil,' she warned, reading the instructions on the back of the little yellow box, in which he had placed the used roll of film. 'Remember to save some for Trafalgar Square.'

In theory walking down the Mall seemed a good idea, particularly since they had passed a troop of Lifeguards on horseback, their helmets festooned with long cream plumes, very different from the sentries who wore the famous black bearskins on their heads. But, by the time they reached the famous square, a good sit-down with an ice cream suddenly became much more interesting than snapping Nelson, high up on his column.

Liz took a bite out of her choc-ice letting it melt slowly in her mouth. She lifted her head skywards to inspect the dark figure of the famous admiral. 'It's like he's staring out to sea from the top of a mast,' she said.

They had also visited the wax works at Madame Tussauds, where Winston Churchill and Charlie Chaplin were on display, and Tower Bridge. Here, they were lucky enough to watch the two halves of the bridge rise slowly and majestically into the air to let a ship pass through. Everything quite magical. And, what was even better than the sights, Phil had not had a single nightmare in three nights.

'Sleep well?' Alison smiled as the two children erupted into the dining room.

'Like a top,' Phil reported, sliding into his seat at the table. 'So what are we doing, today?'

'No nightmares?'

'Can't you tell, Mother,' Liz laughed. 'He's back to being infuriating again.'

'I'm so glad, Phil. Perhaps all you needed was a rest.'

It was Monday morning and, after an extra-long sleep to recover from the rigours of sightseeing, they had just ordered breakfast.

The door swung open and a tall red-haired man appeared, carrying a heavily laden tray. A waitress propped the door open with her foot, to let him go through first, her arms busy with pots of tea and coffee. He stopped at their table and Liz became aware of his glance homing in on them.

'When I arrived back this morning, Mrs Howard told me we had some new guests. I figured I'd better come along and introduce myself. I'm Tom McFaddean. I own this place.' He placed the heavy tray down on a corner of the table and proceeded to unload three plates. 'Egg, bacon, sausage, tomatoes, fried bread – you name it – for …?' He paused, glancing meaningfully at Liz.

She glanced up into eyes that were deep blue and so searching, it felt like diving into a bottomless lake. They made her feel oddly embarrassed. Confused, she dropped her eyes, staring down at the tablecloth.

'Elizabeth,' her mother said, all of a sudden sounding rather stuffy and rather pompous, exactly like Mrs Paluski, if someone ever accused her of being a foreigner. 'I am a British citizen and proud of it,' the housekeeper would retort, drawing herself up to her full height.

'Same for your brother, er …'

'Phil,' he broke in, exchanging a friendly grin with the owner.

'Twins?'

'No! Though my sister thinks we ought to be. I'm the oldest.'

The man's forearms, neck and face were deeply tanned, a rare sight in England where it was frequently so cold and wet that almost everyone, unless they came from Africa or Jamaica, had permanently white skin; often so densely white it developed a greenish tinge from lack of exposure. His face was marked by deep lines running down either side of his mouth and a long scar across one cheek.

'Kidneys.' The tall man placed the hot plate down on the table. 'Just the way you like them, Dr Shaw.'

Apart from the scar, which made him look older, Tom McFaddean might have been about the same age as Dr Shaw who, at thirty-eight, was considered by both her children to be positively decrepit. 'Old,' Mrs Lucy had snapped, overhearing their conversation about their mother's age. 'May I remind you two, if Dr Shaw is as ancient as you think, why is she always being mistaken for a fifth-year medical student by visitors to the hospital?'

The hotelier leaned back on his heels and passed the empty tray to the waitress, waiting patiently at his elbow. Sliding the salt and pepper to one side, he arranged the pots of tea and hot water neatly on the table. Liz noticed her mother staring at the man's hair, which was shoulder length and tied back with a thick band, her face set in disapproving lines.

'Enjoying the sights?' he smiled.

Phil nodded.

'Have you made any plans for the day?'

'Not at the moment.' Alison's voice remained frosty. 'We were just about to discuss what we were going to do when you came in with breakfast. It smells delicious. Eat up, you two, while it's hot. Tea, Liz?' she said, deliberately picking up the tea pot.

Liz screwed up her mouth, raising her eyebrows at Phil as if to say: *what's got into Mother?*

Phil replied with an almost invisible movement of his head, to tell her he didn't know.

Tom McFaddean took no notice, simply shifting from one leg to the other. 'I thought as it was teeming with rain, you might like to visit my collection – things I've gathered on my travels.'

'You're an explorer?' Phil paused his chewing.

'Sort-of. I've visited Asia and the Far East quite a bit.' Mr McFaddean leaned his broad shoulders against the wall replying to Phil's question.

Liz concentrated on her breakfast. Even though the man was chatting to her brother, she could feel his eyes continually flicking back to her. It was a horrid feeling.

He seemed in no great hurry to get back to the kitchen, leaving the waitress to serve the other guests in the dining room and clear away empty plates. 'I believe you've visited Asia, Dr Shaw?'

Alison glanced up from her plate of kidneys and gave a loud impatient sigh – instantly translated by her children into: *oh why doesn't this man go away and let me eat my breakfast in peace.*

'No,' she snapped, shaking her head.

32

'That's strange – I've just been reading about you in a medical journal.'

'Didn't you say you'd *just* got back from a trip, Mr McFaddean?' Her voice crackled with ice.

Liz, embarrassed, buried her head more deeply in her plate, wondering what had happened to make her mother so tetchy.

'I'm a fast reader.' He smiled, the blue of his eyes flaring with mischief. Phil grinned back. 'The article mentioned that you had once worked in Asia.'

'For a week maybe,' Alison retorted. 'So long ago, I'd forgotten about it.'

'Sounds reasonable. So kids – come upstairs after breakfast, the door marked private on the fourth floor.'

'Can we, Mum?'

Alison hesitated then gave a reluctant nod.

'Right!' Mr McFaddean pushed open the door. 'I'll leave you in peace to eat your breakfast. Ring when you need more toast.'

'What a dreadful man.' Alison kept her voice low. 'And so embarrassing. He never spoke to the other guests. I can't imagine what they must think.'

'They've probably already seen his stuff.' Phil flew to the hotelier's defence. 'Anyway, I think he's nice. He was only teasing about being a fast reader. I expect he's heard of you.'

'I think he's a bit strange.'

'Oh, come on, Liz, he's great. I bet he's done some amazing things. Did you notice the scar on his arm? It's massive. I wonder how that happened.'

'When he looks at you,' Liz whispered. 'He *really* looks.'

'Exactly!' Alison reached for a piece of toast. 'We will go and see his collection although I expect it's rubbish – and, afterwards, we'll go to the pictures.'

FIVE

The lift, its concertina gate built from lengths of steel bolted together, ground its way up to the fourth floor as if surprised to be moving at all. Most guests didn't bother with it preferring to use the stairs, leaving the lift to rumble up and down carrying suitcases or laundry for the chambermaids, who found traipsing up and down four flights of stairs exhausting. With a loud grunt, it jerked to a stop. Alison pulled back the heavy gate and stepped out.

'So who won?' she said, seeing the two children perched on the topmost stair.

'He did, by a mile.' Liz said and uttered a realistic groan as if she really had a bad stitch. Phil grinned and, jumping to his feet, knocked on a door marked private.

'Come in.' A voice floated down from somewhere above them.

The door opened onto yet another flight of stairs, the narrow staircase spilling out into a brightly lit room, its walls and ceiling painted white. Phil, taking the steps two at a time, dashed on ahead, leaving Liz and their mother to follow.

Alison caught her daughter's arm. 'He has to learn sometime.'

Liz jumped and flushed guiltily. 'It's much easier this way. Besides, he hates losing to me.'

'Mrs Lucy was only saying the other day that you're likely to be the stronger …'

'Crikey!'

The loud exclamation came from the room above.

Liz spotted her brother rooted to the top step as if he had been turned into stone, his hand frozen in the act of reaching for an imaginary sword or pistol.

Startled, she flew up the stairs straight into a battlefield. All round the room fights had broken out. Swaggering bullies of men, with top knots, square jackets and wide trousers, waved their swords in anger, the air rent by shouting and gunfire. Facing them were armour-clad warriors, some wielding a battle-axe, others with long-barrelled pistols. It took a moment or two for her brain to work out that the swords weren't moving and the men were only full-sized models, while the soundtrack came from a speaker cunningly hidden behind one of the beams near the ceiling. Although the menace in the face of the nearest warrior was so lifelike, Liz joined her brother on the top step reluctant to approach closer.

'Do close your mouth, Phil,' Alison said catching up with them, her voice quite sharp. 'You're not catching flies.'

'They are rather spectacular though aren't they, although it pays to be a little wary of their swords.' Tom McFaddean rose to his feet. He'd been working at a table tucked behind the stairwell, daylight entering the room through a nearby dormer window, its view obscured by the narrow parapet.

'Why?'

'Because, Phil, I keep them as close to the original as possible, which means they can easily take your hand off.'

Jumping back out of range, Phil tucked his hands safely inside his trouser pockets, before leaning forward again to examine the figures more closely. Liz slipped an arm through her mother's content to inspect the models from a distance.

'I don't think I'm going to like this,' she whispered. 'I've never seen anything so violent.'

'I agree it's violent, but I have to admit, Mr McFaddean … ' Alison slowly examined each corner of the room, its steeply pitched roof creating a feeling of space. 'This is most impressive,' she said, her tone grudging, 'although I sincerely hope you don't expect guests to sleep up here when the hotel is full.'

Tom McFaddean laughed. 'To be honest, I can never make up my mind if I like them or not. The models cause so much trouble, they might as well be alive. Some visitors like Phil think they're fantastic, others gruesome. One of my guests actually fainted. You're not intending to do that, Liz, are you?'

She shook her head.

'Good. Then I suggest you start here.'

He indicated the Japanese samurai, whose savage expression had so alarmed Liz, which had been placed for dramatic effect at the head of the staircase.

A framed print had been fastened to a nearby beam. In the drawing, the samurai wore an identical set of robes, a heavy squared-off jacket with, what closely resembled, pink fabric wings sprouting from his padded shoulders. Below that he wore a voluminous green garment, similar to a divided-skirt, the material falling in folds round his legs, cuffs of white trousers poking out below, and slippers on his feet. He also carried two swords, both of which were tucked into his wide sash.

'Don't worry, it's authentic,' Mr McFaddean confirmed, watching Alison peering closely in an effort to read the tiny print, 'although I discovered the two pieces on separate occasions. They date ...'

'From 1811,' Phil exclaimed, studying the small brass plaque. 'Wow! That *is* old. But he didn't fight in those clothes, did he?'

The tall man smiled. 'If he did, I bet his wife had something to say when he got home. No, in the eighteen hundreds they mostly used armour.' He pointed to the warrior wielding his curved sword like a battle-axe. He was wearing a coal-scuttle type helmet, with a long chain-mail fringe running down over his shoulders and back, and a separate piece of metal (rather like a detachable beard) covering the front of his neck. 'Although, this piece is even earlier.'

The chain-mail figure reminded Phil of Hollywood films, in which the armour appeared so weighty knights had to be winched onto their horses before a fight. Naturally, Liz always spoiled his fun by saying it was only cardboard or tin – and the actors were simply pretending it was heavy.

'Edo Period 1603 – 1868.' Phil gave a surprised whistle. 'But how does he see out?' He touched the edge of the helmet which protruded down over the eyebrows. 'He'd never spot anyone coming up behind.'

'It's not that bad. I've tried it. You can see quite well enough to fight – even run if you have to.' Tom McFaddean lifted the edge of the heavy silk skirt, its hem falling to just below the knees, showing Phil the chain-mail greaves encasing the warrior's calves.

'Is that all he did, fight?' Feeling slightly more at ease, Liz crossed the room to examine a collection of embroidered costumes displayed on a tailor's dummy. The silk fabric had faded and become stiff with age although, up close, it was still possible to make out the original colours in its design of birds and flowers. 'Four.' She counted the number of garments overlaid one on top of another. 'Is it cold in Japan?'

'It can be bitter in winter, Liz, and paper houses don't provide much protection ...'

'Paper?' Liz exclaimed.

'As good as. Japan has always suffered from earthquakes and the people sensibly built houses light enough not to crush them when they fell.' The hotelier showed them a second picture; a family group sitting in a room, empty of furniture except for a table in one corner, on which stood a small vase with a single flower. 'The framework of the house was wood, strong enough to support a tiled roof. Unless families were wealthy, they only had the one room, which was heated by a wood stove, and a tiny outhouse for cooking. Actually, fire was an even greater risk than earthquakes.'

'Are they all Japanese?'

'Absolutely not, Liz. These are Mongolian.' Tom

McFaddean showed her two warriors clad in thick leather from top to toe, even their long hair bound with leather thongs, one of the models about to shoot an arrow from a bow. 'And these are Burmese.'

Up close, the three Burmese figures reminded Liz of toads with bandy legs, their fish-scale armour so clumsily fashioned it stuck out at all angles – like a collection of sardine tins stuck together. She frowned at the dozen or so figures in disgust. 'They're all men. Aren't there any ladies?'

The blue eyes twinkled. 'Sorry, Liz. Ladies rarely featured as warriors in those days – except in books. They stayed at home and did embroidery.' He pointed to the elegant garments displayed on the dummies.

Alison bent down to examine one of several paintings dotted along the wall, flinching as she caught sight of the severed heads bouncing about amongst the fighting men.

'Are you interested only in people that kill, Mr McFaddean?' she said, her tone disapproving,

'Absolutely not, Dr Shaw.' He sounded amused. 'My father started this particular collection. My interest is much more peaceful. I research myths and legends. Although, if you've got a minute, I'd quite like to show you something even more bizarre than this little lot. It's over here.' He waved a hand at the specimen table, a microscope in its case almost obscured by a heap of oddly shaped objects, a row of empty cardboard boxes ranged along the skirting board under the window. 'I've just begun cataloguing my latest discoveries.'

Taking Alison by the arm, he headed back to his desk, side-stepping a line of glass cabinets featuring a display of antique guns. Liz and Phil wandered along behind, occasionally stopping to inspect something that caught their eye.

'This chap was delivered first thing this morning. The friend who sent it said they had dug it up in Tibet. I've not a clue what century it is, so I'm sending it over to Will Rutherford at the British Museum.' He glanced down at his watch. 'I'm waiting for the carrier right now. He said eleven and it's gone that.'

An oblong wooden crate had been propped against the wall. Beckoning Phil to take one end, they lifted off the lid. Inside it, and partially covered with straw, was the statue of an old man. Dressed in a long black robe with a close-fitting hat on its head, the silk material had rotted with age, like the velvet slippers on its feet, and lay in tatters. And where the garment fell away, the skin of its face and neck was coloured brown and scored with fine wrinkles. The whole thing seemed ready to fall to bits, except for the hands which remained white and unblemished.

Liz took a hurried step backwards, clinging tightly to her mother.

Concerned, Alison patted her hand. 'What is it?'

Liz shook her head. 'I'm not sure. I feel a bit funny. *Phil*, *don't* …' she exclaimed, her hand shooting out as though to stop him moving.

'Gosh, isn't it lifelike, Mr McFaddean?' Phil's shout of excitement drowned out his sister's soft voice. 'I bet it's ever so old.'

Liz gazed at her brother, surprised and distressed to discover that he couldn't even recognise something out of one of his own dreams. Far from running from the room at full tilt screaming, he leaned forwards wanting to examine it more closely. Liz let go the breath she'd been holding. Perhaps she was mistaken?

'It feels solid,' Phil exclaimed prodding the figure gently. 'I didn't expect that. It's not stone though, is it?'

'Shouldn't think so,' Tom McFadden swept aside a collection of carved figures and perched on the edge of his desk, idly rubbing the palm of his hand against the corner of the wood as if it itched. 'It's not heavy enough. Most likely some sort of wood … although, until we get it properly examined, I can't be sure what. Possibly resin?'

'Resin, Mr McFaddean? You said it was old.'

'It's possible, Dr Shaw, though I agree not very likely. The Chinese knew about resins centuries before the rest of us.'

'But you said it was found in Tibet?'

'On the border. That's right, I did.' Tom McFaddean smiled down at Phil who was eagerly studying the figure. 'The borders in that part of the world, Phil, are somewhat indefinite. You never know from one minute to the next if you are in India, Tibet, or Burma. Over the centuries they've changed quite a bit. In the north-east of India, around Arunachal Pradesh, there are tribes with Mongolian features.'

The statue had unusually long arms and fingers, the nail on its index finger almost four inches in length. Phil screwed up his face in disgust, wondering how people managed to write, or even eat, in those times. The face stared impassively, though every so often the glare from the florescent lights caught at the black-button eyes, making them sparkle as if alive.

'*What?*' he said, spotting his sister's anxious expression.

'Liz, you shivered. Mr McFaddean ...' Alison tucked her daughter's arm under her own. 'We should be going. Thank you.' She took a step towards the stairs.

The telephone sparked into life, its harsh ringing-tone making Liz jump. Tom McFaddean picked it up.

'Hang on a minute, Mrs Howard,' he answered the receptionist. Grabbing Alison's arm, he pulled her back. 'Don't go yet, Dr Shaw, there's something I wanted to show you first. It's the reason I invited you up here.'

She swung round frowning and tapped the dial on her watch.

He held up five fingers, mouthing the words *five minutes*. 'Tell him to come straight in,' he spoke into the phone. 'It's the carrier.' He replaced the receiver. 'He's on his way up now. Phil, give me hand to close the lid.'

Fascinated, Liz found her eyes drawn to the statue lying motionless in its box, convinced if she watched it long enough she would see it move. *Perhaps even sit up and climb out of its box.* She tried to recapture the picture taken from her brother's thoughts – but it had gone, the figure faded away.

The lid of the box dropped into place.

Tom McFaddean ferreted about in his desk, pulling out a large ball of coarse twine. Cutting off a length, he handed one end to Phil.

The whine of the approaching lift stopped and was replaced by the clatter of the gate crashing back.

'Mr McFaddean?' a voice called. 'You, there? *Cor-blimey*! *I didn't expect that*!'

The cheerful face of the carrier appeared at the top of the stairs. He took off his cap to scratch his head, whistling his astonishment at the groups of fighting men.

'Ferocious blighters, ain't they?' He nodded his head at the figure at the top of the stairs. 'Wouldn't like to come across him in a dark alley.'

'You get much worse than this at the British Museum.' Tom McFaddean signed the completed despatch-form on his desk and handed it over. 'I've seen them.'

The man replaced his cap, a haulier's logo emblazoned across its peak. 'More than I 'ave, guv'nor. Do the occasional job that's all, never bin inside.' He attached the sheet to his clipboard. 'Right! It says 'ere, one box and contents. That it?' He thumped the wooden crate with the toe of his boot.

Tom McFaddean grimaced and sprang to his feet. 'I'll give you a hand into the lift. It's not heavy. But it's *fragile*. Finished, Phil?'

Phil tied the last knot, pulling it tight. 'All yours.' He stood up out of the way.

Lifting the crate, the two men carefully manoeuvred it round the displays. Phil nudged Liz to watch the bulky figure of the carrier carefully side-stepping his way round the room. As he passed between the warriors he rolled his eyes nervously, obviously terrified of bumping into one, in case it was only pretending to be made of wax.

'It's been a long five minutes.' Alison pursed her lips, frowning.

Noticing his mother glance at her watch for the third time

41

in as many minutes, Phil pulled her arm down. 'It doesn't matter, Mum, we're on holiday, remember,' he whispered. 'Besides, you're always on about us experiencing new things.'

'If that's what this is.' Liz watched the crate vanish down the stairs, feeling the heavy sensation of menace beginning to lift. She smiled, suddenly feeling hugely better. 'When Mother said that, she wasn't talking about you learning how to tie reef knots.'

'They weren't reefs, they were grannies, clever clogs,' Phil retorted.

The lift gates rattled and the whining noise broke out again.

'Sorry about that.' Tom McFaddean called, coming back up the stairs. 'This way.'

A collection of black and white photographs were tucked under the eaves on the far wall to protect them from daylight. A few showed a tropical landscape with tall ferns and palm trees, although most were black and white stills of a small mountain village. Its houses, built of wood, had neatly tiled roofs, quite different in style from the Japanese house that Tom McFaddean had described. The rest were portraits of a tall man standing among a group of people, dressed in the traditional black cotton tunic and trousers of the villagers who lived in the mountains of Burma and Tibet.

'I promise you *these are quite friendly*.' Tom McFaddean grimaced, his scar bestowing the right side of his face with a mocking expression. 'I have to confess that chappie was a touch gruesome even for my taste. I'm glad it's gone. But since it was my father who built this collection, if you want someone to blame, blame him.'

The photographs were obviously old and, where they had been exposed to sun, faded into monotones of sepia. One of them was of young boy dressed similarly to the villagers; although the rest were undoubtedly Mr McFaddean senior at various stages of his life, always surrounded by people whose faces never changed from one photograph to another. The father appeared not dissimilar to his son, only his clothes and hair marked him out as a different generation; wearing a pith helmet and plus fours as if he was about to play a game of polo or golf. In the background, running water crashed down over rocks.

'Is that you?' Phil pointed to the small boy.

'Yes. I was probably around ten or eleven when that was taken.' Tom McFaddean indicated the villagers in the photo. 'Have you heard of the legend of the Javean, Dr Shaw?'

'No,' she replied tartly. 'Should I?' As if bored, she swung round staring back at the fighting men dotted round the room, their sword and battle axes glinting brightly in the fluorescent lighting.

Aware her mother had hated every minute of their visit and was desperate to leave, Liz took her arm. 'Can we watch a comedy at the pictures, otherwise I'll get nightmares too after all this violence,' she said loudly, hoping her brother would catch on.

Ignoring the hint, Phil continued to stare fixedly at the photos. 'Who were the Javean?'

'They were a race of warrior-magicians. You *must* have heard about them, Dr Shaw?'

'I told you. I spent a week in a hospital somewhere,' she snapped. 'Can't even remember where, it was that long ago. In any case I'm a scientist; I never bother with such things.'

Tom McFaddean regarded her intently, his eyes drilling into hers.

Liz felt the atmosphere change becoming tense, their mother staring rigidly at the hotelier, her face expressionless. Even Phil had noticed it, shifting uncomfortably from foot to foot.

'This particular legend came out of China and is hundreds of years old. The story goes that a powerful sorcerer used magic to try and overthrow the emperor.' Tom McFaddean kept his eyes trained on Dr Shaw. As if she couldn't be bothered to listen, she had moved away and was now examining a glass case full of jade ornaments, the polished stone worn smooth with age. 'According to the legend, the resulting war lasted one hundred years ...'

'Wow! Was there anyone left alive?'

'Surprisingly, yes, Phil. A group of warriors, called Javean, took on the fight and they won. The interesting thing about this story is that the evil magician couldn't raise an army of men willing to confront the emperor. Instead, he created an army of magical beasts – half-animal, half-bird...'

Liz saw her mother flinch, the arm resting on the glass case containing the small jade figurines absolutely rigid.

'Well, thank you, Mr McFaddean,' Alison interrupted loudly, withdrawing her attention from the jade pieces, 'for giving us this tour. But we *really must be going*. We only have today. As you know, we are returning home tonight and there's still a lot we want to do.' She held out her hand. 'Thank you,' her smile remained cold. 'It's been most interesting.'

'*Mu-um?*'

'No, Phil! We really must go if we want to catch the start of the film. We can walk up to the picture house at Notting Hill. A drop of rain won't hurt us.'

As she spoke, she herded the two children towards the stairs as if Tom McFaddean was the beast he'd been about to describe. He said nothing, only raising his hand when Phil glanced over his shoulder to say good-bye, a thoughtful expression on his face.

Back in their room, Phil rounded angrily on his mother. 'I wanted to hear that, Mum. It could have been my beast.'

'I doubt it very much, Phil.' Reaching into her suitcase, Alison tossed over a small travelling dictionary. 'If you search for the word chimera, spelled with a c-h not a k, you will find a description very like the one you gave me.'

'*Fire breathing monster, with the head of a lion, body of a goat and tail of a serpent,*' Phil read out. 'That's not a bit like it,' he protested.

'Possibly not.' She bustled about, rapidly tidying clothes into the waiting suitcase. 'But the Oxford dictionary gives only one version. Greek mythology contains dozens of examples, some of them very strange indeed. This was simply another version. As I told Mr McFaddean, I'm a scientist. I don't believe in myths. In any case,' she said, her tone of voice brooking no argument, 'we came here to stop your nightmares, not create new ones.'

Liz kept quiet, wishing her mother had waited just a little longer. Phil was right; it could have been his monster. Another minute and they'd have found out. Did their mother know that? Is that why she left in such a hurry? And what about the statue? Why didn't Phil recognise it?

'Phil, you know …' she began.

'Not now, Liz,' Alison snapped impatiently. She bent down to put on her outdoor shoes. 'Get your coats on and let's get out of here. I suggest we give Mr McFaddean a wide berth for the rest of the day.'

FIVE

The picture house in Notting Hill was a majestic, white-fronted building that resembled the prow of an ocean liner, a vast stained-glass window patterned in purples and green looming over the street. Smaller versions of the window had been sited at ground level, some already replaced with plain glass, despite being covered by a metal screen meant to deter boys from using them as target practice. There was an early matinee on a Monday and a queue had formed up outside, umbrellas shielding their owners from the rain while they waited for the doors to open. In a nearby street, workmen from the council were busily erecting rows of stalls for the market and covering them with green-striped plastic sheeting to keep them dry.

Liz wandered about admiring the gold-painted scrolls on the walls and the crystal chandeliers dangling from the ceiling, the lavish decorations reminding her of a film set. Elegantly long couches lined the walls and gold-rimmed cases displayed photographs of famous film stars, the black and white publicity shots arranged artistically across all four corners. And the carpet! Even Queen Elizabeth in Buckingham Palace couldn't have anything nicer than the red and gold swirls covering the floor.

She still felt troubled by her mother's anger. She rarely lost her temper, so what was it about Mr McFaddean that had so upset her? Wondering where her brother had vanished to, Liz spotted him outside on the steps. Oblivious to the commotion, as people flapped their umbrellas up and down to rid them of rain before entering the cinema, he was studying a picture of Alistair Sim, the main star of the St. Trinians' caper.

The cinema was busy and very noisy. A long line of people crowded round the glass-sided booth, impatiently waiting to buy tickets; pink and grey rectangles, like thick blotting paper, emerging from the machines as fast as the staff could take the money. On one side of the foyer, a crowd of children were besieging the confectionary counter. Their hands stretched out in the hope of being served first, they were pushing and shoving, uttering boisterous exclamations of: 'Watch it you, that was my foot,' and 'Please, miss, I'm next.'

'Liz, Phil. Upstairs,' their mother called, waving the pink tickets over her head.

Bursts of excited chatter came from the little groups of people as they drifted slowly up the stairs or made their way to the stalls. Hidden behind a pair of soundproof doors, these were guarded by an usherette, quick to pounce on the newly bought tickets and tear them in half. Like the foyer, the twin staircases that led up to the balcony had been designed to conjure up a magical atmosphere. Lit by gold-coloured wall lights, they circled the buttress on the ground floor. Shallow treads created a sensation of floating rather than walking, stronger and more magical at the end of the film, when the audience emerged still gripped in the enchantment of the celluloid reel.

Once inside the heavy doors, seats thumping down into place brought the audience back to earth long enough to remove their coats and open boxes of chocolate and sweets. The family had fortunately arrived in good time, the rows around them filling rapidly. After a few minutes, a massive chord announced the start of an organ recital. It swirled up out of the ground in front of the stage, launching into a medley of popular dance tunes that kept the feet tapping and held the audience spellbound throughout their long wait. Gasps of astonishment were followed by rapturous applause, as the lights eventually dimmed for the start of the film. With a final triumphant chord, the instrument descended below ground again, leaving usherettes with torches to guide latecomers to their seats.

By the time they emerged several hours later, blinking slightly in the daylight, the fine drizzle had ceased and the sun had dried the pavements. It was a little warmer too, although the days had grown both shorter and colder with the approach of winter.

'That was so smashing,' Liz giggled, 'especially the bit when Phil fell off his seat. The noise it made crashing back up!'

'You *would* think that funny,' he retorted. 'I didn't. The people behind spent the next half-hour poking me in the back every time I laughed, in case I'd done it on purpose. I wish we could have stayed on though, and watched it again,' he added wistfully.

'Another time,' Alison agreed, putting on her mackintosh. 'Coats on, you two.'

'But I'm still boiled,' Phil moaned.

'You don't have to do it up.'

Obediently, Liz shook out the creases in her coat, which she had tucked under her seat, the cinema very warm. Automatically, Alison stretched out an arm to help her.

'Honestly, Mother, I'm twelve not two,' she frowned. 'Don't you think it's about time you remembered I can use a knife and fork and put on my own coat?' She side-stepped her mother's hand about to ruffle her hair. 'Not in the street,' she hissed. 'It's so embarrassing.'

'Hurry up, you two. I'm starving, we didn't have lunch yet.'

'I noticed a Wimpy Bar over there, Phil. That do?'

'Yes! That's brilliant, thanks, Mum. What a super time we're having. I wish we could be on holiday always and not bother ever going to school.' He caught his mother's frown and smiled innocently. 'Just joking. So, Liz, which was your favourite bit, besides me?' He fell into step with his sister.

'Mine was definitely the headmaster. The expression on his face!'

Laughing and joking, brother and sister linked arms to cross the road, heading for the red façade of the restaurant, leaving their mother to follow.

The market was now in full swing and its passageways had become congested with old furniture; tatty-old armchairs, still hopeful of finding an owner who loved recovering things, deckchairs with ripped canvas seats, and brass gongs on broken stands. Remnants of curtain fabric had been piled high on a trestle table, waiting for customers who lived in small houses with even smaller windows. A heap of lace and velvet squares had been wedged against the rolls to stop them spilling off onto the ground.

Fascinated by their array of colours, Liz trailed her fingers over the pile pulling out a length of dark ochre velvet with a long fringe. She held it up. 'What this?'

'It's an antimacassar,' her mother said.

Liz pulled a face. 'A *what*?'

'Antimacassar. Dreadful word, I know. They were used a lot in Victorian times. Still are, especially since men took to using hair grease – Brylcream and the like. They stop chair backs getting dirty.' Alison began to laugh, exactly as Liz had done a few minutes earlier. '*And that's an aspidistra,*' she spluttered, pointing to a spiky, long-leafed plant, poking out from a brass coal scuttle.

'*Mum!*'

'Honestly, Phil, I'm not making it up. Have you never heard the word before?' she said, aware that Phil was rapidly becoming a keen gardener under Mrs Lucy's watchful eye, and now possessed his own little plot for growing vegetables.

'I promise you, it's true. My grandma used to have one. What with that, privet hedges full of dust, and being forced to sit still and not talk, how I hated visiting her. I used to sit there thinking she looked exactly like her plant – all spiky. Thank goodness that's all changed; it's spider plants today.'

She nodded in a friendly fashion at a large-busted lady from Jamaica, who was selling guava jelly, tamarind balls and sorrel juice, the trailing-tendrils of a green and white striped spider plant decorating one corner of her little stall. Next door, an Indian gentleman was selling poppadums and spices, the acrid scent of cardamom, turmeric and curry powder filling the air – the accents of the two stallholders outstripped by a barrage of cockney pouring in from all sides.

'Come on, Mum, I'm hungry.'

Dragging his mother out of the market, Phil made a bee-line for the burger bar. A few minutes later, carrying their food on brown plastic trays, they climbed up onto high stools next to a narrow red counter built across the window; most families preferring the Formica-topped tables with their black plastic chairs.

'Brilliant,' Phil muttered. He leaned down propping his empty tray up against the wall. 'Tall stools are so much nicer.'

'But not as comfortable,' Liz complained, curling her feet round the legs of the high stool to stop herself slipping off.

'I do love cheeseburgers.' Alison reached for a giant-sized plastic tomato sitting on the counter, a hollow stalk poking out between a couple of leaves. 'If darling Lucy has a single fault …'

'Mu-um!' exclaimed Phil.

'I only said *if*, Phil … that's her refusal to let us have tomato sauce in the house.' She squeezed a large dollop of the famous ketchup onto the sizzling meat of her burger.

The Wimpy Bar proved the perfect spot for watching the world go by and, straight after eating, Liz and Phil sped out into the market, leaving their mother to enjoy her cup of tea in peace. Spotting a stall selling gem stones, Liz ran over leaving Phil to follow.

The stall-keeper watched the girl heading in his direction with mixed emotions. Business so far that day had been brisk and he had been gasping for a cup of tea for at least half an hour. Reluctant to lose even one customer, even though it was highly unlikely the girl wanted to buy anything, he called over to the lad who was manning the stall next door.

'Keep an eye for ten minutes while I get meself a cup 'a char to wet me whistle. Everything on the stall, five and ten bob – okay.'

Overhearing, Phil said, 'Ten shillings – that's expensive, Liz.'

'I thought we might buy Mother something for her birthday. It's on Wednesday, remember?' Liz trailed her fingers slowly through a necklace made of coloured stone, which was hanging from a wooden rail. The long string caught the rays of sun, darting showers of rainbow-coloured light over the stall.

'Good idea, but not sparkly. You know Mum, she'd hate that.'

Reluctantly, Liz withdrew her hand letting the gently swaying rainbow fade away.

'So what?'

Jimbo, whose real name was James Bower, helped out on his dad's fruit and veg stall every chance he could. He hated school. He could read, write, and add up, and had already decided to follow in his father's footsteps and take a stall in the local market, so what was the point in learning French or anything else for that matter. Besides, he was nearly fourteen and quite old enough to get a job. So far he hadn't paid much attention to the boy and girl by the jewellery stall, except to register they weren't English. Not that that bothered him; his best friend, next door in Wandsworth, came from Jamaica. He was more interested in keeping an eye on two urchins, not a day over seven, who were lingering near the apples at the front of his stall, their eyes constantly flashing towards Jimbo to check if he was watching.

'She likes green and it would go with her new suit,' Phil volunteered.

'Green's not popular.' Jimbo broke into the conversation, still keeping a wary eye on the two small boys. 'Mr Smith says, people think it's unlucky.' He jerked his head in the direction of the van selling tea. 'He keeps the green stones under the counter. See!'

He fished under the folds of the cloth covering the wooden counter. Sensing his attention was elsewhere, the two small boys instantly filched a couple of apples, quickly darting behind a neighbouring stall before Jimbo could raise his head again. In his hands were half-a-dozen small boxes. He lifted their lids, displaying the opaque green-blue stones perched on a bed of cotton wool. A miniature Buddha blinked up at them, while a dolphin tried to swim out of its box and a Japanese geisha knelt on the ground, her hands raised as if pleading or praying.

'I like this one.'

Phil pointed to a circular stone shaped like a medallion. Within a circle of jade, narrow bands of silver were linked to a single bird. He picked it up, feeling its weight on the palm of his hand, noticing that it was meant to be worn round the neck, a neat hole punched through the rim. He handed it to his sister.

'Mum'd like that.'

Liz fingered the smooth stone, admiring the way the silver bands were moulded over the outer edge; five of them like the points of a pentagon. It was beautifully carved, the feathers on the bird's plumage crisp, every detail standing out, its beak sharply hooked. 'It reminds me of an eagle.' She flipped it over, both sides of the jade bird identical.

Jimbo shrugged. 'Wouldn't know one if I saw one,' he admitted.

A doubtful expression crossed his face. Raising his head, he checked across the market for the stall-keeper. He was nowhere in sight.

'I know he said ten bob but these look a bit special. I'll have to charge more.'

'How much more?' Phil squeaked in alarm.

'Fifteen bob – is that too much?'

'It's a bit steep.'

Liz slapped his hand. 'Don't be so mean. It's for Mother, remember. Besides, she'd really like this.'

Phil gave a reluctant nod and, fishing in the pocket of his duffle coat, pulled out a handful of coins.

'If you say so. But I've only got seven shillings and some coppers. I spent the rest on the film.' He trawled through the little pile of coins on his palm. 'What have you got?'

Liz checked her purse. 'Almost eight shillings. Remember, we have to buy a card.' She counted the coppers on her brother's outstretched hand and smiled wistfully at Jimbo. 'I don't suppose you'd let us off sixpence so I can buy one. It's for our mother.'

'Well, miss, as it's you. Go on then. Fourteen and sixpence and I'll throw in the box. Can't say fairer than that, can I?'

Liz beamed and handed over the coins. 'People in London are so nice,' she smiled. 'Thank you. Come on, Phil, let's buy her card now, then we won't need to bother after school tomorrow.'

Waving goodbye, they dived across the market to a stall where stationery and cards were being sold and quickly picked one out, hoping their mother hadn't spotted them through the window of the burger bar and guessed what they'd been up to.

Alison, having finished a second cup of tea, wandered out into the market – the sun warming the air. Spotting two familiar figures in duffle coats in front of a stall selling toys, she strolled in their direction. As usual Liz and Phil appeared to be arguing and she guessed Phil wanted to blow his pocket money on yet more Meccano, his bedroom cupboard already bulging, and Liz was trying to convince him to wait until after his birthday.

She was right. As she came within ear shot, it was to hear Liz's voice.

'Honestly, Phil, you know Mrs Lucy always gets you a football annual or Meccano.'

'But I'd like to buy something to remind me of this trip.'

'You haven't got any money left and you can't ask Mother.'

'No, you certainly can't.'

Phil swung round grinning. 'Hi, Mum. How long have you been standing there? Gosh, there's Mr McFaddean.' He raised his arm. 'Hi!' he called.

'*Phil*!'

Phil gave a wry smile. 'Sorry, I forgot.'

The hotelier nodded but didn't come over, staring round the market as if seeking something.

'No harm done. Are you coming with me, Liz, I'm off to buy a bag? Phil can stay here if he wants and decide which piece he'd like us to buy for his birthday.'

Alison waved her arm vaguely over the counter with its stack of small cartons, containing steel rods, nuts and bolts, pictures of the finished product displayed in brilliant colour on both front and back. 'But that's all you can do, Phil.' She glared at him over her glasses. 'You have a birthday in a month – and a special one.'

'I haven't got any money anyway, Mum. That reminds me.' Phil dropped into step beside his mother. 'I know my birthday's December the first, but it never feels right somehow. I wondered if this year I could postpone it and celebrate on Christmas Day, instead.'

'Not a chance,' Alison responded cheerfully. 'Ah, here's the bag stall.'

'Dr Shaw?'

Liz felt her mother tense up, her arm go completely rigid. It reminded her of the lioness they'd seen in the newsreel protecting its cubs.

Alison swung round on her heel, her face stony.

'I was hoping to bump into you,' Tom McFaddean said, his tone serious. 'I was just having a chat with a pal of mine.'

He pointed to the tea van, where a burly individual was drinking a cup of tea. Liz glanced across, recognising the man from the gem stall.

'We have this understanding that if he buys any pieces of jade, he'll offer them to me first as I collect them.'

'Do you collect *everything*, Mr McFaddean?'

The sarcasm in Alison's voice met its mark and his tanned skin flushed.

'Not everything, no,' he said, adding cautiously, 'but jade, yes. Mr Smith said they sold a piece to a couple of kids a few minutes ago. I wondered if it was you. If so, I'd like to buy it.'

Liz caught her brother's eye and shook her head warningly.

Phil smiled. 'Can't help there.' He glanced over to the tea van. 'Never seen him before in my life. In any case, I'm more interested in Meccano. I wanted to buy some but Mum told me I'd got to wait till my birthday.'

'When is that?'

'*Oh, for goodness sake, Phil*, Mr McFaddean doesn't want to know about your problems,' Alison snapped, her voice dripping venom. 'Pieces of steel rod won't be of interest to a man who collects such impressive artefacts.'

Feeling uncomfortable, Liz fixed her gaze on the ground. Her mother was never rude, what was it about the hotelier she disliked so much?

'*Psst?*'

She glanced over her shoulder, surprised to find the boy who had sold her the jade bird peering round the corner of the bag stall. Relieved to get away from the angry vibrations spiralling up from her mother, she stepped out of the little group. 'What is it?' she whispered.

''Ere, thought you ought to know. There ain't 'alf been a ter-do over that stone.'

'Did you get into trouble about the price?' Liz said anxiously. 'I'm ever so sorry.'

'Nah! He was pleased as punch about that. No, it was this geezer. A minute ago. Said I 'ad a piece 'a jade with a bird on and 'e wanted it.'

Liz pointed to where Mr McFaddean was still talking with her mother and Phil.

'Not 'im,' Jimbo blurted out 'This geezer was foreign. An' covered all over in a big coat like he worked in a ware'ouse. 'E 'ad funny eyes too ... *oh, I don't mean no disrespect, miss.*'

'None taken,' Liz smiled. 'Anyway, I'm as English as you. About this man?' she said, trying not to sound concerned.

'Right weird 'e was,' Jimbo gabbled on hastily. Liz knew he felt embarrassed at his gaff. It didn't really matter. She and Phil had got used to being stared at years ago. There was a Chinese restaurant in Salisbury but, apart from that, the entire population of the Cathedral city had to be English through and through

'Had this long nail,' Jimbo confided. 'Kept scratchin' it on the cloth coverin' the stall. You know like chalk on a blackboard makes yer teeth go funny? Well, like that. Proper gave me the wigwams, I can tell ye.'

Recognising the description, Liz began to tremble. She tucked her hands out of sight. 'So what did you tell him?' she said, trying to keep her voice calm.

Jimbo grinned and wiped his nose on his sleeve. 'Told 'im, someone 'ad bought it and described that bloke.' He indicated Tom McFaddean. 'I mean, it could well 'ave bin 'im, 'e's always 'ob-nobbin' with Mr Smith.'

'Liz?' Her mother called, her tone frosty.

'Thanks.' Liz patted Jimbo on the arm, the sleeve of his jacket shiny with wear.

The boy touched his cap. 'You're welcome, miss.' He disappeared round the corner of the stall.

'Do excuse us, Mr McFaddean, but I really must get to Kensington before the shops close. And hadn't you better continue your search for those children? Goodbye.'

Almost frog-marching her children out of the market, Alison strode off towards the bus stop in the high street, the pavements bustling with afternoon shoppers.

'Mu-um, slow down. Whatever's got into you to-day?'

'*Nothing*! I don't like that man. But that still doesn't excuse your lie, does it, Philip?'

SIX

No one talked much on the journey home. Alison read the newspaper, which she'd not bothered with over the weekend. 'We were having such fun,' she remarked, before becoming so immersed it would have taken a volcano erupting to gain her attention.

Thankfully they'd not bumped into Mr McFaddean again. Mrs Howard, the very pleasant receptionist, had wished them bon voyage, saying she hoped they would return for another visit soon.

'It would have been so embarrassing if he had been there,' Liz whispered across the carriage. 'I'm positive he guessed. Did you notice the way he stared at us? It was like his eyes were drilling right into our brain.'

'You're imagining it,' Phil scoffed. 'I thought he was great.' He buried his head in a copy of Beano he'd picked up at the station with the last of his pocket money. 'I hated lying to him.' He flicked his head in the direction of their mother, making it clear he knew she was waiting for one of them to confess, although she'd not mentioned the subject again.

It was late by the time they arrived back in Salisbury, the train delayed for half an hour by a signals' failure at Waterloo. Phil, eager to discover what was happening, had lowered the strap on the carriage window and stuck his head out, leaping back as an oncoming train rushed past, leaving black tendrils of soot on the front of his beige duffle coat. Quickly brushing them off, he pulled up the window, fixing the leather strap back into place, hoping his mother wouldn't notice the smear of black on the lapel.

After a quick supper, worried their mother would start on about the jade piece again, Phil and Liz rushed upstairs saying they were tired and would have a bath and go to bed.

Now they were both curled up on Liz's bed, staring at the small box lying on the counterpane as if it was an explosive device.

'I might be dim but even I can see there's something wrong.' Phil peered closely at his sister's face, worry lines furrowing her forehead.

'I've been trying to tell you all day. I couldn't believe when you didn't recognise it.'

'Recognise what?'

Liz stretched out a hand, timidly touching her brother on the arm. 'Promise you won't get all huffy?'

'How can I promise that, if I don't know what you're going to say,' Phil retorted indignantly. 'Tell me.'

'Well, you know how we finish each other's sentences,' Liz launched into her story.

'Yes, so?'

'Well, recently I've found I can see into your thoughts,' she admitted, gabbling the final words of the sentence as if hoping Phil wouldn't pay them any attention.

'*See?*'

'Not all the time,' she added hastily. 'Like right now, I haven't a clue what you're thinking. So far, it only happens when you're troubled about something. At first, the images were a bit shaky and I passed them off as imagination. But, recently,' she said, 'I've seen things you haven't told me about … at least, not in detail. Like those monsters. You only said they were animals … nothing more.' Liz stared down at the bedspread, her finger aimlessly drawing patterns on it. 'The other night, when you were telling mother about your nightmares, I saw this dark figure. It tried to grab me. I was so scared.' Her tone changed as she tried to convey exactly how frightened the figure had made her. 'And that statue in Mr McFaddean's office, the one he sent off to the British Museum, it was the one from your nightmare, except in my thoughts it was alive.'

'I don't …'

'There's more.' Liz raised her head, holding her hand in the air like a policeman. 'And this is *really* scary. I didn't get a chance to tell you in the train because mother was listening. In the market, when you were talking to Mr McFaddean, that boy Jimbo appeared. He said he'd come to warn us.'

'Warn us! About what?'

'That someone strange was asking about the jade. A foreigner.' She repeated what Jimbo had said, describing the man in the long black coat, his nail restlessly scratching the cloth on the table top. 'Jimbo said it made him squirm, like when you watch Mrs Lucy wringing out cotton. It sets your teeth on edge.'

She lapsed into silence, hoping her brother wouldn't scoff. Although, even to her, it sounded like something out of a book – pure fiction.

'You can read my dreams – honestly?' Phil said, after a long silence.

'Yes,' she sighed, relieved he'd taken her seriously. 'That's how I saw the animal.'

'Oh, so that's why, I did wonder. It's good to know I'm not going barmy.' Phil sat silently, his fingers counting in the air as if he was working something out. 'So everything I think – you think the same?'

'No, Phil, I told you, it only seems to happen when you're worried or scared. That's why I couldn't understand you not recognising the figure.'

'But I never saw it,' he protested. 'That had to be your imagination.'

'You *really* didn't recognise the statue?'

'No, course I didn't. I thought it ...' He shrugged, 'A bit scary but fascinating – like those samurai.'

'But what about the man in the market, asking about the jade?'

Phil scratched his head. 'Mmm! Forgot about him. Could be a coincidence, except ...'

'Except what?' his sister pounced on the word.

'Mr McFaddean asking about it too,' he admitted a little reluctantly. He lifted the lid off the little box. 'Do you think it's valuable? That would explain why they both wanted it. How can we find out?'

Liz shrugged. 'No idea.'

Phil's tone changed suddenly becoming indignant. '*So how did Mum know I was lying?*'

'You've got this special smile.'

Phil leapt to his feet and rushed over to the mirror examining his reflection. 'What special smile?' he said, trying different expressions.

'Not like that,' Liz retorted. 'It's more like you've just eaten a large box of chocolates and are about to be sick.' She stared at the face gazing back at her and shook her head. 'Don't bother with it now, there's no time. Mother will up in a minute and we need to decide what we're going to do. We can't give her this, it's tainted – she'd hate it.'

Phil glowered at his sister through the mirror. 'It's all your fault. Why did you make me lie?'

'I didn't want him to have it.'

'Why ever not?' He flopped moodily back down on the bed. 'We can't keep it and Mum'll kill us when we do own up. You know what she's like about fibbing.'

'But she lied about never visiting the Far East,' Liz argued. 'She's been there a couple of times.'

'Grown-ups are different,' Phil said, pulling a face. 'Haven't you ever noticed they operate under different rules? Kids have to tell the truth but, as soon as you're an adult, you can tell as many porkies as you like. Doesn't seem very fair, does it?' he added bitterly. 'We'll have to get her something else.' He nodded at the small box. 'You'd better do it straight after school tomorrow. I can't, I've got football training.'

'And I've got gymnastics.' Liz grimaced accepting the inevitable. 'All right, since it was my fault I'll pop out at lunch time.' She reached for her money box, a tin with a round lid and a slot cut in it, painted red like a letterbox. 'I was saving this for Christmas.'

At that moment, they heard footsteps on the landing. Hastily, Phil shoved the little jewellery box into his sister's satchel.

Their mother's head poked round the door. 'I thought you were going straight to bed?'

'We are.' Liz flushed guiltily, snatching her hand back. 'We were just saying what a marvellous weekend. Thank you.'

'I know the conference was a bit boring ...'

'Not really,' Phil said loyally, adding, 'Besides we were awfully proud when everyone clapped you.'

Alison laughed. 'Go along now or you'll be tired in the morning.'

Phil raised his eyebrows, staring intently at his sister from behind their mother's back.

Tomorrow, she mouthed.

SEVEN

Liz gazed through the brightly lit bus window at the dark streets, a light drizzle beginning to dampen the air. 'I hate it when the hour goes back. It's like the sun runs away leaving everything wet and miserable.'

'I never noticed it this year,' Phil said. 'Well, you wouldn't in London, would you? What with all those neon signs in Piccadilly, it was as bright as day. Besides, we were having too much fun. Even when it was dark, there were loads of people about.'

Liz gazed out at the empty pavements, only the odd person waiting for a bus and a man walking his dog to be seen. Quite different from London with its theatres and cinemas, hundreds of people milling about when the theatres emptied at ten o'clock at night.

It wasn't late but putting the clocks back to wintertime had brought darkness down very early. By the time football training had finished and Phil had showered, making his way to school reception where Liz was waiting for him, it was already dusk. Now it was fully dark, with the moon not yet risen and the evening star invisible behind a heavy pall of swirling cloud.

'Did you get Mum something?'

Liz took out a paper bag showing him the spectacle case she had bought, the outside covered in fabric, prettily patterned in green and blue stripes.

'It only cost four shillings but I couldn't think of anything else. It's nice; Mother will love it.'

Quickly folding up the bag, she pushed it back into her satchel, leaving Phil to jump up and ring the bell for their stop.

It wasn't a very long journey from their school, only a couple of miles, and had it been summer Alison would have been quite happy for them to walk. At the outset, the bus route followed the main road, with streets of houses packing the pavements on both sides, accompanied by the steady hum of traffic both in and out of the small cathedral city. Crossing the wide bridge over the river, there, abruptly, the houses petered out. For a short distance the river ran alongside the road, its far bank a dense woodland, where wild primroses and violets had seeded among the trees. In spring, these carpeted the ground in swathes of delicate colour. On the near side, a strip of waste ground had been left between the river and the road, which was flooded every time the river burst its banks. It was overgrown with brambles and stumps of rotting trees, and remained empty and brown even in spring.

'It's not that I worry about anything happening to you,' Alison explained. 'But that stretch of road isn't very nice at the best of times and when it's dark, I'd prefer you to take the bus and always come home together.'

'Mrs Lucy worries.'

Alison laughed. 'To Mrs Lucy, Phil, you two are the most precious objects in the world. She's always thought of you as her own. If I'd allowed it, she'd have moved in lock, stock and barrel. You might be different from me,' she said reverting to her original theme, 'but I always found darkness very spooky. As a child, I regularly checked under my bed before I climbed in. Even then, I was scared stiff and slept with my head under the blankets. My mother said it was a wonder I didn't suffocate. I may be a scientist and understand how the brain can play tricks but I still see gruesome shadows lurking behind every tree.'

The bus pulled away continuing its journey, taking with it their only source of light and company. The narrow road leading up to their small village, with its long parade of houses, was shadowy and dark and tall chestnut trees overhung the footpath. Alternating bands of brightness and shadow flowed along the pavement, where the glass globes of the street lamps had become tangled in the branches. The fierce autumn winds had already stripped the trees of their leave and gleaming russet-coloured pools lay heaped across both gutters.

Behind them, a string of amber-coloured lights floated in the air showing the location of the main road, but the glass-covered bus shelter was no longer visible. The stillness of the early night was broken by a distant engine and a car sped past, silence instantly falling again.

'I don't remember it ever being this dark, Phil.'

'That's because the hour's gone back,' Phil reminded his sister. Keeping one foot on the pavement, he dragged the other through the dry leaves making a harsh rustling sound. 'You can't be scared? Thought that was just Mum and me.'

'I'm not. I was just saying – *it's dark.*'

Phil stared round, catching sight of the lamppost on the far side of the road, its light flickering on and off. A faint gleam of light flared briefly before being extinguished.

'Street light's out, that's why. It'll stay like that for ages before the council gets round to fixing it,' he grumbled. He glanced up at the sky, thick clouds scudding past in the blustery wind. 'No stars either. *What's that?*'

The sound of pattering footsteps came from the pavement behind them. Spinning on his heel, he caught sight of a dark shape slinking into the hedgerow.

'Did you see?' his voice cracked nervously.

Liz stared into the now empty darkness, a dense thicket of hazel and ivy filling the space between trunks of taller trees. 'I expect it was a cat.'

'Not possible. It was far too big.'

Liz shrugged. 'A dog then. I didn't catch more than a glimpse.'

Phil caught at his sister's hand. The darkness had expanded his pupils, giving him a frightened expression. 'It was bigger than a dog,' he insisted, his voice dropped to a whisper. 'I saw claws – like my monster had.'

'That's ridiculous, Phil. Stop it!' Liz said sharply. 'You're letting your imagination run away with you. Your nightmares have stopped, remember.' She tried to make her voice reassuring. 'Don't start seeing things now. Come on,' she began walking again. 'Let's get home. If it was anything, it was a dog. And, if it wasn't that, it was young Fred from next door playing Indians and trying to scare us.'

The thought had only just occurred to her, but Fred and his tricks had to be a distinct possibility. He might only be eleven, but he was still considered by most of the residents in the small village to be a holy terror.

One time, the small boy had crept into their house and, despite the housekeeper's watchful eye, had removed the skeleton that hung in Alison's study. Phil and Liz still didn't know how he had managed it, because Mrs Lucy had eyes in the back of her head. Whenever they tried to hide things from her, she always found out. Fred had carried it into the village street and, late at night when no one was about, had hung it from the sign outside the fish and chip shop. According to the local bobby, it had dangled there all night, 'in a most life-like manner with the wind rattling its bones something chronic.'

Since it was the only takeaway in the small village, quite half the adult population had arrived on his parents' doorstep to complain. Only the children had sided with Fred, saying it served the chippie right. And, if he didn't want the villagers to starve to death, he ought to make his portions bigger. Alison, who had found the whole incident rather amusing and sympathised with the younger members of the population, now kept the offending object locked away in a cupboard, in case Fred should ever become tempted again.

'I don't know why I'm so freaked out by this dream,' Phil said, increasing his pace slightly to keep up with Liz's hurrying footsteps. 'You know me, I don't usually get scared.'

'Come off it, Phil,' Liz scoffed. 'Not get scared? That

Quatermass thing we watched on television at the hotel – you spent half the time hiding behind the sofa.'

'But not like this, Liz,' Phil argued. 'I went to bed all right, didn't I? When I was having those nightmares I was too terrified even to close my eyes. And now it's got me jumping at shadows.'

'Don't ask me to explain it,' Liz shook her head. 'I can't. It's one of those mysteries.'

There came a sudden disturbance of air and something moved in the hedgerow. Claws flashed in the dim light and Liz sprang backwards. She stumbled, treading heavily on her brother's foot. It had to have hurt, she was wearing her school shoes with rigid leather soles and heels, but Phil seemed unaware, his eyes fixed on the hedgerow. A sudden burst of wind fluttered the branches overlapping the nearby lamppost and making the shadows shift. Liz caught sight of two beady eyes protruding from a furry face, pointed ears and a short snout. Then the light moved away in the swirling wind to be replaced by darkness. There was a snuffling noise. The creature leapt from the hedgerow, its claws raking the air to reach her eyes. Instinctively, she raised her free hand to ward it off. In the same moment Phil grabbed her, pulling her back out of harm's way. There was an explosion of green light and a sudden pain in her hand as if it had been caught in the blast. The pool of light moved again as the wind eddied, tearing aside the thick canopy, and a gentle shower of ash drifted down onto the road.

Liz reeled and grabbed at her left hand, nursing it against the lapel on her coat. She laughed shakily.

'That had to be someone playing a trick and throwing fireworks. How stupid. I've burned myself.'

Phil took a step forward. 'Well, I'm going to find out who,' he said, anger taking control. 'What a crazy thing to do. You could have been badly hurt and *not* just your hand.'

Liz grabbed his arm. 'No, Phil, leave it,' she begged. 'I want to get home. Let's do it in the daylight.'

A car swung round the corner, noisily changing-down to

tackle the slope. It headed towards them, its headlights illuminating the scene brightly. The two youngsters turned, staring like terrified rabbits, and it screeched to a halt.

'Liz? Phil?'

'Mother!' Liz let out a shriek of relieved delight. '*You're driving a car.*'

Alison laughed. She opened the passenger door for them to climb in, pulling the seat forward for Phil to get into the back.

'It's my birthday present to myself. My very own Ford Anglia. It's too dark to see but it's pale blue and I *love* it. I drove it all the way home from the garage,' she boasted. 'Bit scary, I can tell you – but I made it.'

Liz glanced back at her brother. As white as a sheet, he was craning forward gripping the passenger seat tightly – obviously still preoccupied with trying to work out what had attacked them. Behind her the dense undergrowth seemed deserted. Nothing moved. No sign of Fred either, hurrying home after playing a successful trick.

Houses came quickly into view on both sides of the street. Alison slowed and was about to indicate, when she spotted the police car parked outside their house. With her bumper almost scraping the kerb, she screeched to a halt, the car stalling with the force of her foot hitting the brake.

On the doorstep, two men, dressed in the navy-blue uniform of the local constabulary, were talking to Mrs Lucy. Both were bare headed, their helmets politely removed and tucked under their arm.

'What's happened?' Alison gasped. Opening the car door, she leapt out in time to hear the housekeeper say, 'Here she is now.'

Forgetting about her new birthday present, she pelted up the driveway. Grabbing her mother's bag, Liz followed, leaving Phil to remove the keys from the ignition.

'What's going on?'

'Oh, Dr Shaw, thank goodness you're home. We had a ...'

'That's all right, Mrs Paluski,' the taller of the two men broke in. He held up his hand to arrest the flow of words spilling from the housekeeper. 'We'll take it from here. Now, Dr Shaw, we don't want you getting upset.' His voice sounded theatrical, as if he had practised how to break bad news to people, and he patted Alison gently on the shoulder.

She shrugged his hand away. 'I'll be getting *very* upset if someone doesn't hurry up and tell me what's going on,' she stormed, 'and why I've got two policemen ...' She swung round on her heel, suddenly noticing the second of the two men and smiled automatically. 'Oh, good evening, Constable Barnes,' she said, her voice quite calm again. 'I didn't recognise you in the dark.'

'Good evening, miss.'

Constable Barnes was a big, friendly man, whose well-padded shape was always much in demand at Christmas time, when a volunteer was needed to play Santa Claus at the old folks home.

'This is Sergeant Fisher,' he explained, indicating the man who had spoken first. 'He's recently come down from central station to take over our little patch.'

'So, Doctor,' the sergeant took up the tale again. 'You've had a burglary.'

'In broad daylight too, Dr Shaw,' Mrs Lucy sniffed.

'I think you had better both come in. Phil?' Alison said, suddenly noticing the keys in her son's hand. 'Would you be a dear and lock the car. Oh, thank you, Liz, you've brought my bag. How kind.'

'I suggest starting upstairs, miss,' Constable Barnes nodded towards the staircase as if apologising. 'Then, if it becomes too upsetting, you can come down and have a cup of tea, and do the rest when you feel better.'

Alison brushed past the two policemen and, stopping only to glance into the study and living room, headed for the stairs with Liz in hot pursuit. Hastily, Mrs Lucy pressed herself into the hat stand to avoid being trampled on in the rush.

'Very upsetting.' Sergeant Fisher said to the ceiling. 'It makes me wonder sometimes.'

Leaving their helmets on the hat stand, he and Constable Barnes, in single file, mounted the stairs, following the hurrying figures. They used exactly the same pace as they did when patrolling the streets, a steady plod guaranteed to cover two miles every hour – and standard police policy – convinced they got to where they were going pretty much the same time as people who always dashed everywhere.

Stopping only long enough to peek into her brother's room, Liz ran along the landing to her own. Drawers lay on the ground, their contents spilled onto the carpet, her clothes and shoes pulled from the wardrobe. Leaving her door ajar, she joined the little group gathered outside Phil's room, staring at the chaos. No one said anything, simply turning and moving silently towards the front bedroom where Alison slept.

Both bedrooms had been torn apart. Every drawer systematically dumped on the floor and every shelf swept clear of its contents. Even the beds had not escaped; sheets and pillows had been tossed onto the floor, the mattress pulled away from its base and left leaning against the bed frame.

'Whoever would do such a crazy thing?' Liz put her arm round her mother, who was gazing at the chaos a bewildered expression on her face.

They heard Phil's footsteps on the stairs. He wandered in, his face a mask of horrified shock. 'Are they all like this?'

'Mine's not as bad,' Liz said.

Mrs Lucy sniffed. 'The study's the worst. They didn't touch the kitchen otherwise I'd have seen it straight off.'

Alison said in a shaky voice, 'What happened?'

'I came back as usual this afternoon to fix your tea.' Mrs Lucy stared round defiantly, as much to say it wasn't her job to check upstairs for burglars. 'I was doing some cooking in the kitchen when I heard footsteps overhead in Liz's room. I guessed right off it had to be a burglar, so I tip-toed into the study to ring the police. That's when I saw the mess.'

Sergeant Fisher coughed. 'Redoubtable woman, Mrs Paluski … though, by rights, she should have waited for us. Decided to tackle the burglar herself and came up here armed with only a frying pan.'

'Good as a truncheon any day. If you get hit with that, you don't get up in a hurry,' Mrs Lucy boasted. 'He was in Liz's room. Didn't half give me a fright, I can tell you. I'm ashamed to say I screamed. That scared him good and proper and he ran out of the house then. I heard the front door slam behind him.'

'What was he like?'

'That's the strange thing, Dr Shaw. I don't remember.'

'Shock, ma'am,' Sergeant Fisher explained good-naturedly. 'Seen it many a time. Takes people like that, but she'll remember after a few days.'

The housekeeper burst into noisy tears. 'I know you're hungry but I haven't done a thing about tea. I've been too upset.'

'There, there, Lucy.' Alison comforted the older woman and, putting her arm round her, led the way back along the landing. Sergeant Fisher followed closely as if they were suspects he didn't want to escape. 'Come along with me. We'll get you a nice cup of tea. I can always get supper later.'

Phil flopped down on the stool next to his mother's dressing table, his head propped in his hands, and stared blankly into space. 'As if it isn't bad enough getting burgled,' he muttered after a bit. 'Now we've got Mum cooking supper. If we're lucky it'll be cheese on burned toast.'

Liz erupted into giggles. Constable Barnes gazed at her in astonishment, his eyebrows drawn together in a disapproving frown. He gave a small reproachful cough.

'It's the shock. I always giggle,' Liz hastily explained, aware the policeman would think her laughter unseemly on such a serious occasion. 'Can we tidy up?' she added, hoping to make up for her shocking behaviour. *But it was so funny.* Phil's room would take absolute ages to get tidy again, and all he was worried about was their mother cooking supper. Although, to be fair, he was right. Put a piece of toast in her hand and it was guaranteed she'd burn it.

Constable Barnes nodded. 'But if I were you, Miss Elizabeth,' he said, sounding concerned. 'I would go downstairs and get some sweet tea in you. It's very good for shock.'

'Not until we've sorted the beds.' Collecting the sheets and blankets, Liz dropped them onto a chair. She picked up the mattress, which had slumped down on one side like a drunk leaning against a wall. 'Here, Phil, grab hold.'

'I'll give you a hand, Miss Elizabeth.' Constable Barnes lifted the mattress back onto its base, as if it was of no more bother than a bag of potatoes, and squared it off. 'But, before you do anything else, we need a list of what's missing.'

'I know, but it's such a mess we'll never know what's gone unless we tidy up a bit, first.'

'Mrs Paluski had a quick look,' Constable Barnes continued in his steady way. 'She doesn't think they've taken anything.' He moved his head slowly from side to side as if he was watching a game of tennis. 'That can't be right, burglars are always after something.'

'I agree,' Phil chimed in. 'But only by putting everything back can we discover what's gone. Come on, Liz. Let's do your room first. We can help Mum later with hers.'

After performing the same trick with the mattress in Phil's room, Constable Barnes headed downstairs, where the faint chink of teaspoons against china cups could be heard.

Phil closed his door on the mess, walking down the corridor to Liz's room.

'You got off lightly.' Collecting a little heap of jumpers and cardigans, he passed them over to his sister. Then, kneeling down, gathered up the contents of her desk drawer, which were spread over the carpet. 'What were they searching for, I wonder?' he said.

Liz picked up one of her drawers, edging it onto the

runners, the slots where the drawers fitted gaping emptily. 'Can't say.' White powdery smudges daubed the face of the drawer. 'They already tested for finger prints – it's all greasy.' She picked up the duster she kept for cleaning her shoes, and rubbed at the marks. Then, folding her woollies neatly, she arranged them tidily in the drawer. 'But why did the burglars choose us?'

'Because the house is empty all day.'

Liz bent down and picked up her piggy bank, giving it a shake. It rattled. 'They've not taken my money.'

Phil sank back on the bed, his chin propped on his fists. 'That's what's worrying me. Why bother with upstairs anyway? Kids like us don't have anything worth stealing. They might have done Mum's room, hoping there was some jewellery, but why ours? There's a couple of good paintings in the front room downstairs and a set of silver cutlery, her parents left her. They could have pinched that. Only, according to Constable Barnes, they didn't.' He jumped to his feet. 'Let's go and talk to Mrs Lucy and Constable Barnes, perhaps they can shed some light on it. How's your hand, by the way?'

Liz inspected her hands, holding them up in front of her.

'It's fine,' she said in astonishment. 'I'd forgotten about it to be honest, what with all this happening.' She sighed loudly, aware it would take an entire evening to get the house back to normal, and even then it wouldn't feel normal. You couldn't expect that, she thought, not after being the target of burglars.

'Well, I haven't,' Phil said, his voice as grim as his face. 'Even if it was a trick, we have to discover who was behind it.'

'Stop worrying, I'm absolutely fine. In any case, all sorts of weird things go on at this time of year, what with Halloween and Bonfire night.'

'That's true. But tomorrow, we'll go and see young Fred. Find out what's he's been up to.'

EIGHT

Tom McFaddean had just finished cooking breakfast for his guests and had poured himself a cup of coffee, when Mrs Howard called him out of the kitchen for a phone call.

'It's the British Museum,' she whispered, keeping her hand firmly over the receiver.

'Good, they must have got the statue.' He took the telephone. 'That you, Will? Package arrived okay, then?'

'That's why I'm calling.' The line was so clear, the curator, who sounded rather irritated, might have been in the same room. 'Someone hijacked it.'

'What do you mean, hijacked?'

Tom McFaddean mimed drinking a cup of coffee. Mrs Howard nodded and hurried back into the kitchen.

'I mean, Tom,' the voice snapped as if his friend was particularly dense, 'the statue never reached me. I thought you'd like to know, since I've no doubt the police are on their way to talk to you even as we speak.'

'Not my responsibility. Have you contacted the carrier? What does he say?'

'He's not involved. He delivered it all right. Monday afternoon. It was even signed for.'

'You've lost me … you said it never arrived.'

'Oh, it arrived all right. Witnesses said the van drew-up, the carrier got out, and he unloaded the box. Got a signature. Got back in the van and drove off. With me so far, Tom?'

'Yes.'

Mrs Howard returned with his coffee, placing the cup on the reception desk. She tugged at his arm to get his attention, grimacing urgently.

'What?' he said absentmindedly, rubbing the palm of his hand on the knob of the topmost drawer.

'Your coffee. Drink it while it's hot,' she hissed. She glanced down at his hand. 'That's supposed to be lucky. Means you're coming in for money.'

'What does?' he said startled.

'When your left hand itches.'

Tom McFaddean made a face and waved her away. Taking a sip of the hot liquid, he turned his attention back to the telephone, once again listening intently.

'Right!' the curator continued his tale. 'So our stockman takes it into the building. Forget the carrier. His name's Wiggins – by the way – *our stockman not the carrier*. He's on his own while his mate goes to the canteen for lunch, which accounts for why no one much was about. You know that long passageway leading to my office?'

'Course I do, Will. Been there often enough. So?'

'That's where he vanished. Never reached my office.'

Tom McFaddean sat up straight. 'That's impossible,' he snapped.

'I know.' Will Rutherford gurgled. 'Isn't it a great story? You know my job, Tom. Dull as ditchwater. How often do I get something this interesting?'

'Not since our last little trip.'

'*Exactly!*' The voice at the other end of the line took on a gleeful quality, the curator wallowing joyfully in the drama of his little story. 'So when Mr Jenson, he's our main stockman – he's worked for us for thirty years – got back from lunch, he found his mate missing. He wasn't particularly bothered since he could easily have been called away to do a job somewhere in the building. You know how big the British Museum is?'

Tom McFaddean nodded carelessly and picked up his cup again. 'Go on.'

'It's easily done,' the curator excused their employee. 'At the end of the day, he locked up and went home. Got in next morning – still no sign of Wiggins. The man doesn't call in sick *but again* Mr Jenson wasn't that bothered. At least, not until today, when he received a frantic phone call from the man's mother, asking where her son was because he'd not come home. That's when Mr Jenson got the spare key to his assistant's locker and discovered his jacket still hanging on the peg. He called the police and they began searching the basement. Half an hour later, a constable heard noises coming from one of the stockrooms and discovered poor Wiggins inside a box. Tied and gagged. Missing his overall coat, too. Been there two nights! What do you say to that?'

'The man's a lunatic.'

'That's what we thought at first, but not now. *Listen to this.* After several cups of sweet tea for shock and biscuits for starvation, Wiggins told us that he was pushing the trolley down the corridor when he heard a noise coming from the box. He lifted the lid and something leapt on him. Next thing, he's tied up, gagged, and in the box. Poor man, he had to be sent home on sick-leave to get over his shock.

'Anyway ... to cut a long story short, the police had already begun questioning staff when one of the secretaries on the second floor heard about it. The girl was on her lunch break and remembers seeing a man in a long black robe, clutching a brown overall coat, run from the building.'

There was long and hushed silence.

'Tom? You there?' Will Rutherford shouted down the line.

'I'm here.' Tom McFaddean said, his voice suddenly very grim. 'You don't happen to know when Toby Adams gets back, do you?'

'He's back now. I rang Cambridge the other night and spoke to him. Why?'

'He found that piece, Will, and I need to know precisely where.'

'I'll give Cambridge a ring. Tom ...' the voice hesitated. 'You don't sound very surprised. Is it what I think it is?'

Tom McFaddean paused before answering, all the while staring down at his left hand, a dark mark obscuring the centre of it. 'A spirit created by a powerful sorcerer? Has to be. It's more than twenty years since we found the last one, remember?'

The curator's voice slowed as if the words he was saying bore a special significance. 'If it is a yuppy, getting itself in and out of a box would be child's play.'

Neither of the two men said anything for a moment, the silence deepening until Will Rutherford finally broke it.

'But who?'

'That's why I need you to speak to Toby. I have a feeling it might be Zheng-Li. I've been expecting something of the sort for years now – ever since I left the village. Find out what you can and let me know. If I'm right, there are some people out there who are in very great danger.'

NINE

'I thought you'd be round.' Fred's gaze brightened amazingly at the sight of a large piece of cake in Liz's hand. 'That for me?'

Liz nodded. 'But only if you tell us the truth.'

Fred was a small, red-headed child who, if they ever thought about it, Liz and Phil both liked and admired. Like them he was an orphan, fostered by Mr and Mrs Reid, their neighbours, when he was five. Unlike them, hardly a day went by without his foster mother threatening to send him back, *if he wasn't more careful* – which in general terms meant behaving himself. Unfortunately, keeping out of mischief was something Fred found impossible to do, for more than a day or two at a time. He was well-known both to Constable Barnes, following a series of pranks, and the village shop-keepers, who held him solely responsible for the increase in bad language amongst local children.

Liz particularly liked him because none of his japes ever set out to harm anyone and, despite frequent punishment, he maintained a cheerily optimistic view of his future.

Earlier that year, he had spent the whole of one evening painting a life-like portrait of the fishmonger on the rear doors of his van. The shopkeeper was a bad-tempered miserable man who was frequently rude to his customers, so that the majority had taken to bussing into Salisbury to buy fish. Sadly for the elderly and infirm, who found the bus journey difficult, they had no choice but to use his shop. Most of the week, they could make do with chops or even a bit of corned beef. But when Friday came around, it was tradition to eat fish for your dinner. And, it was very hard when the fishmonger was un-obliging, refusing point-blank to swap the piece of haddock he'd picked up, for a bit of plaice that smelled fresher.

The painting bore an uncanny resemblance, even to the straw boater Mr Jones wore in the shop. Rumour had it, that the cause of the fishmonger's bad temper was his nightly habit of hitting the bottle. Fred had drawn the figure on the back of the van with crossed-eyes and a broad toothy smile, his tongue lolling out of one corner of its mouth as if very drunk. He had also written the words: *A Merry Xmas – hic – to all my customers*, across the doors, even though it was late-spring when he painted it.

His prank wouldn't have worked had it been a wet night because the paint was designed to wash off easily. As it was, it stayed dry. The following morning, the fishmonger had driven right through the village, unaware that everyone was laughing at him, until he arrived at the wholesalers. There, he left his driving seat to open the back doors. His rage was alarming for everyone that witnessed it, jumping up and down and swearing volubly, threatening to kill the little worm responsible.

Fred, who happily confessed to Constable Barnes that he loved drawing and took every opportunity to practise his art, was confined to his room for a week, although privately Constable Barnes thought he deserved a medal.

Their admiration came about because Fred was able to swear and use bad language – out of his foster mother's hearing naturally.

Liz and Phil loved their mother dearly but considered her awfully old-fashioned. So far she had refused to even consider buying a television set, saying it was a waste of time. And they couldn't even listen to the radio until all their homework was done. Pocket money depended on keeping their rooms tidy, and the tiniest fib was frowned upon. So, despite Mrs Reid's constant threats to send him back him to the orphanage, they had come to the conclusion that Fred's life was actually a great deal more exciting than their own.

'It was a rotten trick,' Liz said. 'I nearly got my hand blown-off.'

Fred's face was a mass of freckles. Whenever he was puzzled, these formed a straight line across his forehead and over the bridge of his nose, rather like a pince-nez.

'What are you talkin' about?'

'The firework you let off in my face last night.'

Fred screwed up his nose. 'Wasn't me. I was in dad's shed all evenin' makin' a guy. I thought you'd come about the burglary.'

Liz studied the younger boy's face. Despite having the freedom to tell lies Fred rarely did, always owning up to his trouble-making.

'If it wasn't you, who else would do something like that?'

'Tell me what happened?'

Phil told him, the story about weird creatures and explosions no longer alarming in the daylight.

Fred scratched his head. 'No one I know has brains enough to do that, 'cept me. It would be a good wheeze though – might try it myself one year. So if it wasn't me, can I have the cake now?'

Liz handed it over. Fred took a huge mouthful and started chewing.

'Wish I could live in your house. I'd eat cake every day,' he mumbled, his mouth full. He jumped to his feet and, carefully wrapping the half-eaten slice in his hanky, put it in his pocket. 'Let's go an' see, while it's light.'

In the daylight everything appeared normal. Cars swished by, their tyres splashing water up from puddles where it had rained in the night. Brown shiny buds, sticky to the touch, decorated the branches of the chestnut trees, and the pavement was covered in empty husks from the hazelnut bushes.

Identifying the spot from the broken light on the far side

of the road, the three friends trawled slowly over the ground. The leaves no longer rustled, the rain having compacted them into a squelchy mass. Beneath the hedge, on the spot where Liz had been confronted by the animal, they spotted deep gouges in the soft earth.

'Like a tiger pawing the ground,' suggested Liz.

Fred shook his head. Ducking under the tangle of branches in the hedgerow, he traced the footprints back into the wood. They arched round, emerging by the gap lower down in the hedge where Phil had first heard the leaves rustle.

'That, most definitely, is not me.' Fred pointed down at the prints, plainly visible in the soft ground. 'Some sort of bird, I think.'

'Bird?'

'Yep. Definitely a bird, Phil. See, three talons at the front and a spur at the back – like a chicken.'

'It wasn't a chicken.' Phil shook his head.

'Turkey – Ostrich?'

'It wasn't a bird,' Liz argued. 'What I saw was an animal. It had ears. Birds don't have ears.'

'Owls do,' Fred insisted. He shrugged. 'I give up. It has to be someone playin' the fool.' He nodded at the tangle of trees and bushes that made up the little copse. In spring and summer, this was filled with the scent of cowslips and wild garlic. Now it was the aroma of rotting leaves, the ground snarled up with straggling lengths of ivy and small branches, blown off by the autumn wind. 'I know this place backwards. No hidin'   places – more's the pity.'

They started back up the road. Dusk was now beginning to fall, the brightness of the day rapidly dissolving into damp grey mist, which would shortly lose colour altogether and fade into the dull blackness of a November night.

'See you tomorrow, Fred,' Liz called as they reached his mother's house.

'Don't you want to know about the burglar then? I saw him clear as day.'

'*You did what?*' Phil stopped dead. 'But it happened in school time.'

Fred rubbed his ear. 'I wasn't actually in school. I sort of left a bit early. So do you want to hear or not?' He grinned at the nodding heads. 'Thought so. Came out of nowhere. I didn't see no car nor nothin'. Thought it was a salesman first off.'

Liz took hold of Fred's arm and dragged him up the path. 'Sit,' she ordered pointing at the step. 'And?'

'He goes up to the porch and goes in. Never thought nothin' about it 'cause Mrs Lucy's always there. Then, about ten minutes later, I spotted her walkin' up the road. That's when I began to think it might be a burglar.' Fred's voice rose dramatically. 'Next thing I know she goes in and, before you can say Bob's your uncle, I hear a scream. Real loud it was, too. Then he comes runnin' down the path. Only ...' Fred beamed triumphantly. 'It wasn't the same man as went in.'

'There were two of them?'

'No, only one.'

'Then how?'

'That's exactly what I said to meself. *Fred, old chap. You might skip school but I know you can count...*' Liz erupted into giggles. '*So how does one and one, make one?*'

'Can you describe him?' Phil broke in.

Fred scratched his head. 'Well, the one that came out – I took particular notice of him in case the cops wanted a description. I was real disappointed when they never came round to ask.'

'But why would they?' Liz said seriously. 'You were supposed to be at school.'

'I could have been ill,' he protested. 'Anyway, he was tall – posh suit – smart except for his hair. Same colour as mine and he wore it long in a ...'

'Ponytail!' Liz and Phil burst out together.

Fred's mouth opened in astonishment. 'You know him?'

'It's Mr McFaddean,' Liz nodded.

'He came for the jade,' added Phil.

'What jade?'

'It's a long story.'

Fred shuffled round on the step. 'You see me wantin' to go anywhere,' he grinned.

'Well ...' Liz paused trying to sort events into some sort of sequence. 'Remember, we told you we were going with Mother to a conference in London.' Fred nodded, listening intently. 'We stayed at this hotel which was owned by this man – the one you saw – Mr McFaddean. He's supposed to be an explorer. Right from the start, I didn't like him – he was always asking questions. Now, we know why.'

'Come off it, Liz. He was great. I can't believe ...'

'He's a thief?'

Phil set his face stubbornly. 'No, I can't.'

'What else would you call him?'

'Hello?' Fred interrupted patiently.

'Sorry, Fred,' Phil took over the story. 'It's just that we bought this piece of jade as a gift for Mum for her birthday. It was in the market. We'd been to the cinema ...'

'Cor! What did you see?'

'The new St Trinians.'

'Any good?'

'Phil fell off his seat laughing.'

Fred grinned at Liz. 'That good, eh! Per'aps Dad Reid'll take me when it comes to Salisbury. Go on.'

'We'd just bought it when Mr McFaddean appeared. He told us he collected jade ...'

'Which is true,' Phil jumped in again. 'He showed us his collection. I tell you what, Fred. You really ought to go and see it. It's so life-like. Gave me the shudders all those warriors with real swords and guns ...'

'*Phil!*'

'Sorry. So where was I? Yes! Mr McFaddean said the man at the gem stall told him some children had bought a piece of jade, and he asked if it was us. If so, could he buy it?'

'And we said no,' Liz confessed. 'He must have come looking for it.'

'Cor!' Fred whistled in astonishment. 'It must be ever-so valuable if he wanted it bad enough to steal it. What's it like?'

'It's a green stone with a bird carved on it, about this size.' Liz circled her two thumbs and middle finger. 'It's really pretty but ...' She shrugged not knowing what to say.

'Problem is Mum knows we told a fib and we haven't admitted it yet.' Phil glowered. 'It's like the sword of ... sword of ...'

'Damocles?'

'Thanks, Liz, hanging over our heads. We meant to do it yesterday, but what with the burglary – we forgot. And today's her birthday.'

'At least she won't threaten to send you back to the orphanage.'

'Mrs Reid doesn't mean it,' said Liz, trying to help.

Fred picked up an empty flowerpot, stamping viciously on a little colony of woodlice that had taken up residence under its base. '*She does*. But one day, I shall pick up my stuff and really go back, *you see if I don't* – that'll show her.' He stood up. 'Right then. I'll go down later and watch the wood. You never know – they might try it again.'

Just then Alison passed, driving her new car. Noticing her children outside the neighbour's house, she waved. Indicating right, she swung into the little road adjacent to her house, parking a short way down next to a lamppost.

'Enjoy the cake – and thanks.'

Waving goodbye, Liz darted down the path leaving Phil to follow.

'I made enquiries today about building a garage,' Alison called, getting out of the car. She locked the driver's door, immediately opening it again to check the passenger door. 'I understand you have to get planning permission, first. I thought you could just go ahead and build it. Anyway, one of my colleagues gave me the name of an architect who does that sort of thing. Remind me to phone him tonight, Phil.' She crossed the road. 'What's up,' she said, noticing their serious expressions. 'Not another burglary?'

Liz linked her arm with her mother's, leaving Phil to carry her brief case into the house.

'Happy Birthday,' she said giving her mother a kiss. 'But, before we give you your present, we need to tell you something.'

Alison took off her coat and led the way into her study.

Despite not getting any sun, this was everyone's favourite room. A small window, set half-way up the wall, overlooked the garden fence, where strands of clematis scrambled, huge purple flowers covering up the bare wood panels in summer. And while Alison had considered having French windows, she hadn't got round to doing it yet. For much of the day, especially when it was gloomy outside, a lamp burned, giving the room, with its stacks of books and papers, a homely feel.

'If it's about the piece of jade, I should apologise. I forgot it was my birthday. But it was still a fib – although on this occasion, an excusable one.'

'Honestly, Mum, couldn't you have told us straight off you weren't cross? We've been in agony, worrying about it,' Phil groaned.

Alison laughed. 'A bit of agony never hurt anyone. Besides, I didn't notice it affecting your appetites.'

He grinned. 'It'll take more than that for me to lose my appetite, you know that, Mum. But I wish you'd told us because we had to rush out and get you something else.'

'You mean I rushed out!' Liz said sternly.

'Well, *you* made me tell the lie.'

Alison laughed, holding her arms wide to arrest the slanging match before it began. 'Save the other present till Christmas. Come on, let's celebrate my birthday and you can give me my present now. I'm dying to see it.'

Noticing their sombre expressions hadn't altered, she asked, 'There's something else?'

Liz nodded. 'Fred saw the burglar. It was Mr McFaddean.'

'*What?* He might be the most awful man, overbearing and arrogant. But no!' Alison sprang to her feet pacing the carpet. '*Absolutely impossible*. People like him don't need to steal. Fred was mistaken.' She fixed Phil with a stern look. 'Unless, it really is valuable?'

Phil shook his head. 'Don't think so, Mum. But whoever it was, they didn't find it, Liz had it in her satchel all the time. But there's something else. You know my nightmares ...'

Liz's hand shot out to stop her brother continuing. 'Mother doesn't need to hear about that now,' she protested. 'We've done what we set out to do – apologise. It's her birthday remember, and I bet Lucy's left us a nice tea.' She frowned. 'Anyway, we agreed they're not connected and it was all a trick.'

'That was before Fred saw the footprints.'

'*No!* That was *after* Fred saw the footprints,' Liz insisted. 'That's why Fred said he'd go down there tonight, in case someone tried it again.'

Alison took off her glasses. She stared at the two faces; the one red with anger, the other white as if its owner felt sick. She put them back on.

'What's not connected, Phil?'

'It's not fair on her birthday,' Liz warned.

Ignoring his sister, Phil quickly explained what had happened to Liz. The words tumbled out, needing to convince his mother that the incident was somehow connected with his dream, whatever his sister might say to the contrary. 'The creature went for her eyes. Then, all of a sudden, you came along in the new car – and it was gone.' He shook his head in bewilderment. 'I know we only got a glimpse but it was definitely the animal I saw in my nightmare. It's *got* to be connected.'

'You're right, Phil, it is.' Alison sighed, her blue eyes tired and worried looking. She removed her glasses yet again, dropping them into her lap, her fingers fiddling with the ear pieces. 'I think now would be as good a time as any other to explain how I came to adopt you,' she said, in the sombre tone of voice she only ever used in church.

Getting to her feet, Alison opened a large cupboard, almost the only piece of good furniture left by her mother. Built of walnut, its curved sides were made of bevelled glass, with glass shelves in them for displaying ornaments. The amber-coloured wood sparkled in the lamp light, adding to the comfortable atmosphere of the room. Neatly fitting double doors opened up to display shallow drawers, which her mother had used for storing embroidered tablecloths and napkins. Alison had tidied away most of the cloths, except for a couple which were brought out at Christmas and Easter, using the drawers for important documents needed at a moment's notice, without tearing the house apart first. The thief had searched here but fortunately nothing had been damaged. She pulled out the bottom drawer, carefully lifting out a flat parcel neatly wrapped in brown paper, before sitting down again.

'I believe your ancestors came from Tibet or China.' Liz and Phil knelt down on the floor staring at the parcel on Alison's lap as if it was about to explode. 'I was newly qualified and, to gain experience, I had answered an advertisement for the United Nations to work in a hospital in the Far East. They sent me to Bantu.'

'Where's that?'

'It's a village in the far north of Burma, Liz. It's set high in the mountains on the borders with north-east India and Tibet. To this day, I maintain it was all a mistake because the only transport in and out was by bus. And the population was minute. But there was this brand new hospital and it needed trained staff. And there I was – all keen and eager, determined to make my mark on the world. It was a nice place. The villagers were really friendly. And so grateful for what I was doing for their children, I was inundated with gifts,' Alison remembered dreamily. 'It was because of that village I became a paediatric surgeon, specialising in children.' She laughed suddenly startling the two children perched on the floor next to her. They stared up at her enquiringly. 'By today's standards, it was a disaster. Only the hospital, hotel and cinema had electricity. And even that broke down every other day. I got pretty good at operating using only an oil lamp. Anyway, this particular night it was late. I'd checked on my patients to make sure they were comfortable, before leaving the hospital. The hotel was not far and I decided to walk along the river to get some air.' Her face changed becoming grave. 'You can imagine my concern … and fright … when I was suddenly accosted by this strange figure. I didn't pay it much attention except to notice it was badly injured. Before I could react, it had thrust a bundle at me and run off.

'When I got to the hotel, Chang, the night-porter, and I opened the parcel.' She smiled lovingly down at the two children, sitting in hushed silence at her feet, and stroked their hair. 'Imagine my surprise when you two rolled out.' Liz gasped with astonished. 'You'd been wrapped tightly together in this.' Quickly undoing the package, she showed them the length of coarse black cotton folded into a neat square, two tunics of emerald-coloured silk nestling on top. 'These were the clothes you were dressed in.'

'Who was the person? A man or a woman?' Tentatively, Liz put out a hand to touch the smaller of the two gowns, gently fingering the heavy fabric. It felt stiff to the touch, as if Mrs Lucy had starched it like their shirts. 'It's impossible to imagine being that small.'

'A woman.' Alison began to wrap the parcel up again, smoothing the material carefully into place.

'Our mother?' Liz whispered

'I don't know.' She stared at the face of her daughter, with its mop of straight hair and wide eyes. 'Of course she was,' she exclaimed, remembering. 'She looked exactly like you.'

'So what has this got to do with the monsters in my dream?' Phil said.

The phone began to ring, loudly and harshly. Everyone jumped. Phil grabbed it.

'Salisbury one-two-one-seven. Philip speaking.'

'*Phil?*'

'Fred!' he exclaimed. Putting his hand over the receiver, 'It's all right, it's only Fred. What are you whispering for?' he said into the mouthpiece.

'Mum'll kill me if she catches me usin' the phone. We're only supposed to use it for emergencies.'

'Then why risk it, you'll only get into trouble.'

'Because you've got *things* in your garden.'

Phil frowned into the phone. 'What are you talking about?'

'Mother, can Fred come for tea tomorrow?' Liz put out her hand to attract her mother's attention away from Phil's conversation. There was no point trying to listen in; you could never hear what the person at the other end was saying. Besides, if it was important she'd know by the expression on her brother's face or he would tell her afterwards. 'He loves cake,' she added, 'and Mrs Reid never buys any, says sugar's bad for him.'

Alison nodded and tapped Phil on the arm.

'Ask Fred ...'

Liz felt the atmosphere in the study change as swiftly as a coin flipping over from heads to tails. She caught sight of her brother's face. It was ashen, as if someone had drained all the blood out of his body. Slowly, he replaced the receiver.

Liz didn't need to ask. She already knew. She jumped to her feet.

'What is it?' Alison said. 'Fred's all right, isn't he?'

'It's not that.' Phil spoke slowly then stopped as if his brain was trying to shut down.

Liz said the words for him. 'He rang to say our garden is full of monsters, that's right, isn't it, Phil?'

TEN

Making up in length for what they lacked in width, each of the gardens at the rear possessed a long narrow lawn edged by flower borders. Number 57 also boasted a neatly dug vegetable patch, which produced a crop of potatoes and carrots in summer, with broad beans planted out in early autumn ready for spring. In the dusk, spindly silhouettes of blackcurrant bushes poked spiked fingers at the sky, and compost heaps created mounds like burial plots, while left-over cabbage stalks became alien figures from a far-distant galaxy.

When the houses were built, cars had only just been invented and, although there was plenty of room for a garage, only Alison's house at the end had access to a road. A narrow cul-de-sac bordered her garden with a line of terraced houses on its far side, where she had left her car. Neighbours, lucky enough to own a motorcar, left them parked against the kerb, storing engine oil, wash leathers, and buckets for cleaning, in the shed at the bottom of the garden. Alison had employed a local man to build her a shed, and this had a neat stretch of paving stones leading up to it, with posts for a washing line. At the far end of the lawn was a swing, which she had bought for the children when they were little. Now it stood idle, its seat hanging down like some species of bat.

In the centre of the lawn a pond, shaped like a four-leafed clover, was filled with frogs and goldfish. Astride its stone edge sat a dozen or more brooding figures. At first glance they might easily have been mistaken for vultures, although exceedingly large vultures. A sudden movement came from one of them and claws struck at the water. A shower of droplets flew into the air, caught in a beam of light from the street lamp. The claw reappeared grasping a wildly flapping fish.

A stone flew over the fence, striking one of the creatures squarely on its head. It reared to its full height and, swinging round, hissed angrily. The watchers at the window saw an animal head with furry ears and a snout, its jaw a vicious snarl, its white teeth with long canines bright in the lamplight.

'We'll see about this ...'

'*No!* Please don't go out there, Mum. It's far too dangerous,' Phil begged.

'I may be all sorts of things but I'm not a fool. I'm calling the police,' Alison stormed.

'What can they do?' Phil grabbed her arm. 'They're monsters.' He shook his head helplessly.

'*Well, somebody's got to do something.*'

A loud thumping noise came from hallway and someone hammered on the front door.

Liz and Phil spun round gazing back down the landing, only the bottom edge of the door visible from upstairs.

The knocking came again, louder.

'It can't be those things from the garden,' Alison tried to smile but only succeeded in looking as if she was suffering from toothache. 'I'm sure they don't go around knocking on doors, unless they're cleverer than we think. I'll go.'

'We're coming with you,' Liz said, suddenly finding her voice.

'Put off the light as you come down. No sense wasting electricity even if strange creatures have invaded our garden.'

Liz hurriedly switched off the bedroom light, clicking the switch on the landing before racing downstairs, all the while listening to the banging which was growing steadily louder.

Alison reached the door and clicked the latch back.

'*About time, too.*'

The door was blasted open and the tall figure of Tom McFaddean swept into the hall, a large bag in one hand and Fred's coat collar – with Fred still struggling wildly – in the other. 'And get those lights on,' he snapped.

Without stopping to ask why, Phil tore upstairs again, running back down almost immediately.

'What on earth are you doing here, Mr McFaddean?' Alison said, sounding astonished.

'Saving your bacon.'

'I'm sure we don't need your help,' she replied tartly. 'I'm just about to call the police. They can deal with these creatures. After all, it's their job.'

Fred stuffed the handful of stones he'd been carrying back in his pocket. He shook his head as if arguing about the wisdom of calling in the law.

Tom McFaddean confirmed the thought. 'I shouldn't bother if I were you. If I know the local constabulary, you have one constable and a sergeant.' Kicking the door shut behind him, he dropped Fred and the bag on the floor. 'Do you know this lad? I found him halfway up a lamppost throwing stones. Five minutes more and the street cleaner would have been sweeping up his carcass in the morning.'

'Of course! That's Fred, he lives next door.' Alison nodded at the boy. 'Fred, don't you know it's wrong to throw stones?'

'But I wasn't throwin' stones, Doctor. I was usin' me catapult. I'm a dab hand with that,' Fred added proudly.

'Oh well, that's all right then,' Alison said in a distracted tone.

Fred grinned triumphantly. 'Can I stay then?'

Ignoring his request, Alison swung round on the tall men her voice stern, like a teacher reprimanding a badly-behaved pupil. 'If you think you can do a better job, removing those objects from our garden, than our British police ...' She jerked her head towards the back of the house, 'Then you are welcome. But, first, we need to clear up the small matter of a burglary.'

'Burglary.' The tall man exclaimed. 'What burglary?'

'Our home was ransacked by someone who looked remarkably like you.'

'Not exactly like him, Doctor, if this is the real Mr McFaddean,' Fred butted in. 'It sort of did but it didn't, if you see what I mean. The bloke was shorter, definitely shorter.'

Phil beamed.

Alison seemed taken aback. 'Oh, well, in that case...'

'But what are they?' Liz said.

'They're called Shantu – which is spelled with an X and an h.'

'You knew!' Tom McFaddean gaped at Alison in amazement.

'Of course I knew, Mr McFaddean,' Alison retorted still sounding angry. 'If you think, for one moment, I would remain in ignorance of *anything* that involved my children then you'd better think again. What I don't know ... is what they're doing here and how to deal with them.'

'That's easy. They've come after the jade. You do have it, don't you?'

It took a moment for Liz to realise the question had been directed at her. She glanced up at her mother, who nodded back as if giving permission.

'Yes, I'll get it. I'm sorry we fibbed but it was for Mother's birthday ...'

'And the other piece, Dr Shaw?'

Alison sighed heavily, both children interpreting this as: *I do wish people wouldn't ask awkward questions.* 'I've lost it,' she admitted.

'You can't have.' Tom McFaddean frowned down at her. 'This little lot wouldn't have gathered here otherwise.'

'*Then I've mislaid it,*' Alison snapped, waving her arms about as if conducting an orchestra. 'I've searched everywhere – on several occasions.'

Fred nudged Phil. 'Got a paper bag?' he said, patting the pockets of his blazer, which were bulging with missiles for his catapult.

'In a minute,' Phil hissed. 'I don't want to miss this.'

'Okay.' Fred sat down on the bottom step, piling the small pebbles into a heap against the skirting board.

The sound of the door-knocker crashing down once again froze everyone into statues.

'What now?' Alison hurried back across the hall and opened the door. '*Constable Barnes?* Whatever are you doing here?'

The large figure of the policeman stood on the doorstep, his helmet under his arm. 'Evenin' Doctor. I came to check if everything was all right?'

'Er …' As if unsure, Alison swung round glancing at Tom McFaddean. He shook his head in warning. 'Of course it is, why?'

'Well, ma'am, one of your neighbours has phoned in to say you've got some very funny goings-on in your garden.'

Alison laughed awkwardly. '*Oh is that all!* Aren't they just the most adorable things you've ever seen?'

Liz shook her head in disbelief, unable to understand how this person lying so skilfully – and to police – could possibly be her mother.

Alison swung round pointing at Tom McFaddean. 'This is Mr Hitchcock. He's a famous film-director from London. He's come down here to try out some props for a horror film, would you believe? Be an absolute angel, Constable, and warn our neighbours, if they hear a few screams it's just us play-acting.' Smiling brilliantly, she stepped back a pace, her hand on the latch. 'We'll try not to make too much noise.'

Fred elbowed Phil. 'Isn't she great – should have been an actress.'

Liz caught sight of the constable's face, totally mystified by the flood of words battering him. His hand crept up to scratch his head. 'Well, if you're sure …'

'Absolutely,' Alison beamed, cutting off the rest of his speech. 'I can understand anyone being alarmed they're so life-like. Can you imagine what a scary film it's going to be? It will

93

have us all hiding under our beds.' She began to close the door. 'Goodnight, Constable, and thank you for your concern. But, I assure you, we're fine.'

Closing the door firmly, she leaned back against it smiling triumphantly, and dusted her hands together as if wiping away the problem.

'*Hitchcock!*' exclaimed Tom McFaddean. 'Why ever did you say *Hitchcock*? I'm not a bit like him – he's fat and bald.'

'If it had been left to me, Mr McFaddean, I would have told him the truth,' she retorted. 'Besides I couldn't think of anyone else. I should have said David Lean, only I didn't remember his name in time.'

'Mother, you're amazing.'

Alison grimaced. 'I've had lots of practice, Liz. Right! The jade. But first things first – I'm putting the kettle on. I don't care how dangerous those things are …'

'Mu-um, how can you possibly …'

'Because, if I don't get a cup of tea pretty soon, Phil, I shall be dead from thirst. Are we likely to be attacked in the next five minutes?'

'Hopefully not, as long as we've got the lights on,' Tom McFaddean camouflaged a grin.

'I'd like a cup 'a tea, Doctor,' Fred piped up, 'if that's okay.'

'Of course it is, Fred, dear. Then you really ought to get off home. I'm sure it's almost time for bed.'

She swung round pointing upstairs. 'Liz, fetch the piece you bought. Phil, you go with her. Mr McFaddean, please make sure we aren't attacked while I'll get the tea.'

Excited now brother and sister dashed upstairs again, Fred chasing after them.

'I tell you what, your mum ain't half a character.' He peered admiringly at Liz's bedroom. 'Cor! How can you be this tidy?'

Liz examined her room as if seeing it for the first time. 'It's not usually this neat, Fred. I tidied it up after the burglary and I expect Mrs Lucy gave it a good clean this morning.'

Perching on the end of her bed, she rummaged through her

satchel searching for the small box, which had fallen down behind her English exercise book and her pencil case. Catching sight of the glasses' case wrapped in pink paper, she suddenly remembered her mother's birthday. What a strange sort of day. But at least no one would ever forget it.

'Have you ever seen Mother like this, Phil? She's not a bit scared is she, she's more excited.'

'Now Mr McFaddean's here, I'm not scared either.' Phil crossed to the window peering out. 'Isn't that weird.' A loud yelping noise greeted his words.

Liz quickly dragged him away. 'Honestly, Phil, you should know better than that,' she scolded. 'Now it's dark, they can easily spot us with the lights on.' Ducking her head below the window sill, she stretched up a hand to tug the curtains across. 'Come on, Fred, let's get downstairs.'

'What's that noise?' Alison called from the hall.

'It was Phil.' Liz paused mid step, her hand on the banister. 'He wanted to look.'

'You can do all the looking you want when we go out to confront them.' A whistling noise came from the kitchen. 'They won't leave until we do. Ah, the kettle's boiling.'

'What does confront mean?' Fred said.

'I think it means fight.'

'*Fight? Us!*' Liz stared at her brother, her stomach churning.

'Mum was joking,' Phil searched for a laugh and gulped instead.

Tom McFaddean glanced up at the three children running downstairs. He raised his eyebrows. 'I've come to the conclusion Dr Shaw knows a hell-of-a lot more than she's letting on. What an astonishing woman.'

ELEVEN

Liz lifted off the lid on the box taking out the little jade medallion, its silver links glinting in the lamplight. She passed it on to Phil, who gazed at it intently.

'So what's so important about the jade?'

Alison paused, then slowly replaced her cup on its saucer. She stayed silent for a moment as if listening. In the distance a car revved its engine and, nearby, a neighbour put out some rubbish, the iron lid of the dustbin clanking noisily. From the garden came a steady plop-plop of water, ample evidence that by morning the pond would most probably be empty of goldfish.

'Apparently, you are descendants of the Javean, the race of magical warriors Mr McFaddean referred to.'

Fred, determined not to be sent home, had crawled under the table to escape notice. He gasped loudly and the paper ball, he'd been about to send speeding across the room from his catapult, dropped lamely onto the carpet.

Not the slightest bit surprised, Liz glanced across at her brother sitting cross-legged on the carpet. Like Fred he seemed stunned, rather like the goldfish in the garden. Yet the announcement made by her mother was not news to her, she'd been expecting something of the sort ever since she'd touched the little emerald tunics. It was horrid feeling as if her head no longer belonged only to her, and was being shared by other people.

'Why didn't you admit all this back at the hotel …' Irritably, Tom McFaddean got to his feet. He unzipped his bag pulling out a couple of swords, which he leaned casually against the wall.

Phil stared at the blades glinting in the lamplight and nudged Fred. He craned his head, peering out over the top of several pairs of legs.

'Cor, I bet they're sharp,' he whispered, slumping down again.

The hotelier gestured towards the garden. 'We might have avoided all this.'

'I can see you don't have children, Mr McFaddean,' Alison stirred her tea briskly, her tone rising; its edge as keen as the swords glinting in the lamplight. 'If you had, you'd realise that a parent's first duty is to protect, not announce to young children, they are descendants of a race doomed to guard a crazy old sorcerer for all eternity.'

'Wow!' came the muttered exclamation from under the table.

'You still here, Fred?' Alison said. 'I thought you'd gone home ages ago.'

Fred frowned, his freckles creating a solid ridge of colour on his otherwise pale skin. 'Too scared to leave the house, Doctor, with all them creatures about.'

'I quite forgot about that, Fred, dear,' she said. 'It is rather scary isn't it? Never mind, I'll take you home in a minute and explain to Mrs Reid why you're late.'

Fred poked Phil in the ribs. '*She will let me stay, won't she?*' he hissed.

'If you keep quiet, she'll have forgotten all about you again in a jiffy. Mum never remembers ordinary things … like bedtimes,' Phil whispered back, 'too busy thinking about work. That's why we have Mrs Lucy. You're quite safe.' He raised his voice. 'About these warriors, Mum? Are there any others?'

'I don't know,' she gazed enquiringly at Tom McFaddean. 'Only me,' he agreed. 'And I'm adopted.'

'The Javean clan,' Alison began again, 'took it upon themselves to protect the Mongolian Empire from Zheng-Li. To do that, they were given five pieces of jade, powerful enough to stop him ever escaping from his prison.'

'You *have* done your homework, Dr Shaw.' Tom McFaddean stretched out his arm to take another biscuit.

'Research is child's play for a scientist,' she retorted. 'And I gather, since you are wearing one of the pieces ...' She pointed to the open collar of his shirt. A black ribbon was tied round his neck, an edge of green jade showing below it. 'And Liz has another – somehow the collection was broken up?'

He nodded. 'Japanese soldiers stole them, just before the end of the war. We only recovered the one piece – and that was given to the children.'

'And we are the children,' Liz confirmed, her voice suddenly very grown-up.

Tom McFaddean smiled. 'Indeed you are, and I'm overjoyed to have found you. I've spent most of the past eleven years searching. But what happened to your real mother?'

Alison's face changed. 'She died,' she admitted reluctantly.

The tall man's face changed. 'When?'

'Did you know she'd been injured?'

'Yes, she was attacked by one of the Xhantu but I thought ...'

Alison got to her feet. Opening the walnut cupboard again, she took out the brown-paper parcel, sitting back down to open it. 'I came across her on the river road. She handed me this bundle of cloth; the children were wrapped in it.'

Tom McFaddean stared down at the little emerald robes resting on their black cotton shroud, his eyes sombre and filled with pain.

'I'm so sorry,' Alison put out a hand. 'She died shortly after from loss of blood.'

Tom McFaddean nodded abruptly. 'I searched Bantu – even spoke to the mayor. Nobody had heard of her. Or the children.'

'Well, I like that. *Of all the devious ...* Of course the mayor knew.' Forgetting, Alison jumped to her feet, the fabric cascading in a storm of light and dark onto the floor. Hurriedly, Liz gathered it back together, folding it neatly. 'He's the one that bulldozed through the adoption,' she fumed. 'And Chang, the night porter at the hotel, he helped me care for them. Although probably,' she added more calmly, 'since the mayor owned the hotel and pretty much everything else in the village, the young man feared he'd lose his job if he spoke out. Thank you, Liz.' Lost in thought Alison carefully replaced the brown-paper parcel in the chest and, closing the drawer, resumed her seat. She frowned suspiciously at Tom McFaddean. 'It was almost a month before the adoption papers came through and I could leave, so why didn't you find me?'

Tom McFaddean showed her the scars on his left arm. 'I sort of blew myself up.'

Fred, forgetting what Phil had said about keeping quiet, stuck his head out from under the table again. 'You mean like dynamite?'

Tom McFaddean smiled ruefully, 'Exactly like dynamite.'

Fred gasped and quickly ducked back out of sight.

'Really, Mr McFaddean, I would have thought you to be more sensible than that. You could have been killed.'

'Normally, Dr Shaw, I am.' The tall man got to his feet. 'Could we leave the rest of the talking till later.' A distant yelping came from the garden. 'That lot out there will storm the house any minute now, unless we stop them.'

Alison cuddled her cardigan more firmly her. 'By that, I suppose you mean the third jade piece. I told you, I can't find it.'

'Besides, we want to know about our parents?' Phil said.

'And I want to know how you blew yerself up?'

Tom McFaddean grinned down at the head poking out from between the carved oak legs of the table.

'Bloodthirsty little creature you are, Fred. To answer you first, Phil.' He laid a friendly hand on the boy's head. 'Telling you about your family will take time, and that is something we don't have right now. I have a collection of photographs at the hotel. I'll show them to you when we get back to London.'

'London?' Alison picked up on the word. 'I've no intention of taking my children to London.'

Tom McFaddean raised a hand like a policeman stopping the traffic.

'We can argue about that afterwards.' Picking up the edge of the tablecloth, he peered down. 'As for you, young Fred, Zheng-Li's creatures, the Xhantu, hundreds of them attacked the village. I used dynamite to stop them and blew myself up too. Some of the villagers escaped and when eventually they returned, they found me. But it was months before I was fit enough to leave.' He dropped the cloth back into place. '*The jade piece, Dr Shaw?* Phil told me about his nightmares. He said he didn't have them at the hotel.' He frowned thinking, the edges of the scar on his cheek puckered, a parallel row of discoloured dots still visible where the wound had been roughly sewn back together. 'That might have been from the jade I've got lying about – I'm not quite sure why it happens. When I was a boy, the headman of the village told me all jade has the power to repel evil spirits.' Tom McFaddean fixed his eyes on the green bird – the smooth surface of the stone glowing faintly in the lamp light. 'That's why I collect it.'

'If the jade is as powerful as you say, Mr McFaddean,' Alison said, 'then reluctantly I have to agree. It certainly might account for Phil's good dreams in London.'

'But he didn't get nightmares in my room either,' Liz argued. 'And we don't have any jade in our house.'

McFaddean leapt to his feet. 'You must do. And that's where we'll start. Come on.'

Once again, piece by piece, Liz's room was dissected and searched; the bed pulled out, the carpet lifted, the wardrobe's contents taken out and scrutinised.

Tom McFaddean glanced at the trap door in the ceiling. 'What's up there?'

Alison frowned. 'Nothing that I know of, except the cold water tank. I never go up. Besides, I don't even have a ladder.'

'Well, it's here somewhere, Dr Shaw,' the tall man snapped. He grabbed hold of the edge of the dressing table and heaved it across the carpet. 'Will this bear my weight, Liz?'

'I think so.'

Leaning his shoulders against the heavy wardrobe, he attempted to push it away from the wall, wanting to use it as a stepladder to reach to the trap door. It swayed but remained stubbornly unmoving. There came a rustling noise, as if something had been caught between the piece of furniture and the wall and the movement had dislodged it. Impatiently, he put his weight against the solid wooden side shifting it a fraction. An edge of a thick webbing strap poked through the gap.

'Good gracious! It's my old bag,' Alison exclaimed. She bent down tugging at it. 'It's stuck.'

Using all his strength, Tom McFaddean levered one side away from the skirting board.

Pushing him out of the way, Alison pounced on the strap and began seesawing it up and down. No one said anything, waiting with bated breath. Gradually, a grey canvas shoulder bag came slowly into sight, the fabric on its outer side faded by the sun.

'How extraordinary!' Alison exclaimed excitedly, pulling it free. 'This is what I used for my trip. I thought I'd lost it.' She rummaged in the pockets, turning them inside out in her haste. 'There's nothing here.' She shook her head. '*Wait!* Scissors, anyone?'

Liz grabbed some from her dressing table; the four figures crowding impatiently round as Alison cut through the seam of the lining. Triumphantly, she pulled the jade ornament from the bottom of the bag, where it had lain for eleven years.

'So that's the reason you slept well, Liz, and you didn't. Poor Phil.'

Different from the piece they'd found in the market, the

narrow silver strips formed liquid streams of light, an eagle floating in the air its wings outstretched and hovering, an identical image carved on the reverse side.

Liz touched it carefully, feeling the jade vibrate against her fingers as if it was alive. She bent down and, pulling out one of the laces from her school shoes, threaded it through the hole pierced in the rim.

'May I wear this one, Mr McFaddean?'

'May I see?'

She passed it over. He examined it critically, rubbing his thumb slowly over the edges. 'Good choice. This was worn by your mother, Mei-Xui. It has a slight dent in the jade – right on the edge.' He took her hand, rubbing her finger across the minute flaw on the surround, invisible to the naked eye. Liz sniffed, her eyes welling up with tears. Slipping the lace round her neck, she tied it at the back.

'After the villagers got it back, fearing that Zheng-Li would escape it was guarded night and day,' the tall man continued his story. 'They were right. Singly, it did not possess sufficient power to stop him.' Removing the jade piece from around his own neck, he handed it to Phil. 'What about this one, Phil?'

Liz watched nervously as Phil took it in his hand and carefully examined it. Again, the bird was airborne, its wings outstretched, its head tilted, its gaze riveted on its twin now hanging from a ribbon on Liz's neck.

'What am I supposed to be looking for?' he said, a puzzled expression on his face. He handed the medallion to his sister.

'Perhaps Liz can explain.' Tom McFaddean said.

Liz frowned, her hand clasping the jade ornament. 'The one I'm wearing feels alive when I touch it. Have another go, Phil.'

He leaned forward his hand outstretched and grasped the green medallion. Then, his face a mask of misery, he flung the little jade ornament onto the carpet.

Without saying anything Tom McFaddean picked it up. 'What about the piece you found in the market? Try that.'

Phil shrugged and picked up the jade medallion they'd found in the market, still resting on its bed of cotton wool, dropping it instantly back down as if it burned him. 'Nothing! *It's not fair*,' he burst out at his sister. 'I'm the oldest, and you do everything better than me. You even run faster – and boys are expected to be better at sport than girls. Besides, you know plenty more things than me. *And you can read my thoughts*,' he hurled the words across the room.

'I can't run faster than you,' Liz countered.

'I'm not a dope,' Phil shot back. 'I know you let me win – and it infuriates me.' He glared. 'And now it's you again with the jade. Why can't it be me for a change?'

A loud yelping came from the garden. Tom McFaddean edged back the curtain a notch and peeped out.

'It's time to go,' he said closing the curtain again. 'Wear it anyway, Phil, it will keep you safe. Don't worry, there's a piece belonging to you, too. As each generation takes its place guarding the tomb of Xheng-Li, the jade picks out its true owner. We'll find it, I promise.'

Leaving the chest in the middle of the floor, he headed down the stairs, leaving the atmosphere in the little bedroom frosty like ice. Unrepentant, Phil stared stubbornly at the ground, the little jade circlet dangling from his fingers. Liz gazed beseechingly at her mother.

'*Honestly, men!* Why can't they put things back?' Alison said, her voice a shade louder than necessary. She crossed the floor, pulling futilely at the chest. 'Phil, give me a hand, there's a dear. We can't leave it in the middle of the room, someone will catch their foot on it.'

His expression still mulish, Phil hurriedly tied the ribbon round his neck, the silver bars of the little ornament catching the light. Hooking his fingers under the rim of the chest, he lifted it up and swung it back into place against the wall.

Nodding her thanks, Alison opened the door to the wardrobe and peered in. 'I keep meaning to buy you some slacks, Liz. Oh well, you'll have to make do with your old games skirt. Wear your gym knickers under it for extra warmth – and your old shoes.' She hurried out of the door. 'I'll go and change. *Quickly now*. Oldest trousers for you too, Phil, no sense getting your best things muddy. Fred, dear, I am going to be a bit too busy for a minute to take you home. If you stay in the background, you'll be quite safe – and wrap up warm, it's cold outside.'

Fred's eyes lit up. 'Wouldn't miss it for the world, Dr Shaw.'

'I'm sorry, Phil,' Liz said and put out her hand. 'But I didn't ask for this to happen.'

'Come on, Fred, let's get going,' he said, ignoring her.

Liz collapsed down on to her bed gazing forlornly at the mess their searching had made, the wardrobe left on the skew a few inches from the wall. Now she'd have to tidy it all up again. She fingered the little jade ornament round her neck. Phil was right. It must be really horrid being lumbered with a younger sister who could outdistance you in everything. She felt the jade beating against the palm of her hand as if it had a heart, and wondered what else she could do.

'Please, *please*, let Phil do something extra-special too,' she whispered to the jade bird. 'I promise I won't mind whatever it is.'

Reluctantly, she got to her feet and dragging her skirt off its hanger, pulled her thick socks out of the toes of her shoes where she'd left them. Quickly changing, she raced downstairs to the study. Tom McFaddean was alone, the two boys and her mother still upstairs. He had changed into a black-cotton tunic and trousers, his feet encased in black plimsolls with thick white soles. He picked up a coarse cotton jacket figured in red, securing it with a narrow sash.

'Phil's right. It isn't fair,' Liz said. She caught sight of herself in the mirror, noticing a large hole in the heel of one of her knee-length hockey socks. Obviously, Mrs Lucy hadn't spotted it, otherwise she would have whisked it away for darning. Impatiently, she tugged at the hem of her hockey skirt trying to pull it down. She'd grown since the previous year and it was now too tight, riding up over her bottom in a double crease and exposing the legs of her navy gym knickers with their elasticated bottoms.

'If Phil is to become a true warrior, he has to lay jealous thoughts aside.' Tom McFaddean picked up the medallion Phil and Liz had bought for their mother's birthday. Threading a piece of string through the hole, he replaced it carefully in the box. 'At least that is what Tung Wei always taught me. Once he has mastered his temper the jade will respond.'

'But it's hard, especially if you're the eldest *and* a boy.'

'How clearly can you read his thoughts?'

Liz hung her head, reluctant to admit she could see everything.

'*Everything?*' Tom McFaddean said the word for her.

Liz glanced up smiling timidly. 'Would you think I was crazy if I told you it was like having a head full of roads, all running in different directions.'

'No, I wouldn't – that's exactly how your mother described it.'

'She did!' Liz smiled excitedly.

'She'd have been about your age. She said my thoughts were like a pathway through the forest. As she walked along it, it stretched out until she could see for miles.'

'It makes you sad, when you think about her.'

'You can see that?' Liz's smile reflected the pain of his thoughts. 'I always prayed I'd find her alive,' he added.

The study door swung open and Phil appeared, wearing a thick pullover over his gardening trousers, the knees torn and stained with mud. Fred followed closely, draped in Phil's yellow plastic mac, which reached down almost to his ankles. He had tried on Phil's balaclava too but had pulled it off again immediately, saying it made his ears feel like scrambled egg, and had plumped for the matching sou'wester.

'It's more than my life's worth to get my blazer dirty,' he said, buttoning his coat. 'Ma Reid'll send me back to the orphanage for definite if I do. Says I'm skatin' on thin ice already and I haven't done anythin' – well, not *really* bad.'

'I thought you were supposed to be watching?' Tom McFaddean reminded with a grin.

'*Me,* Mr McFaddean?' Fred raised his eyebrows in astonishment. 'Whatever gave you that idea?'

Hearing Alison's feet on the stairs, Tom McFaddean glanced up at her, a broad smile on his face. She had changed into a pair of neatly pressed slacks with a matching twin-set, and was wearing a beret on her head. In her hand, she grasped an old hockey stick.

'Really, Dr Shaw, with the best will in the world, I think you must leave this to us.'

Alison bristled fiercely. 'If you think, for one moment, Mr McFaddean, I intend leaving *my* children to face this threat alone – you've got another think coming.'

He nodded and, picking up the jade medallion from its box, held it out.

'Then wear this.'

Alison waved it away. 'I don't need a talisman to keep me safe.' She brandished the stick in her hand, waving it purposefully through the air, 'My hockey stick is quite good enough, thank you. But thank you, anyway,' she added politely.

The door knocker sounded.

'*Really!*' Alison swivelled round on her heel, glaring. '*Now who could that be?* You'd think people could mind their own business. I'll go. They will definitely think us odd, if they catch sight of you lot. You look like you're playing charades,' she muttered, hurrying down the hallway.

'Constable Barnes,' she exclaimed, recognising the stout figure. 'Whatever's wrong now? I've told you about the film making. We were just about to start.'

Liz, peering round the edge of the study door, smiled at the uniformed figure. He was such a nice man, nothing was ever too much trouble; going out of his way to help old ladies across the road and sort out kids fighting. He was often to be found marching the miscreant home by his ear, rather than bother the sergeant at the station. *Kids will be kids*, he'd explain away the incident to an angry parent. *But a drop of bread and milk for supper won't go amiss either* – his favourite remedy for all mischief. They'd known him always, although it was strange how grown-ups started out really huge, like giants, and shrank every year as she and Phil got bigger. That had happened both to her mother and Constable Barnes. Even with his helmet on, he was scarcely taller—

Liz watched the policeman's hand rise up to scratch his head, the way it always did when he was puzzled about something. Without thinking, she reached out for the floor with her hands. Her legs followed in a wide cartwheel, whipping swiftly forwards into a second, and faster again into a third, her feet rising up high. Cannoning into the door, they blasted it shut. She flipped back upright, hastily pushing the bolt across.

'*Liz!*'

Liz tossed her hair back into place. 'That wasn't Constable Barnes,' she announced firmly as Tom McFaddean, closely followed by Phil and Fred, flocked into the hallway.

Alison stared at her daughter as if she had never seen her before. 'You cartwheeled fifteen feet!'

'Did I? *How amazing!* I've often dreamt about doing cartwheels in a row like that but I never thought I could actually do it.'

'You sure it wasn't the constable?' Tom McFaddean said, his piercing gaze scrutinizing Liz as if inspecting the inside her head.

She flapped her head vigorously from side to side, her mop of hair swinging round her face. 'He *always* takes his helmet off when he knocks at a door and puts it under his arm – and he didn't.'

'Well done for spotting the difference. That must have been our yuppy, who I guess was also responsible for the burglary.'

'Yuppy?' Alison exclaimed.

'Evil spirit – didn't I mention him?'

'No, you certainly did not. Too busy warning us to leave everything to you. Is there anything else we should know about?'

Tom McFaddean laughed. 'You really are quite fearless, Dr Shaw.'

'Fearless? Not at all. It's simply that I find it difficult to believe in ridiculous things like evil spirits.'

'So what happened to the real Constable Barnes?' Phil broke in, his face rigid as if trying to control his temper.

'I expect he's tied up somewhere, Phil.'

'Ouch,' Liz exclaimed. She peered down at her hand and rubbed it furiously. 'I must have hit it on the tiles. Golly, it does hurt and there's a bruise.'

'That's not a bruise,' Tom McFaddean said. 'That proves you're Javean from the magical side. Whenever danger looms your palm will glow with the mark of the bird.'

Fred grabbed Phil's hand. 'Nothing on this one. Sorry, chum, you're not magic.'

Angrily, Phil snatched his hand away and tucked it behind his back, glaring furiously at the floor.

'Not his right.' Tom McFaddean held up his left hand. 'His left. See! I have one, too.'

Anxious to make amends, Fred seized Phil's other hand and yanked it up into the air. 'Stone the crows! Look at that, Phil?'

In the centre of Phil's palm was the dark brown imprint of a bird. He jerked his hand free.

'So what can I do, Mr McFaddean?' he said, his tone still peevish.

'Excuse me.' Alison ran upstairs and they heard the bathroom door close.

'I don't know, Phil, that's something you alone will discover. Everyone is different.' Liz noticed the hotelier examining her brother's face, his expression still set obstinately.

'I am hoping you will take after your father,' Tom McFaddean said. 'He was a brilliant swordsman.'

'Mr McFaddean, are cartwheels part of my magic?'

'Do call me Tom.'

The bathroom door clicked open and Alison ran downstairs again, rubbing cream into her hands.

'Absolutely not, Liz. I forbid it,' she said overhearing. 'You're only twelve and, in my book, children do *not* go round calling grown-ups by their Christian names.'

'Dr Shaw, in general I agree with you, but we're heading for a fight. By the time Liz has shouted: *Mr McFaddean you're in danger* – I'll be dead!'

Liz giggled and quickly put a hand over her mouth, glimpsing the indignant expression on her mother's face. She glanced at her brother relieved to find he was trying not to laugh too. He grinned at her his temper forgotten, and she sighed thankfully.

'How about a compromise? Friends call me Mac.'

Alison screwed up her mouth. 'I suppose, but I'm still not happy. Now, we'd better get going,' she said, sounding exactly like a Sunday-school teacher proposing a walk in the countryside. 'We've wasted quite enough time already. I don't know about you but I want my dinner. Mrs Lucy has left it warming in the oven, and it'll be ruined if we don't hurry up.'

Tom McFaddean laughed. 'Dr Shaw, you're incorrigible.'

'What does that mean?' Fred hissed, stuffing the little pile of stones into his pockets. Phil shrugged. Pulling out his catapult, Fred twanged the elastic. 'I'm ready.'

Tom McFaddean ducked into the study, handing Phil the shorter of the two swords.

'This belongs to you, Phil,' he said.

'But I don't …'

'Trust me, you will know how to use it when you need to.'

'Don't I get one?'

'No, Liz. Unfortunately the person with the clearest thoughts has to be the watcher – and that's you.'

'So what does a watcher do?' she said, with a disappointed frown.

There came the crash of breaking glass and the lights

sparked out, leaving the house dark and silent, except for the breathing of the five friends and a harsh panting emerging from somewhere at the back of the house.

TWELVE

In the conservatory a loud yelping broke out and plantpots crashed onto the tiled floor.

'I wondered why they waited so long to attack, they were waiting instructions from the yuppy, blast them.' As if he could see through the gloom, Tom McFaddean left the safety of the hallway at a run. 'Use your left hand.'

'But how?' Liz shouted, following closely behind.

A snarling animal leapt out of the darkness straight for her throat. She flinched back screaming.

'Like this!'

A flash of light erupted from his outstretched hand, like a spark from a fuse box, a stream of green particles arcing through the air. With a flutter of ash, like burned paper swirling about in a breeze, the animal vanished.

Phil stopped dead. 'Did you see that?' he exclaimed, his mouth dropping open in surprise.

'Pull yourself together, Phil.' Alison gave him a little push. 'And concentrate, please. We've got a fight to win.'

'They're on the roof,' Tom McFaddean shouted. 'We need to get into the garden. We can't fight in here – too cramped – someone will get hurt.'

Liz found herself struggling to see, the darkness in the conservatory solid, opaque, with the moonlight trapped behind fast-moving clouds. A moment later, to her surprise, her vision cleared, the gloom no longer bothersome as if her eyes had sliced a pathway through it. She spotted a hunched furry form, half-hidden behind Mrs Lucy's washing basket, the feet and claws of a second animal clinging to the wooden struts either side of the smashed window. A body and head dropped down. Up close the Xhantu resembled a large and vicious bat, its lower canines narrow and sharp like a stiletto, a row of four glistening teeth like white marble tombstones between them.

'I'll take this one,' Alison shouted out. She swung her hockey stick in a blur of speed, aiming it straight at the hanging shape. It tumbled to the ground. For an instant Liz hesitated, mesmerized by the closeness of the drooling mouth with its rank stench of fish. As if on auto pilot, she raised her left hand and a shaft of light punched a hole in the animal's chest. She watched the light fizz, like acid, and then a flutter of powdery dust as the body of the animal disintegrated.

'They're not real,' she exclaimed.

'I promise you they are, if they catch you off guard. Their claws can rip out your throat, so watch yourselves.' A shaft of light from Tom McFaddean's hand hit the glass at the corner, missing the animal by a whisker. It rose clumsily into the air unable to fully extend its wings in the cramped space. Instinctively, Phil raised his hand and it disappeared in a blaze of light.

'Fred? You any good with that catapult?' Tom McFaddean picked up a broom, smashing the glass above his head.

'Yes, Mr Mac.'

'Then dislodge this little lot.' He aimed the broom at another pane of glass and jerked his head at the brooding figures. 'So we can get into the garden.'

'But my roof,' Alison wailed.

'For Pete's sake, woman, I'll buy you another one.'

Liz ran over to the garden door, watching the little stones from Fred's catapult fly upwards with deadly accuracy. The Xhantu flew off with a loud screaming hiss and landed in the garden.

Tom McFaddean dropped the broom and pulled out his sword.

'Ready, Phil?'

Liz saw her brother's face chalk white and felt his thoughts wing their way across the space, sensing his reluctance to use his sword in case he failed yet again.

'It's okay, Phil,' she called, unable to stop herself. 'You can do this.'

Tom McFaddean shot her a single glance. Then, muttering instructions as fast as he could push them out, dived into the garden. Phil, still glancing over his shoulder as if for re-assurance, timidly followed.

The Xhantu had formed a dense semi-circle on the far side of the pond, their clawed feet kneading at the ground like a bull about to charge, the air so thick with menace that Liz found herself stretching out an arm to touch it. Only a short while before, there had been perhaps a dozen shapes round the pond. In the space of less than an hour, this had doubled – even trebled. The hissing figures jostled together, like a bunch of impatient bargain hunters waiting for the doors to open on the first day of a sale, their wings concealed within the long fur of their body. Liz stared round the garden in astonishment, wondering how it could possibly happen

At the far end of the garden, she spotted a tall dark figure, exactly like the one in her thoughts, its body like a tree trunk in a gale, swaying first one way and then another – never still.

'Ignore it.' Tom McFaddean shouted following her line of sight. 'Clear the garden, first.'

As he spoke the animals attacked, a furious beating of wings and scratching of claws on the stones of the pond, lifting her attention away from the figure.

Thwack.

Alison's lunged with her hockey stick at the snarling animal which was aiming for Liz's head, its mouth agape, its claws reaching out, and sent it hurtling back over the fence.

'No time for day-dreaming, Liz,' she reprimanded.

Behind them, Fred was discharging stones as fast as he could. Liz heard the whine of the projectiles as they flew through the air – and his voice keeping score.

Out of the corner of her eye, she saw her brother standing back to back with Tom McFaddean. Shafts of light criss-crossed the garden, their swords battling a mob of teeth and claws, their blades never still for a moment – parrying and thrusting – a deadly blow followed by a screaming hiss. The green flash from Tom McFaddean's hand missed its target and hit the swing, making its chains spin wildly.

'Damn!' he swore.

'Mr McFaddean, your language,' Alison rebuked. 'There are impressionable children about.'

'What's going on out there?' yelled an angry voice from an upstairs window.

'We're having an early fireworks party,' Alison called back. 'Be done in a minute.' She aimed her hockey stick at the animal crawling towards Fred. The force of the blow somersaulted it backwards. 'Fred, dear, tuck yourself behind the rain barrel and use the broom if you need it. Mr McFaddean will always buy me a new one.' She darted forward slashing at everything within sight.

Liz gazed down at her hands. Of them all, she was the only one without a weapon. Sensing a presence close by, she raised her hand and, swivelling on her heel, angled it into the sky, a beam of light pulsing upwards to strike the animal full in the chest. In the same moment, her mind registered danger to her brother. He had moved out from the safety of Mac's broad back, unaware that Xhantu were creeping across the ground, his sword occupied with an attack by flying animals.

The words, *get up high*, penetrated the confused whirlpool of thoughts milling round her head. The words stuck refusing to pass on – rather like the traffic jams that built up in Salisbury high street whenever the traffic lights failed. Shaking her head to clear it, she leapt for the top of the fence balancing as easily as if it had been a solid bar, not a series of fragile inter-lapping panels little thicker than a pencil.

'Phil, behind you!' she screamed, watching her words gobbled up in a cacophony of noises; a rustle of wings, the deadly thump as a light beam struck its target, the hissing and growling of the creatures, a solid thwack as the wooden hockey stick struck its target to the ground.

Without stopping to think if it was possible, she flitted along the fence, her toes scarcely brushing the tops of the wooden panels. Level now with her brother, she tossed a stream of light from her hand.

'Thanks, sis,' Phil panted. His head swung round briefly to acknowledge her action. He lunged forward, his sword carving through the wing of the animal attacking him as if it was butter. Without bothering to watch the dust shower settle, he spun round, his blade moving at the speed of light.

Liz touched the jade piece round her neck. 'Thank you,' she said aloud.

She paused for a moment to watch the fight. From her post high up off the ground, everything was clear – as if it was being acted out in slow motion. Closest to the house was her mother, protecting the backs of the two men, both she and Fred aiming their weapons at any animal trying to crawl behind them unnoticed. Another burst of light and two more Xhantu vaporised into harmless droplets. Yet the number of attacking figures had scarcely altered. If anything there were more than when they began. Yet another creature disintegrated into a shower of ash. Alarmed, Liz tried to count the flying and crawling shapes.

She stopped at twenty, noticing that the Xhantu had, all at once, changed tactics. Now, instead of hurtling into the attack, they were beginning to back away down the garden, the two swordsmen pursuing them. Immediately, Liz sensed the danger. Once the stone rim of the pond stood between them and the safety of the house, the animals were free to circle round behind it. She felt her eyes drawn to the far end of the garden, aware of the intelligence directing the fight, even though the yuppy appeared to be taking little interest. Mac was right. Real or not, something was organising them. Even as she thought the words into sense, the animals began to divide into two distinct groups pulling Mac one way and Phil the other, trying to separate the two fighters.

She had to warn them before it was too late. But how? Once down on the ground, she'd be in danger too – even though instinct told her that speed was on her side. Only in the air were the Xhantu faster than her, their angle of attack hurling them downwards onto their victim like a buzzard dive-bombing its prey – their heavy bodies no deterrent to speed. Even so, she'd never reach them in time, the press of animals too solid. Her thoughts began to spin wildly. She took a deep breath trying to clear them. Closing her eyes, she flew a single sentence of warning down the roadway of thoughts to Tom McFaddean, hoping he would hear her.

Nothing happened, the progress of the two fighters towards the pond relentless, both convinced they were winning the fight and the monsters fleeing.

Forcing herself to stay calm and block out every other thought, Liz tried again, imagining the words bursting down the road like a speeding bullet.

Tom McFaddean's head jerked up. He swung round.

'Phil,' he yelled and grabbed the boy's arm. '*Get back*, they're trying to split us.'

Liz felt tears of relief trickle down her cheeks and, hastily, wiped them away. Reluctantly, she switched her gaze from the fight, directing it along the concrete slabs and past the shed to the far end of the garden, where spider-like runners from a bed of strawberries pushed out tentacles into the newly dug earth. The dark shape was still there but it's fingers and arms had become quite grotesque – twice the length they originally were. Like stretched rubber, they swirled about performing some sort of weird ritual. Then she saw he was using his hands as a butterfly net, scooping up the flakes of dust whirling through the air. Moulding the bits between his long fingers, he arranged the miniscule wads of dirt on the ground where they instantly began wriggling about like worms. Shocked, she watched them change, growing at an alarming rate, until the earth around the yuppy's feet was thronged with the jostling figures of the miniature creatures – like young birds not yet able to fly. At the speed with which they were growing, in a very few minutes they would be fully fledged, unless someone stopped them.

Letting go the breath she'd been holding, Liz dropped down off the fence and ran back to where Fred was crouched. Having run out of projectiles for his catapult, he was now lobbing stones from the rockery bowling them over-arm.

A green flash directed at her feet stopped Liz dead. She glanced down, all at once aware she'd given little thought to her own danger, so immersed in the need to stop the yuppy. She simply hadn't noticed the animal crawling low across the ground. She swung round calling out her thanks but Phil and Tom McFaddean had their backs to her and didn't hear, only her mother close by.

'You weren't watching,' Alison rebuked her daughter. 'Do try and be more careful.'

'Sorry,' Liz said the words automatically. 'But it's the yuppy. He's re-creating the Xhantu in an attempt to wear us out.'

'And he's succeeding.' Alison wiped her hand across her face, her hair dishevelled.

'Fred?' The boy grinned at Liz, his face still bright and cheerful, as if he was having the time of his life. 'I have to get down the garden – and I need your catapult.'

'Then you need me.' The small boy got to his feet, the plastic of his mac so rigid he might have been wearing cardboard. 'But how?' He pushed back his sou'wester. 'We'll never get past that little lot.' He pointed to the dense mass of animals, clearly working under instruction, alternate ranks crawling and flying into the attack, keeping the two men at full stretch, their arms never still for a moment.

'If you can climb over the fence, we can get to him that way. Can you do it?'

'Is it goin' to be dangerous?'

Liz nodded.

'Then I'm all for it.' Fred grinned. Grabbing the top of the solid water butt, he hoisted himself up the side, his feet scrabbling for a purchase on the slippery wood. He stood up, balancing gingerly on its rim. Comfortable now with her new-found agility, Liz sprang to the top of the fence.

'Cor,' the small boy exclaimed. 'Wish I could leap about like that, I wouldn't half have some fun.'

Relieved, for the sake of the more elderly residents in the village, that Fred didn't possess her particular gift, Liz leaned down to help him up. Straddling the top of the fence, he swung his legs over before dropping feet first onto the pavement, his plastic mac crackling loudly with every movement.

Skimming across the pavement Liz ran for the shed, its slanted roof clearly visible thirty yards away. It was up to her to stop the fledgling creatures before they became strong enough to join in the attack. If she failed – no way could they beat them off. She swung round, astonished to find the road empty behind her. Scared that something might have happened to Fred, she was about to go back and check when he came round the corner.

'Get a move on,' she beckoned. 'We've haven't got time to waste, they're in danger.'

'I needed ammunition,' Fred patted his bulging pockets. 'The roadmen left a pile of gravel when they mended a hole last week. It's perfect. Right, what's the plan?'

'This isn't funny, Fred. 'We'll could all be dead in a minute – you too.'

'Nah! Constable Barnes says I was born to be hung.'

Liz paused. 'Don't you ever get scared?' she said curiously.

'Nope,' he boasted. 'Don't know the meaning. Dad Reid says I'd make a good soldier. He was in the war, got injured,' Fred said, referring to his foster parent.

'Yes, I know. But tell me later. Quickly, now. Remember, when you get up on the roof, keep down. The yuppy mustn't spot you – *that's vital*. Then, when I say, you fire stones at him and I'll try and zap him.'

Hastily unbuttoning his mac, Fred dropped the yellow garment on the ground, stuffing a handful of stones into his blazer pocket. 'Give me a leg up, then.'

He lifted his foot, the sole of his shoe encrusted with dirt.

Liz squealed. '*Yeeoh!* I'm not touching that, you stepped in some dogs' muck. You'll have to take your shoe off.'

'Sorry, didn't notice it. Must have been left by the gravel.'

Hopping on one foot Fred pulled off his shoe, carefully scraping it on the kerb edge to clean it. Leaving it on the pavement, he fitted his sock foot into Liz's cupped hands.

'I've got heavy bones,' he apologised as she struggled to hoist him up. Grabbing the top of the fence, he crawled up the steep side of the bitumen-covered roof like a Red Indian through pampas grass. Liz leapt up beside him. Lying flat, she peeped over the edge.

In the time it had taken her to gather Fred up, the fledgling monsters had grown enormously and were already streaming down the garden to enter the battle. Neither of the two swordsmen had spotted the sudden increase in the enemy's ranks, too busy obliterating the animals in the front row, but Alison had. Liz saw her gaze at the solid mass of snarling shapes, her shoulders beginning to droop.

Liz felt her stomach gripe with nerves, something she had rarely experienced before. She took in a deep breath, trying to remind herself that being nervous was good for you. It produced adrenalin which made you move faster – and become fearless.

'Ready, Fred,' she quavered, not feeling at all brave.

Fred eased himself up till he was kneeling. Pulling out a handful of stones, he gave them to Liz to hold. Fitting a stone into the little cup, he loosed the powerful elastic aiming at the swaying figure, reaching out immediately for another missile. The torso of the oriental figure stretched over backwards, collecting particles of ash from the ground, and the little projectile sailed unnoticed over the head of the newly created Xhantu, landing in the soft earth. Fred fired again and again – the figure never still long enough to make contact.

'Come on, Fred,' Liz muttered. Despairing, she watched the little pile of stones dwindle rapidly till there were only a few left.

'Don't worry, I'll get the blighter if it's the last thing I do,' Fred grunted.

Pursing his lips with determination, his eyes glued to the target, he drew back his hand releasing a stone. Like a bolt of lightning, the sharp edge caught the willowy neck a glancing blow. Spinning round, the figure leapt straight into the air with the speed and agility of a grasshopper. Anticipating his move, the green light, already speeding from Liz's hand, met its target. Even as the yuppy dived towards her like a heat-seeking missile, the light force slammed into it. A sheet of flame engulfed the willowy figure. It spiralled upwards, the heat singeing the leaves of a conifer in the neighbouring garden. Spreading along the ground, the flames swiftly enveloped the struggling shapes. There was a spurt of bright energy as it caught and devoured them, followed by a ferocious fireball.

'*Oh, Fred, we did it.*' Liz flung her arms round the small boy, hugging him fiercely to her. 'You were just *wonderful* with that catapult. Come on – I'll give you a hand down.'

THIRTEEN

Almost too tired to walk, a very weary and dirty-looking party dragged themselves back into the house. At the door to the veranda, Tom McFaddean paused, his hand on the latch. A pungent smell of burning resin and animal fur filled the air, a few spiralling wisps of smoke all that was left of the bonfire. Locking the door, he pushed the bolt across.

'Though what good that will do with so many broken skylights,' he muttered. 'Where's the fuse box? I'll get the lights on.'

'Under the stairs,' Alison said. 'There a torch next to the door.'

The light flickered once before remaining steady and Tom McFaddean, hanging the torch back up, joined the three children and Alison in the kitchen. He glanced with concern at Phil, Alison busily dabbing disinfectant onto a nasty gouge on his shoulder.

'Bad, Dr Shaw?'

'Could have been. It went clean through his jacket and pullover. I don't want it becoming infected, that's all. You'll have a bruise tomorrow, Phil, a beauty I expect. Still, I got the blighter. Anyone else?'

Liz shook her head, not wanting to admit that her legs hadn't stopping shaking yet.

'Ma Reid'll kill me,' Fred intoned, staring mournfully down at his blazer, streaks of green slime from the roof of the shed daubing the front of it. Silently, he dumped the yellow mac on to the back of a chair and sat down, his elbows on the table. 'Still, it was worth it.' A grin broke through the dirt on his face. 'Do it again termorrow if I could.'

'I thought you were supposed to stay on the sidelines.' Tom McFaddean gave an abrupt laugh and patted the young boy affectionately on the back. 'Don't worry about it, Fred, I'll buy you a new blazer. How much did it cost?'

'Three pound ninety-nine from Woolworths, Mr Mac.'

He nodded and, picking up the two swords which had been left on a chair, headed into the study to put them away.

'You come cheap, Fred.' Alison, packing away her first-aid kit, smiled warmly at the small boy. 'A dab hand with that catapult, too. I was most impressed. Proper David and Goliath you were; glad you were on our side.'

Fred beamed with pride. 'Don't suppose I could have some of that dinner Mrs Lucy left then as a reward, I'm starvin'.' He eyed the stove hungrily.

'I'm with Fred,' Tom McFaddean said from the doorway. 'I could eat a horse.' He strolled back into the kitchen, handing Fred four one-pound notes.

Fred beamed. 'Cor! Thanks Mr Mac. Never seen this much money before.' He folded the notes neatly, tucking them away in the top pocket of his blazer.

'If that's okay with you, Dr Shaw,' Tom McFaddean picked up an oven cloth, 'I'll get the dinner on the table. So, Liz, you didn't need me to tell you what your role was after all.'

'Is that why you didn't give me a weapon, Mr McFaddean?'

'*Mac*, remember? So you can get up high and watch our backs? Yes.' Tom McFaddean opened the oven door pulling out a large cottage pie. 'There's plenty of pie, thank goodness, unless anyone fancies dried-up broccoli and peas?'

Spotting a universal shaking of heads, he emptied the contents of the second dish into the rubbish bin under the sink.

'Hate broccoli anyway, Mr Mac.' Fred's eyes gleamed at the sight of the steaming potato crust.

Phil tore over to the dresser and, opening the drawer, reached in to grab knives and forks.

'*Phil – your hands!*' Alison screeched. He stopped dead and swung round. He stared down at his hands, a guilty expression on his face. 'Children, I know you're tired but please wash your hands. They must be filthy. I don't mind you sitting down to dinner with dirty faces *this once* – you can have a bath straight after dinner and go to bed.'

'Mu-um! I can't possibly go to bed. I'm much too excited.' Phil dived across to the kitchen sink. Turning on the cold tap, he hastily rubbed soap into his hands. Then, swilling them under the running water, grabbed the kitchen towel. 'That do?'

He held his hands out and stepped back to make room for his sister and Fred to wash theirs. Alison nodded. He grabbed a handful of cutlery and began spreading it round the table.

'*You* can sit up, Phil, if you like,' she said, 'but I'm worn out. Straight after dinner, I'm heading for my bed. Mr McFaddean, there's no need for you to return to London tonight, you can have Phil's room. You can bunk in with Liz, Phil, the camp bed is made up.' She opened a cupboard door and pulled out a bottle and two glasses. 'There's some Tizer in the pantry or orange squash if you prefer it. I expect you're all thirsty. I know I am. A glass of whisky, Mr McFaddean?'

He nodded and, reaching for a plate from the overhead rack, ladled a large scoop of carrots, meat and potato on to it.

'Traditionally, one of the Javean has always had the gift of being able to throw their thoughts,' he answered Liz's earlier question. 'Hand this to your sister will you, Phil.' Phil took a deep sniff, inhaling the savoury aroma, and smiled blissfully. 'As I said, your mother possessed the gift and I'm thrilled you've inherited it. Some, the most gifted, could also read minds.' The glance directed at Liz was penetrating.

Liz screwed up her face, replying no to his silent question with a shake of her head. 'It's horrible though – like having a storm of angry bees in your head.'

'It gets easier with time. What about you, Phil, happy in your role?'

Phil nodded. 'Very happy. I'm sorry about before, Liz. I behaved like an idiot. But how do you know all this, Mac?'

'When my father discovered the village, at first he assumed they were simple farming folk.' Tom McFaddean sat down beside Fred. 'There are seconds if anyone's still hungry.' He took a mouthful of pie. 'This is good. If your Mrs Lucy ever needs a job...' His eyes twinkled. 'My father was an explorer and, after my mother died, I was sent out to India to live with him. Except when I arrived, he wasn't there.' He paused sipping at his drink and smiled ruefully. 'He may have been brilliant at his job – somebody recently wrote a book about his discoveries – but he was a dreadful parent, forgetting about me for months ... even years on end. So, basically, I grew up there.'

'Wow!'

Tom McFaddean glanced down at Fred with amusement.

'Yes, it does sound rather exciting doesn't it. I promise you it wasn't, especially when the monsoon rains came and everything – including your shoes – went mouldy. Most of the time, I ran around bare-foot. There was no school in the village ...'

'You didn't go to school?' Fred's eyes grew large at the thought.

The tall man laughed. 'Sorry to disappoint you. My father left a great many books and every morning I was made to study. I grew up knowing science, a little maths, but heaps of history, geography and English.'

'Oh!' Fred's face dropped becoming gloomy.

'It was Tung Wei, your grandfather, who taught me everything I know. He was like a proper father to me.'

'Grandfather!' Liz exclaimed excitedly. 'We have a grandfather?'

'I don't know if he's still alive, Liz. He was badly injured in the attack like me.'

'Oh, Mother, can we find out?'

'*Oh, please*, Mum. Wouldn't it be great to have relatives?' Phil grabbed his sister's hand, his eyes sparkling. 'We've simply got to go and see him.'

Alison glanced up at the kitchen clock. 'The only thing, you two have got to do, is go to bed. There's school tomorrow, remember.'

There was a chorus of loud squeaks – Fred joining in. Alison laughed at their outraged faces.

'*But, Mum*, you can't send us to school, not after this,' Phil protested.

'You don't really think I'm going to let a little thing, like a blood-thirsty fight with monsters, prevent you going to school as normal. Besides, I have to work and I'm sure Mr McFaddean needs to get back to London.'

Tom McFaddean helped himself to some more pie. 'I did leave in rather a hurry, yes. Seconds, Fred?'

Fred groaned. 'I couldn't, I'm full right up to here.' He placed two fingers under his chin.

The door knocker slammed down. Still only half way through her meal, Liz laid down her knife and fork, staring anxiously towards the hall.

'Oh no, not again,' Alison groaned. 'Why can't people leave us in peace.'

'Would you like me to go?' Tom McFaddean rose to his feet.

'No, I'd better, but I'd appreciate some back up.'

*

Sergeant Fisher had just finished eating his supper when Mr Sproggett knocked on his front door. As senior officer, he occupied a small terraced house built onto the back of the police station and, although his post carried many perks – like nipping off home after dinner for forty-winks – it did have one drawback. If there wasn't a constable on duty, people took liberties and knocked on his door.

Mr Sproggett, who was always between jobs, yet still managed to have enough money to go drinking in the pub several nights in the week, had been in a furious temper. Blabbering incoherently, it had taken a series of calming words before Sergeant Fisher understood that Constable Barnes was nowhere to be found, the police station had been left open, and there was a riot at Dr Shaw's house.

Having locked the police station, Sergeant Fisher, accompanied by the irate neighbour, headed for the house in question. And since he felt rather aggrieved at being dragged out so late, he had hammered on the door with more force than necessary.

'Sergeant Fisher! What's the matter?'

'I've had a complaint, Doctor, about the noise.'

'Didn't Constable Barnes explain?'

'Well …' the sergeant began.

'I warned him about the noise earlier,' Mr Sproggett broke in. 'He said you'd got a film director here, a Mr Hitchcock.' He stared balefully at Tom McFaddean. 'You're not Mr Hitchcock, I seen him in that film – you know the one about a train.'

Tom McFaddean leant casually against the door. 'He's made lots of films about trains – great director. But you're right. My name's Hasleknock …'

Hidden behind his back, Liz, who had crept into the hall anxious to discover who was at the door, after the incident with the yuppy, stifled a giggle.

'The constable got it wrong. Phil Hasleknock – pleased to meet you, Mr Sprog-itt.' Tom McFaddean switched his voice, producing the nasal tone of an Australian accent.

Alison, recognising the voice from The Goon Show, something Phil never missed if he could help it, brushed an imaginary hair away from her face to disguise her sudden smile.

'The noise kept me awake.'

Alison's glanced directly at the neighbour, his bulbous

nose, streaked with thread-like purple veins, poking over the sergeant's shoulder.

'I didn't realise you went to bed quite so early, Mr Sproggett?' she said. 'But isn't that your television I hear, blasting out every night till eleven?'

'I was tired tonight. No law against that, is there?'

Alison glanced down at her watch. 'You really must have been tired. It's only half-past nine now. And we just sat down to supper. If you'll excuse us, Sergeant.'

'But the noise, Doctor,' the policeman protested.

'Oh, that's all over with. It won't happen again, I promise. All quiet – listen.'

'Maybe ... but I'd still quite like to look round the garden. Mr Sproggett says there was a fire. Dangerous things, bonfires.'

'I agree,' Tom McFaddean smiled. 'That's out as well. Those props didn't work. What a waste of time and money. Off back to London tomorrow to have another go. I'll use a field next time.'

'Well, that's all right then.' The sergeant shifted his weight to his left leg and cleared his throat. 'Er, there is another matter. Constable Barnes is nowhere to be found.'

'That's definitely nothing to do with us.' Alison smiled cheerfully. 'You'll have to talk to our neighbour about that. He's already admitted speaking him earlier in the evening. *Goodnight*.' She made to close the door. 'And do remember your television, Mr Sproggett, I'm sure Sergeant Fisher doesn't want me bothering him with a complaint,' she added, closing the door firmly on the astonished men.

'Mother, you're the best,' Liz hugged her.

Alison smiled. 'Any more complaints and we'll end up moving.' She raised her voice. 'If you've finished your dinner, Fred, I'll take you home.'

*

Sleepily, Liz listened to the murmur of voices coming from the kitchen.

'I wonder what they're talking about?' Phil sat up in bed. 'I wish I could creep down and listen in. I say, Liz, you know that reading-our-minds trick you do?'

Liz leant up on one elbow. 'You mean, do I know what they're talking about? No! I told you, I can't read people's minds – not really,' she confessed, reluctant to say how easily she had sensed the sadness in Mr McFaddean when his thoughts had strayed to the death of their mother.

'You read mine?'

'But only when you're scared or unhappy. Right now, it's all quiet. Mr McFaddean – Mac – says he doesn't know how it works either. In the battle, I sensed what was happening around me and I could throw my thoughts.' She touched her head. 'I don't much like it, though.'

'Oh!' Phil exclaimed. 'It's really unfair. I bet Mac is telling Mum all about the Javean. We should be listening to that. We're the Javean not her. And what about our real names?'

'Mother was Mei-Xui and I'm Mei. It's a bit strange after always being called Liz. But I like yours.'

'Quon – that means bright and shining – like my sword. Father was called Huang-Fu. Does it make you feel sad, Liz?'

'Losing our real parents? To be honest, I'm not sure – everything's happening too fast to take in.'

'But you do think Mac'll take us to meet our grandfather?'

'I hope so.' Liz sat bolt upright, her tiredness forgotten. 'At the moment, none of this feels real – not even the fight. It's like Mac is telling a story about some other children.'

'Well, I'm like Fred. I'd do it all again tomorrow if I could. That sword, it was so amazing, it felt alive in my hand like I was … a real hero. Do you think I could try flying – like you.'

Before Liz could stop him, Phil had climbed up on the edge of the bed waving his arms in the air. The camp bed tilted and he overbalanced, crashing to the floor, the bed on top of him.

'*What on earth's going on up there?*' their mother called from the bottom of the stairs.

'Phil fell out of bed,' Liz called back, trying not to laugh at the pained expression on her brother's face.

'*Is he all right?*'

'His pride's a bit dented.'

There was a pause then: 'Mr McFaddean says, if you're trying out new skills they only come to life when there's danger.'

Manhandling the camp bed upright again, Phil pulled the sheets straight and climbed back in. 'He might have said,' he grumbled, rubbing his elbow where he'd hit it on the wooden corner of the bed.

'I don't suppose he expected you to start throwing yourself off furniture.' Liz paused. 'Don't you think it's all a bit scary?'

'*Scary,*' Phil's tone was scornful. 'It's the most exciting thing that's ever happened.'

'*Not the fight, Phil,* I meant our lives. Everything will be different from now on and Mother knows it. Sending us to school is her way of trying to keep things normal for a bit longer – but they'll never be normal again, because we aren't.'

'I never thought about it like that,' Phil confessed, doubt replacing his usual confident expression. 'I suppose we aren't.' He shuddered and made to get out of bed again. 'We need to talk to Mac. We can't leave it.'

'That's what Mother's doing now. I expect she's giving Mac the third degree. Poor Mother.' Liz lay back down and closed her eyes.

'Why?'

'All she can think of is our future full of danger.'

'But that's why it's exciting.'

'Not for her, it isn't. She never wanted us to be different, that's why she never told us. She wants us to be ordinary, with ordinary lives, and that's never going to happen now.'

FOURTEEN

As she opened the front door, Mrs Lucy gave a loud and ominous sniff. Liz and Phil exchanged glances, sensing the housekeeper was seriously put out about something. Silently, they hung up their blazers. It was rare for Mrs Lucy to get upset. She loved her job and even her employer's vagueness about ordinary things didn't particularly bother her. But when it did happen, it usually meant suffering several days-worth of horrid dinners until she got over it, often serving cauliflower cheese for several days on the trot, even though neither Phil nor Liz much cared for it. And, if she was very, *very* cross, it was leeks in white sauce.

Miserably aware that whatever she cooked their mother would insist they ate, Liz faked a happy smile and, tucking her arm in the housekeeper's, dragged her off down the hall.

'Darling Lucy, we're starving – what's for tea?'

'Huh! You're mother's coming home early, so you'll just have to wait. And kindly remember my name is Mrs Paluski. That other lady went back to Poland where she is appreciated.'

Phil rolled his eyes at his sister, groaning silently. *This definitely was serious.*

'You can have a glass of milk and a *plain* biscuit to tide you over.' The housekeeper relented a little, still maintaining her severe tone. '*She* asked for roast chicken – on a Thursday too. Whatever next! *And apple pie.* Apparently, you are expecting a visitor.'

'Fantastic!' Phil exclaimed. Grabbing Mrs Lucy by the hand, he tried to whirl her round. She planted her feet firmly refusing to budge. 'You know it's my favourite.'

Mrs Lucy gave a stiff nod, her face still rigidly set.

Liz, watching the resentful expression on the housekeeper's face, felt the angry thoughts buzzing around her head. Unless the housekeeper had a chance to voice them, she would explode.

'Darling Lucy, I know you're cross because we left the house in such a mess. But it looks wonderful again now. *You must have worked ever so hard.*'

As if she had pressed a magic button, Mrs Lucy drew herself up, words flowing out in an indignant tirade.

'It's a good job somebody notices. *Your mother never does*, otherwise she wouldn't have asked for chicken. All that glass and muddy footprints. It took me all morning just to clear *that* up – never mind polishing the dining table to make it fit for visitors.'

'We could have eaten in the kitchen,' Phil said unwisely. 'We did last night.'

'*Kitchen! I'll not have visitors eating in the kitchen.* Who is this gentleman, anyway?'

'Oh, do sit down, Mrs Lucy, and I'll make you a cup of tea.' Phil quickly filled the kettle with water, carrying it to the stove.

Liz sat down beside the rigid form of the housekeeper, flashing little sympathetic glances at her still mortified expression. 'He's from London and he knows our grandfather,' she said.

Liz watched the housekeeper's expression change, exactly as if someone had taken a pin and let out all the bubbling steam.

'Your *grandfather*, you say. Oh well, that's quite different,' Mrs Lucy cooed maternally. 'Where does *he* live?'

'We don't know exactly.' The kettle began to whistle. Phil took it off the gas. Carefully rinsing the tea pot with boiling water, he added two teaspoons of tea before filling it with water from the kettle. Placing the teapot on the table, he went to the larder to get the milk. 'We're not even sure if he's still alive. That's why Mr McFaddean's coming tonight – so he can tell us more about our family.'

Liz flashed him a grateful glance.

'I wish your mother had told me.' The housekeeper tapped Phil on the hand. 'It's a good job I made custard then, isn't it, dear?'

'You're such a darling, Lucy.' Phil beamed his delight, carefully pouring the tea into the waiting cups. 'Is the custard nice and thick?'

'Just the way you like it.' She picked up her cup and took a sip. 'Very good, Philip. So how did the glass get broken? Your mother said it was a freak storm.'

'We were in the study when we heard the noise,' Phil said, munching a biscuit.

Realising he was stepping on dangerous ground, Liz twitched her eyebrows at her brother to stop him saying anything further. Besides, it was safer to leave the lies to their mother – she was so much better at it than they were.

Relieved, she heard her mother's key in the door. Leaping up she ran into the hallway, catching sight of Tom McFaddean's tall figure. He was clutching a large bouquet of mauve chrysanthemums, the huge heads protected by cellophane and tied with a matching ribbon.

'Mr McFaddean kindly offered to drive me. Do come along in,' Alison said politely, sounding as if Mr McFaddean was the gas man come to read the meter. Liz thought it most odd especially when, only the night before, they'd been bellowing instructions to one another during the fight.

Tom McFaddean grinned at Liz and headed for the kitchen. 'I'm mending fences,' he whispered. 'Mrs Paluski ...' He gave the housekeeper a neat bow before handing across the bouquet. 'These are for you.'

The housekeeper flushed bright red. 'I've never been given flowers,' she bridled.

'That's a great mistake.' He smiled warmly at her. 'Anyone who cooks as well as you should be serenaded with flowers on a regular basis. Besides, we left your house in a terrible mess ...'

'Oh no, sir,' she gushed. 'When the children were younger it was often dirty.' She stood up, peering over his shoulder at Alison in the hall and gave her an approving nod. 'Did you hear about Constable Barnes, Dr Shaw?'

Alison's face assumed a politely interested expression. 'Sergeant Fisher did mention he was missing.'

Mrs Lucy shook her head. '*Missing! He was set upon.*' She paused dramatically. 'I don't know the world is coming to, really I don't. Have you ever heard anything like it? Attacked he was and hit on the head.' She shook her own from side to side, as if to check it was still working all right. 'The butcher told me when I bought the chicken. 'Keeps going on about some Chinaman taking his clothes. But he was fully dressed when they found him.'

Out of sight of the housekeeper, Alison exchanged a speaking glance with Tom McFaddean.

'What an extraordinary thing. I do hope he gets better soon,' she said, keeping her tone smoothly bland.

'They're keeping him in,' Mrs Lucy added darkly. 'Observation, the butcher called it.' Her tone brightened. 'If you don't mind, Dr Shaw, as you're early, I'll leave now. Everything's ready – except for cooking the vegetables. Of course, I'd be happy to stop and put them on.'

'You've done quite enough for one day.' Tom McFaddean took her elbow and steered her into the hall. 'You should go home and put your feet up. My car's outside, I'll run you.'

'Oh, no, sir, I couldn't let you.' Giving Liz the flowers to hold, she slipped on her coat, a heavy brown cloth with a deep collar and tie belt, which she had worn every winter since Liz was little. She picked up her bag, draping the enormous bouquet across one arm. 'I only live down the road.' She stepped out into the porch then, as if unable to stop herself, buried her nose in the bouquet and inhaled deeply. 'I love the smell of chrysanths,' she said, a dreamy smile on her face. 'Always makes me think of Christmas. Thank you again,' she repeated almost curtseying with delight. 'See you tomorrow, then.'

Alison laughed and closed the door. 'She doesn't live down the road – it's a quite a long walk to her house but she wants to show off her flowers.' Her tone suddenly changed, becoming formal. 'Thank you, Mr McFaddean. That was very kind of you. I would never have thought of doing something like that.'

'Mum,' Phil interrupted. 'Can we ask Fred to come for dinner?'

'You can.' Alison took off her suit jacket, hanging it up. 'I expect Mrs Lucy has set dinner in the dining room but we can change it if you like. Mrs Reid isn't best pleased with us,' she told Phil, who was hovering anxiously. 'Naturally, it was her favourite conifer that got burned up and, despite Mr McFaddean giving her money for a new blazer for Fred, she was muttering about *not putting up with it*. It was ten minutes before she stopped talking long enough for me to get a word in.'

'How did you explain it?'

'Your mother and I decided the horror film scenario was the best. At least, it's consistent.'

Leaving the front door ajar, Liz and Phil ran down the path, swinging round the wall into next door's front garden. Shielded from the road by a dusty laurel hedge, a cotoneaster with bright red berries clung to the shabby brickwork at the front of the house.

Phil tapped cautiously. After a minute or two, they heard a shuffling from the hallway and the door opened. Mrs Reid stood there, her hand ready on the latch to close the door again. A tall stick-like figure, her long flat feet were encased in slippers, which accounted for the shuffling, and her short brown hair clung tightly to her head, permed into rows of tight curls like sausages,.

She opened her thin lips wide enough to let out the word, 'Yes?'

Liz heard Phil swallow. He had always found Mrs Reid

intimidating. When they were little he'd been convinced their neighbour was really a witch and the broom, which she used to sweep the front path, was the one she rode at night about the skies, frightening dogs into barking noisily.

Despite denying she could actually sense what people were feeling, as the day had worn on Liz had found her power growing stronger. At first it was exciting but, by the end of the school day, it had become rather wearisome. On entering the playground, she had experienced a quiver-full of arrows loosed at her head. Snatches of anger, jealousy, sadness, spite, plus a hundred other feelings bombarded her, although it was impossible to tell from what direction they had flown. And there was nothing nice in any of the feelings, as if happiness was a closely guarded secret that never strayed far from its owner's thoughts. By the time the bell rang marking the end of lessons, she was worn out and the only thing she wanted to do was go home and hide away quietly in her bedroom.

Now, she got the impression that Mrs Reid bitterly blamed life for letting her down. Gazing at her thin twisted lips, it was quite impossible to imagine their neighbour ever being young and happy. So different from their mother, who had demonstrated with her hockey stick that she was still youthful enough to enjoy doing madcap things. And, although her mother had been wearing her usual serious expression when she arrived home from work, Liz sensed the excitement bubbling under the surface as if, like Phil, she was hoping there'd be another fight that night.

'Is Fred in, please?'

'He's in the garden.' Mrs Reid snapped her thin lips together and jerked her head backwards. 'Wait there, I'll call him. You're not bringing your dirty feet through my clean hall.'

Phil pushed Liz back down the path. 'That's all right. We can shout over the fence.'

They rushed back through the house. In the kitchen Tom McFaddean, perfectly at home, was pouring boiling water over the vegetables. He raised an eyebrow as they flew past.

'Fred's in the garden,' Liz explained, opening the door to the veranda.

She stared in horror. Even though Mrs Lucy had swept up all the broken glass and earth, and had picked up the flowerpots, it still resembled the aftermath of a hurricane. Wind whistled through the broken panes in the glass roof, making a pile of newspapers in the corner flap noisily. The garden was even worse, if that was possible. Gouged and churned up by the feet and claws of dozens of animals, the lawn resembled a ploughed field and the flower borders had disappeared under a thick layer of ash. At the far end of the lawn, the swing dangled dejectedly from a single chain, where the fierce light had cut clean through the metal.

Keeping to the path they ran down the garden, clambering onto a wheelbarrow, which Phil had placed upside down against the fence for just that purpose.

'Fred, you there?' he shouted.

The shed door creaked open and Fred stuck his head out.

'We wanted to ask you for dinner…'

Fred gazed up at them, the freckles across his face furrowed into deep lines.

'What's wrong?' Liz said.

'I've really gone and done it this time.' Holding the door partly open, he kicked at a stone on the path sending it flying into the vegetable patch. 'Says she's had enough of my mischief. I told her I didn't mean to do it, I said sorry.'

'Oh, Fred,' she groaned. 'Whatever did you do?'

'I was practisin' shooting things, you know in case we had another fight, and broke her new plant pot. Dad Reid told her it was an accident and he'd get her another. But she said, after last night, it was the last straw. Dad Reid's in there now, tryin' to talk her round.'

'Oh, Fred. But that's so unfair.' Liz screwed up her face, wanting to cry. 'You weren't to blame for last night. Why if it hadn't been for you, we might all be dead.'

'Honest?'

'Of course, you were amazingly brave.'

'But you can't tell Mrs Reid that, Liz,' Phil reminded. 'No one's to know, remember.'

'I never mean to get into trouble.' The small boy emerged from the shed and swung the door shut. He stood by the fence staring up at the two heads peering down at him, his expression doleful. 'Dad Reid says that trouble finds me.'

Liz felt angry. Fred and his smile were always together, like Mrs Lucy coming to work every morning – they could be relied on. 'Now, you've got to come over for dinner, Fred. We can't let this happen.'

Fred's expression brightened at the thought of food. 'Okay, I can always do with another dinner. Be with you in a jiffy.' He ran up the garden, disappearing through the back door of the house.

FIFTEEN

'It's not right, Mum,' Phil grumbled, telling Alison what had happened. 'We have to stop her. She can't send Fred back to the orphanage – not now.'

Alison and Tom McFaddean exchanged concerned frowns. 'I agree, but what can we do?' she said. 'Mrs Lucy says, she's a most unpleasant woman and never a day goes by without her threatening to send Fred back where he came from. Let's hope that's all this is – a threat.'

'What happened to his real parents?' Tom McFaddean asked.

'They were killed in a rail crash when Fred was two. According to Mrs Lucy, who knows absolutely everything about the people in the village,' Alison pulled a face, 'his father served with Mr Reid in the army. When he died, Mr Reid tried to adopt the boy but couldn't because he was a bachelor.'

'You mean he married Mrs Reid for Fred's sake,' Phil interrupted. 'Poor Mr Reid. Fancy being married to a witch.'

'*Phil!* She might be quite nice underneath.'

'She isn't,' Liz said quietly.

Alison gazed at her daughter in startled surprise. 'Well, anyway, we'd better keep off the subject – agreed. And no more boasting about last night, Phil, you've done quite enough and worn me out in the process.'

'You mean, we have to sit in silence?'

'That's enough, Phil,' Alison rebuked. 'There's always plenty to talk about. You can start out by telling me what happened in school today.'

'Mu-um!' he groaned. 'How can you possibly expect me to concentrate on Latin verbs after last night?'

'You need Latin, Phil, if you're ever going to amount to anything.'

Tom McFaddean, propped up against the kitchen cupboard, grinned sympathetically. 'I ...' he began.

'Not one word please, Mr McFaddean,' Alison rounded on him. 'You may have survived being brought up in the jungle – *but that's not going to happen here.* My children are going to school.'

'Mother, I know you want to keep things normal ...'

Alison flinched and her voice changed. 'You can read my thoughts, Liz?'

'Not really, perhaps a tiny bit around the edges.'

'Oh!' Alison sat down at the table fiddling with her glasses, her voice suddenly tired. 'Then you know Mr McFaddean and I don't agree on what to do next.'

'I am trying to convince Dr Shaw to move you both to London, where I can keep an eye on you.'

'And leave school?' Phil exclaimed excitedly. 'Fantastic!'

'We've already had this conversation, Philip,' Alison replied sharply, like a turtle snapping its jaws together.

'Zheng-Li won't stop, Dr Shaw. As soon as he finds a way, they'll be another yuppy searching for you.'

'What exactly are yuppies, Mac?' Phil eyed his mother cautiously wondering if she was going to object to the nickname now the fight was over, but she didn't appear to have noticed.

The doorbell rang.

'That will be Fred. Answer it, will you, Phil?'

Tom McFaddean removed the chicken from the oven, where it had been left to keep warm. He began carving, handing Liz the plates to put on the table. She had already cleared the dining room table, carrying the knives and forks back to the kitchen, aware that Fred would feel more comfortable there.

'And we won't have to worry about dropping food on the carpet.'

Glancing anxiously across the table at her mother, she picked up an oven cloth and, carrying the dish of vegetables to the table, placed them on a mat in the centre. Ignoring the activity around her, Alison sat twisting her glasses round and round. Liz felt the whirling thoughts and hoped she hadn't made up her mind to put a stop to their adventures.

Fred bounced into the room, his freckles and smile lighting up the room like a hundred-watt light bulb. Putting her glasses back on, Alison smiled warmly at him.

'Phil says you've already had your tea. You're not – seriously – thinking of eating another, are you?'

'You just watch me, Dr Shaw,' Fred beamed. 'You ain't never tried Ma Reid's cookin'. Her rock cakes are that hard I built a rockery out of mine, and Dad Reid says he was fat when he came back from the jungle.' He grinned at the laughter. 'So what have I missed?'

'Phil was asking about yuppies.' Tom McFaddean pulled out a chair. 'Sit yourself down.' He put a plate down in front of him, helping the young boy to vegetables. 'Carrots?' Fred nodded. 'And I guess you like gravy.' He picked up the gravy boat. 'Over your meat or veg?'

'Both, please, Mr Mac, I like gravy better than anythin'.'

Tom McFaddean chuckled and poured a liberal quantity onto Fred's plate, passing the gravy boat across to Phil to serve himself.

The table, when pulled away from the wall, was big enough for six. Tom McFaddean occupied the seat he had used the night before, nearest the stove, with Alison at the far end. Fred and Liz sat between them on the one side, leaving Phil on his own with his back to the wall.

'But we got rid of it, didn't we?' the small boy said. Smiling happily he eyed the food on his plate, his elbows stuck out at right-angles, his fork hovering anxiously, undecided which bit to eat first.

'For the moment, Fred, but it's likely to return – and not necessarily looking the same. You saw how quickly it could change its appearance.'

'What else can they do?'

'Besides clone themselves into a dozen different shapes at the same time.'

'They can do that?' Fred said, his meal forgotten.

'Definitely. Anything they see, they can imitate. And so well, it's often impossible to tell which is the genuine article.'

'Can they kill, Mr McFaddean?'

He shifted uncomfortably. 'They can, Dr Shaw, if they take possession of someone. I saw it happen. The man went completely mad and jumped off the mountain side. They use a type of hypnotism so, if you meet one, don't for goodness sake look directly at it.'

'You mean you've met up with them before?' Liz said, helping herself to potato. She loved food but only in small amounts, whereas Phil would eat non-stop if their mother let him.

Tom McFaddean nodded. 'I had gone out to Burma for the summer holidays with my friends.' He picked up his knife and fork. 'Will Rutherford, he's curator at the British Museum now, and Toby Adams. He lectures in archaeology at Cambridge. My father, like theirs, was excavating some ruins and they had discovered a treasure trove of ancient gold and jewellery. Only thing was, as fast as they dug it up it vanished. At first, they thought it was one of the porters. It was only when they found the thief could get into a locked room, did they decide it had to be a yuppy.' Tom McFaddean grinned and glanced slyly at his hostess. 'Of course, I didn't believe in evil spirits at that time but I soon changed my mind.'

Liz caught sight of her mother's expression, a disapproving frown on her face.

'Did you get rid of it?'

'We did, Liz, but it took some doing and we didn't get off entirely scot-free.'

Fred scratched his nose, his brow a deep furrow as if a tractor had just run along his forehead. 'You know that sorcerer ...'

'Zheng-Li?'

'That's the bloke. Well, Phil says he's been dead for – like a thousand years. So how come he's still makin' trouble?'

'That's a good question, Fred.' Tom McFaddean paused thinking. 'The villagers believe him still to be alive, his power dormant, waiting...'

'Like a volcano?' Phil jumped in.

'Exactly.'

'That's one of the areas where Mr McFaddean and I can't agree,' Alison said. 'Reluctantly, I now accept that magic exists – only because I saw it happening last night,' she added severely. 'But a sorcerer that can live for thousands of years ...' She shook her head. 'More vegetables, Phil?'

'No thanks. I need to save some room for pudding. The thing is, Mum, if you accept that Zheng-Li is still around then everything fits. It doesn't make sense any other way.'

Alison laid down her knife and fork. 'Logic says you're right but for a person of science that's a big leap.' She leaned forward. 'You're very quiet, Liz,' she eyed her daughter.

'I was listening,' Liz said, unwilling to admit she felt exhausted. Her mother was bound to ask what time they'd gone to sleep the night before, and that would mean admitting Phil had talked non-stop for hours, excited by the knowledge that he belonged to a clan of magical fighters.

'You'd better get off to bed early tonight, you look – what I would call – ropey.'

'I'm fine, Mother, honestly,' Liz protested. 'But you know me, I'm quite happy to go to bed and read.' She caught her brother's glare. 'You don't have to go, Phil, I know it's Paul Temple later.'

'But, Mac ...' Phil pointed with his knife. Alison, noticing, rapped the table loudly with her knuckles. 'Sorry, Mum,' he muttered, hastily laying the offending item on the side of his plate. 'If Zheng-Li is that powerful, why can't he escape?'

'I simply don't know, Phil. It's back to Fred's original question. After a thousand years, does he still exist?'

Liz sat silently, remembering the statue that had been dug up, its clothes in tatters – only its hands unblemished with age.

'I'm hoping the jade, even though it's been removed from the village, is still powerful enough to stop him.'

'Is that why they came after us, to destroy it?'

'Partly,' Tom McFaddean said. '*If* the story is true, Zheng-Li also fears you.'

'Me!' Phil's fork clattered down on to his plate with astonishment, earning him another reproving glare from his mother, his expression wavering between scared and excited.

'You were fourteen, on the third of November.'

'*Yesterday*! *The same as Mum*. I was right,' he crowed triumphantly. 'I always said it wasn't December. But why?'

'At fourteen, a Javean is considered a man.'

'Cor!' Fred exclaimed. 'I only got two more birthdays to go.'

'When's my birthday?' Liz said. 'My passport says March.'

'It's actually the beginning of February, Liz,' Mr McFaddean smiled. 'I am not sure which date. We'll have to ask your grandfather about that. He'll know. But, with you two growing up, Zheng-Li obviously fears the Javean might become strong enough to take on the fight, as they did once before. It makes me think that Tung Wei, your grandfather, is very much alive and in touch with some of the villagers who fled back in forty-seven. Somehow, we have to trace the final two pieces and take them all back to the village.' He glanced out of the corner of his eye at Alison who, head bent, was scowling down at her plate again.

Fred, who had been quietly eating, put his knife and fork down, beaming down at his empty plate, an expression of pure bliss on his face. Undercover of the tablecloth, he rubbed his tummy.

'That was smashin'. Wish I could live here always, Doctor. I wouldn't mind sleepin' under the kitchen table in a dog basket if I could eat grub like that every day.'

'That would be nice,' Alison kept her tone brisk. 'But I promise you, Fred, chicken is a rare event in this house – it's far too expensive to eat every day. I decided you deserved something special to celebrate our victory over those vile creatures.'

Tom McFaddean got to his feet. 'Everyone finished?'

The door knocker sounded. Before anyone else could move, he headed into the hall to answer it. Alison glared at the ceiling and gave a loud and exasperated sigh. Phil glanced under his eyebrows at Liz. She grimaced back at him, both of them understanding the sigh to mean: *typical man, trying to takeover. I'm perfectly capable of answering my own door, thank you.*

'It's Mr Reid,' Tom McFaddean's voice called from the hallway. 'We've just finishing our dinner. Come in and join us for pudding, there's plenty.'

Fred swallowed and glanced at the door, his face unchanged except for its deep ridge of freckles across his brow.

'I don't like to disturb you, sir,' they heard Mr Reid's soft voice. He limped into the kitchen, his right trouser leg flapping loosely.

Alison got up and sat next to Phil.

'Do sit down,' she said, indicating her empty chair. 'Have some apple pie and a cup of tea.'

'A cup a' tea will do nicely, thank you, Doctor.'

'Is it curtains, Dad?'

Mr Reid appeared to be on the brink of bursting into tears. Liz stared at him, shocked at the thought of a grown man crying.

'Mrs Reid can't understand that boys are naturally full of mischief,' he confided, glancing at Tom McFaddean for support. 'But give them a bit of time and they grow out of it. I did – and I was a real handful. My mother had four boys.

Says, I was worse than all the rest put together.' Mr Reid tapped Fred on the shoulder. 'It won't be so bad, lad, I'll come and visit every Saturday.'

'We'll come, too.' Liz screwed up her face, trying to stop herself dissolving into tears. How could this be happening – it was rotten.

Alison reached out across the table, patting Liz on the hand to get her attention. 'Put the kettle on, there's a good girl, I can't get up. But Mr Reid, last night was nothing to do with Fred, I told your wife that.'

'I know, Doctor. And I'm not blaming you. If it hadn't happened yesterday it would have happened tomorrow, if you get my drift. The missus only took him in the first place as a favour to me. We've been living on borrowed time ever since.' Their neighbour shrank visibly in his seat, sniffing loudly. 'Never wanted children. It's the mess, you see; she can't abide mess.'

Fred opened his mouth to say something and shut it again, staring down at the table.

The kettle gasped loudly, the noise accelerating into a sharp whistle. Liz, arranging the cups and saucers on the table, dived for the stove to switch off the gas, pouring the boiling water into the large brown teapot.

'I know, son …' Mr Reid picked up a fork from the table and began twiddling it in his fingers. 'It's not reasonable, but what can you do when the ladies have made up their minds – eh, sir?' Tom McFaddean gave him a sympathetic nod. 'As I keep telling you, Fred, you've gotta keep your head down below the parapet if you don't want it blown off.'

'Fred told me you were army.' Tom McFaddean said, busily cutting the apple pie into six slices. He passed the plates round.

Mr Reid's shoulders went back and his head jerked up as if on parade. 'That I was, sir, served almost five year.' Liz passed him a cup of tea. 'Thank you, miss.' Picking up the sugar bowl, he added two heaped teaspoons to the cup stirring it briskly. He pointed the spoon at his right leg. 'Lost it in Burma.'

'Were you one of Wingate's men?' Tom McFaddean cut into his pie with his fork. 'Oh! This *is* delicious.'

Fred raised his head, beaming proudly round the table. 'Dad Reid got the Burma Star.' He stared down at his plate again, his apple pie lying untouched in front of him.

'So did your dad, lad,' Mr Reid nodded the words out. 'Went right through without a scratch, he did.'

Liz, sitting next to Fred, caught sight of his clenched fists and realised how hard he was trying to cling on to his tears. How horrid it must be, living with the threat of being sent away. She and Phil were so lucky. She twisted round in her seat, staring meaningfully at Tom McFaddean at the end of the table, hoping he might be able to do something to stop it happening.

'I was mostly in India,' Tom McFaddean said, the expression on his face thoughtful as if he was considering something else. 'Interpreter. Know that part of the world well, do you?'

'Indeed I do, sir. Made it to Myitkyina – in the north of Burma.'

'Did you now? Strange we never met. I was attached to General Stilwell's staff. Bad do that. But our victory made a lot of difference in the end.'

'That's where I got shot, sir,' Mr Reid volunteered eagerly. 'The bullet wound wasn't too bad but gangrene set in before they could get me back. Still, I was one of the lucky ones.'

'What did you do before the war?' Tom McFaddean continued his questioning.

'Machine tools, sir. Apprenticed for seven years in the motor industry. Not much I don't know about engines. They refused to take me back after the war, on account of my leg. Didn't think I'd be safe around machinery no more. I'm working part-time in the Lost and Found at Salisbury station, but they're shutting down at Christmas so I'll have to find something else.'

'Interesting.'

The table fell silent, the only noise a scraping of dishes.

'I don't suppose you kept in touch with any of the other chaps?'

'Yes, sir. Through the Burma Association.' Mr Reid smiled proudly at the name. 'We meet every year. Why?'

'Did Fred tell you about last night?'

'Said it was a secret, Mr McFaddean.' He shuffled in his seat.

'That's okay, Mr Reid.' Alison put out her hand. 'I think, in a roundabout way, Mr McFaddean is asking for your help.' She frowned at the tall man.

'You are, sir?' Mr Reid's voice changed, becoming more like Fred's eager tone.

'Mm! When you were chasing the enemy, did your lot come across any jade?'

'Most of the prisoners had a piece on them – good luck charm, they said. Why?'

'We're searching for two medallions, a bit like this one.'

Tom McFaddean untied the ribbon from around his neck, once again wearing the piece of jade that he'd given to Phil for protection during the fight. 'I discovered this in Nepal. One of the Ghurkha's had brought it back with him.' He passed it to Fred. 'Let Mr Reid see it, Fred.'

Fred sat fingering the little medallion and Liz sensed his reluctance to let go of it.

'The pieces aren't identical. If I remember rightly, the two missing are similar to this.' Tom McFaddean pulled the small box, bought from the market in Notting Hill, out of his pocket and placed it on the table, the proud gaze of the bird staring endlessly at its cardboard surround.

'I think we need more tea.' He crossed to the sink to fill the kettle, replacing it on the stove to boil again. 'I lived in a village near Bantu, while my father went off exploring.'

'Never got to Bantu, sir. Too far north.'

To Liz, Mr Reid had always seemed rather shy. He had always been very polite but their mother had often commented she never got more than a *good morning* or *good evening* whenever she met him. It had been a surprise when Fred confided that his dad was ever so good at imitating people on the radio. Now, talking about the war appeared to give him confidence, his voice stronger.

'The Japs did though. Our lot chased them as far as Kuto. Lost them in the mountains.'

'So when are you off?'

'Tomorrow afternoon, sir, after I get in from work.'

Fred freckles promptly vanished, his face chalk white.

Mr Reid leant over and patted him on the arm. 'No, point fretting about it, Fred. What's done is done. It won't be too bad, son, you mark my words. Something'll turn up.'

'Where's the home?'

'Near Amesbury, sir. There's a good bus.'

'Don't worry about that. If Dr Shaw will give me a bed for the night, I'll take you.'

'Can we go, too,' Phil begged. 'Then we'll know where it is, when we want to visit.'

Tom McFaddean patted the small boy on the shoulder. 'I'm not promising anything, Fred, but I'll talk to some people and ... if it's humanly possible, I'll get you out. Wouldn't be right to leave a soldier as good as you in an orphanage,' he added.

Mr Reid grinned widely, exposing the gaps in his teeth, all at once appearing little older than his foster son. Remembering her thoughts about his wife, Liz began to wonder if that's what unhappiness did to you – made you look old.

'Knew you for a gent the moment I clapped eyes on you, sir.'

Fred's freckles burst into life. Flashing a smile, he picked up his spoon and began shovelling apple pie and custard into his mouth as if he hadn't eaten for a month.

SIXTEEN

The three children sat together in the back of the Rover, its leather upholstery creaking mournfully when anyone moved, sympathizing with their gloomy thoughts. Tom McFaddean drove fast but skilfully along the narrow roads as if he wanted to get the whole painful business over and done with. Surprisingly, despite knowing him for such a short time, Liz and Phil felt totally relaxed in his company. It was as if they had known him for ever, like some long-lost uncle. If they couldn't be with their mother, he was better than anyone, except perhaps Fred – and he was just about to vanish from their lives.

Tom McFaddean was the only one to speak during the journey, keeping up a cheerful monologue about London football clubs, particularly Tottenham Hotspur and their chances of winning the FA cup. Mr Reid stared blankly through the windscreen, his expression morose. Only Fred seemed unperturbed, despite his white face, watching the countryside flash past with interest.

Liz envied Fred his cool courage, showing little concern about what was waiting for him now he understood that efforts were to be made to get him out. But the sight of him in his Sunday-best trousers, his blazer newly cleaned, his hair slicked back with water, had made her furiously angry. It was hateful that someone as nice as Mr Reid couldn't be allowed to care for Fred. Yet, if he was married to Mrs Reid, who was

149

unkind and horrid, he could. And their first sight of the home, ringed by a red-brick wall with broken glass on top and gates of iron topped with a fancy monogram, did nothing to help.

The house had been left to the council by a wealthy spinster. Over its thirty years' service to the community, it had undergone so many modifications and extensions that the original structure had all but disappeared. Had Victoria Ellis been able to come back, she would have been appalled to find iron steps climbing its vine-covered walls, bulging windows and a bare brick annexe, giving her home the appearance of a humpback whale.

Like the alterations, there had also been numerous staff changes, and no familiar face came out to welcome Fred back. He recognised a few of the children, loitering in the front yard, as being there five years ago, but it was the sight of one particular youth, craning out of an upstairs window, that caused Fred to utter the only word he had spoken since getting in the car.

'Crikey, *Slasher Harris!*' Grabbing his suitcase from Mr Reid, he dumped it on the back seat. 'Mind these for me, will you,' he said, handing Phil his catapult and dinky toys, hurriedly stuffing a packet of sweets in his blazer pocket. 'He should have been called *Snatcher*,' Fred explained, quickly locking his suitcase again. 'You can bring them when you come, I should have found somewhere to stash them by then.'

'Are you going to be all right?' Liz said, beginning to worry.

'Yeah, he don't bother me none.'

Tom McFaddean frowned. 'You sure? I wanted to give you this.' He passed over a five-pound note and a small card. 'It's for emergencies. That's my address and phone number in London. You never know.'

Fred grinned. 'No problem, Mr Mac, thanks ever so. Slasher won't worry about pinchin' paper 'cause he never learned to read, and I'll hide the money in my shoe.' Carefully folding the crisp dark-blue rectangle, he tucked it into his sock. 'But you will come and visit?' His expression changed, suddenly becoming anxious.

'We promise, every other Saturday,' Phil said.

It was a mournful procession heading back to Salisbury. All at once the car felt very empty.

'I feel like I've been to a funeral,' Phil confided to no one in particular.

Tom McFaddean caught Phil's eye through the rear view mirror and he gave a sympathetic smile.

'I was younger even than Fred when I first went out to India,' he said. 'My father was supposed to meet me in Calcutta. He left a message at the embassy there to say he'd be waiting in Dacca, so I was put on the train by the embassy staff. On my own, mark you. When he didn't appear there either, your grandfather hired porters and ponies to take us back to the village. Afterwards, I was glad because that was a most fascinating trek along the Brahmaputra. Over here, we only ever use the word mighty in hymns. But this was a mighty river. In places so wide, and remember I wasn't any bigger than Fred, it was like walking along the seashore. In others, it wandered along flooding the plains so rice crops could be sown – and there were as many crocodiles as elephants.' His blue eyes twinkled. 'My father wasn't at the village either and when he did arrive, he'd actually forgotten he'd sent for me. So I have a pretty good idea how Fred feels.' Indicating, the Rover pulled out to overtake a row of slower cars. 'It was awful at the time. In hindsight, I think it was the best thing that could have happened. Taught me early on to be independent.'

Mr Reid chortled, the first sound Liz and Phil had heard him make, apart from an emotional farewell, since the devastating news that Fred was to be sent back. 'I don't think our Fred needs to be taught that, sir. Very independent – always has been and that's part of the problem. Like his dad in that respect, he is. He didn't believe in following rules for rules' sake, either – if you get my drift. By the time I arrive there tomorrow, I expect Fred'll have found trouble or trouble will have found him.'

'You're going tomorrow?' Liz exclaimed.

'Might as well start as you mean to go on.' Mr Reid shifted round in his seat and gave her a smile. 'There's a bus at one. I can catch it straight after work.'

'In that case,' Phil replied, 'we'll go next Saturday.'

*

By the end of his first week, Fred had discovered a hut where the gardener kept his tools. Concealed behind a straggling grove of rhododendron bushes, their tough leathery leaves proved an effective barrier against Peeping Toms.

The gardens were substantial and only the area nearest the house was maintained, the remainder dwindling into woodland full of beech and elm, a carpet of bluebells flooding the ground each spring. By the time Liz and Phil made their second visit, Fred was satisfied that he had a monopoly on the hut, not even the gardener bothering to visit during the winter months, preferring to spend his time doing odd jobs round the house.

Spotting his friends on the driveway, Fred dragged them off down a side path, skirting round the kitchen garden, its edges framed with clumps of rhubarb, parsley and mint. 'Slasher hates fresh air. I bet he's never set foot past the end of the terrace,' he said, assuring Phil his catapult would be quite safe buried among the dahlia tubers and empty plant pots until spring. 'And, by that time,' he added optimistically, 'I hope to be gone from here.'

It wasn't a particularly salubrious place but at least it was dry. Searching through a stack of old flowerpots, Fred pulled out the three cleanest. Turning them upside down, he padded their tops with old newspaper from a pile on the shelf. It was a tight fit, a collection of garden tools and an ancient lawn mower taking up most of the space, and both boys sat scrunched up, their knees tucked under their chins.

Phil immediately launched into a story about Constable Barnes attending the village fireworks party in mufti, with his head still bandaged, before remembering he'd told Fred the same story two weeks earlier. Trying to make it sound like he'd done it on purpose, he continued talking, telling Fred about the Catherine Wheel someone had managed to attach to the tail of Mr Sproggett's dog. The dog in question, a demented bullterrier, spent all its time lurching viciously at the front gate, every time anyone was foolish enough to walk past on that side of the street. The justice of the act was never in question – only how it had actually been achieved. Everyone in the village knew it was nigh-on impossible to get near the animal while it was awake, or even asleep for that matter.

'That was my ambition in life.' Fred sighed enviously, hearing how Mr Sproggett had now moved the dog's kennel into the back garden. 'To get that dog.'

'Someone beat you to it,' Phil grinned.

'We still don't know who. Nobody's owned up,' Liz said. 'None of the village kids are brave enough. If you'd been there, everyone would have blamed you. We figured it was the postman. He had big grin on his face for days afterwards. Poor man, he got bitten again just before it happened.'

'At least he can stop wearin' his wellington boots in summer.' Fred sighed regretfully. He switched his attention to an inspection of the lawn mower on which Liz was resting her feet.

Liz caught the direction of his gaze. 'Remember what Mr Reid said,' she warned, 'no trouble.'

'*I know*,' Fred exclaimed indignantly. 'I was only wonderin' if I could take it to pieces and put it back again.'

'That's exactly what Mr Reid meant by trouble.' Liz pretended to be cross. 'You know what you're like, Fred. Every time you see something that interests you, you want to take it to pieces. Remember when you removed the hinges from the back door? You lost your pocket money for a month.'

Fred shrugged. 'But I like learnin' how things work. I tell you what,' he raised his head, his eyes brimming with mischief. 'I know it's borin' without me there but I'm ever so glad you're not goin' to live in London.'

'I'm not!' Phil shifted round trying to get comfortable. 'And you're right. It is deadly boring.' Fred grinned triumphantly. 'All I ever get to do is homework. Exams start next week. And Mum – she's driving me potty pretending that nothing's happened. I almost wish my nightmares would start up again – at least that would mean *something* was going on.'

Liz kept silent. It would only cause an argument if she admitted she liked the peace and quiet, at least a part of her did, although it wasn't exactly peace and quiet. Since the night of the Xhantu, disturbing dreams had plagued her sleep making her understand the anguish Phil had gone through with his nightmares. Except hers weren't nightmares – rather feelings and scattered thoughts jumping in and out like a gymnastics display. Each morning, she woke up in a deep fog of exhaustion that left her sluggish and miserable at school. The weather hadn't helped either. It was wet and muggy, and hardly ever light except for a few hours in the middle of the day. The thought of going abroad somewhere warm and sunny was exciting, even if the idea of flying in an airplane gave her goose bumps.

'Is Mr Mac comin' with you next time?'

'Shouldn't think so. Mum and he had a big fight. We haven't seen him since.' Phil propped his head on his hands, his voice gloomy.

'It was a disagreement,' Liz corrected her brother.

Fred leant forward eagerly. 'Go on, tell me. I'm all ears.'

'Mum wants us to carry on as if nothing had happened …'

'And Mac says it's too late for that,' Liz added glumly. 'We're Javean and that's not going to go away, however much she tries to make it.'

'He's right, you know.' Fred eyes sparkled. 'I'd give anythin' to swap places and do magic and stuff.'

'But I thought you wanted to be a mechanic like Mr Reid,' Phil reminded.

'Can't I be both?' Fred's stomach rumbled noisily. 'Have you got any chocolate left, Liz, I'm starvin'. Tell you the truth, the food's not half-bad here – better than Ma Reid's any day. Best thing about this place.'

Liz fished in her jacket pocket and pulled out a bar of Cadbury's Dairy Milk, dividing its little squares equally.

'Phil and I could go off round the world fighting monsters – there has to be loads of others. Mmm!' The small boy gazed at the little squares anticipating their luscious taste, a dreamy smile on his face. 'Smashin', thanks.' He bit off a corner chewing contently. '*Good stuff!* You could come with us, Liz, if you like. Dad Reid said that Mr Mac was talkin' about his old bus. He wants to fix it up and take it out to India on his next expedition. We could live in that and Dad Reid could drive.' The freckles on Fred's face shone brightly at the visions running through his head. 'We could be like them knights that went off killin' dragons. You know … that King Arthur bloke.'

Liz spluttered with laughter. 'As if that's ever going to happen. Mother wants me to be a scientist like her. She detests the idea of our having magical powers. If it had been left to her, she'd never have told us. Besides, you don't need magic. You and that catapult, you're simply wizard. Even Mother says she's never seen anything better.'

Fred beamed. 'Go on about the fight.'

Phil shrugged. 'That's it really. Mum says we can't decide anything until they discover the missing jade pieces. And, when they do, Mac can take them back. We don't need to go.'

'Bad luck. I know you wanted to ask about your granddad.'

'Mac was furious when she told him,' Phil giggled. 'He called Mum the most irrational female he'd ever come across.' He said …' he hiccupped loudly, 'if she and Zheng-Li ever met up, he pitied the sorcerer.'

'Only Mother didn't think that funny,' Liz finished the sentence.

Phil fished inside the neck of his pullover, pulling out the jade medallion he and Liz had bought in the market square, the eagle staring off into the distance. 'Mac insisted I wore it. Said I was more in danger than anyone else,' he boasted proudly.

A bell rang loudly from outside the back door.

'That's the dinner gong.' Fred stood up and unlatched the door. 'It must be half-past twelve. We have it early on a Saturday, so cook can have the afternoon off. We take it in turns to get tea.'

Phil glanced down at his watch. 'It is.' He got to his feet. 'And we need to go, otherwise we'll miss our bus.'

'Did I tell you,' the small boy said. 'I got a letter from the Burma Star Association askin' me to represent my real dad at their next reunion? I bet that was Mr Mac's doin'.'

'Will they let you go?'

'Hope so, Liz. There's a good chance. When the Director heard about it, he called me into the office. They like stuff like that 'cause it looks good in the newspapers. Dad Reid said he'll take me. It's somethin' to look forward to anyway.'

Despite the fact she knew Fred was being well cared for and had settled down, Liz still felt miserable and spoke little on the bus journey home. Without Fred to liven things up, it felt as if the whole village had been struck down with the plague – the streets silent and empty, nothing happening. Mrs Reid had found a job and, when they passed the house on their way to and from school, it looked deserted. Phil had even tidied away the wheelbarrow from their side of the fence, saying there was no point leaving it there anymore. And, in the last week, solid wall-to-wall rain had finally washed away all traces of ash and levelled the ground. Now it was easy to believe the fight had simply taken place in their imagination. Even the swing had been repaired and, although the damage to the veranda had proved more extensive than at first thought, with half-a-dozen wooden struts found to have rotted and needing replacement, the work was well on its way to being finished.

'You've got to speak to Mum,' Phil burst out. 'I feel as if I was given this great book to read and it's been snatched away from me before I reached the end.'

'Why me?'

'Because you know what sort of mood she's in when she

comes home – and whether we dare mention it,' Phil sounded very pessimistic.

Liz heaved a sigh. He was right. Even Mrs Lucy had commented how miserable their mother had become since the row with Tom McFaddean, snapping everyone's head off on the slightest pretext. Liz wondered if she was stalling for time, hoping the excitement of Christmas, with its parties and decorations and rushing off to Salisbury to buy presents, would quench their curiosity. Except it hadn't. Liz felt a sense of indignation bubbling away inside Phil. The dreams might have terrified him but knowing he had the ability to do something about them – and couldn't – he now found equally frustrating.

They opened the front door and a mouth-watering aroma of steak and kidney pie wafted out. Mrs Lucy, aware her employer was incapable of doing more than open the occasional tin, always left Saturday lunch ready to pop into the oven – with something cold for the Sunday. Quickly washing their hands, they helped their mother dish up.

As usual, Mrs Lucy's food tasted fantastic and, for ten minutes or so, silence reigned. Alison asked about their visit to Fred, agreeing that the village was awfully dull without him. Liz waited quietly, the conversation migrating to the topic of their end of term exams, with Phil complaining that he had both geography *and maths* on the Monday morning.

'Would you like a cup of tea, Mother?' Liz leapt up to put on the kettle, waiting by the stove for it to boil. She could feel Phil's eyes drilling into her back, willing her to get on with it. It wasn't fair, when she was the youngest. It should be Phil tackling their mother. But, if he tried, he would end up frustrated and angry and rush off to his bedroom in a sulk. Carefully pouring the boiling water onto the tea leaves, she carried the pot to the table, concerned that her mother had already started reading the newspaper and might not want to listen.

Pouring out the tea, she sat down again, and a determined expression swept across her face.

'Mother …' her voice cracked. Clearing her throat, she began again, 'I know you hate what's happened, but we are Javean. Ignoring it won't make it go away.'

Alison gave a startled gasp and hot tea slopped over the edge of her cup onto the wooden table top. Ignoring the pool of liquid dripping onto the floor, she burst into tears, quickly pulling a handkerchief from the sleeve of her jumper to wipe her eyes. Phil jumped to his feet and, grabbing a dishcloth from the sink, hurriedly mopped up the mess before it could spread any further.

'I always think it strange, how liquid expands when it's freed from the confines of a vessel,' their mother said, her voice irrationally calm.

Phil made a face at his sister, clearly asking if their mother was having a nervous breakdown. Liz, her fists crammed up against her mouth, gazed back in alarm.

'I'm sorry, Mother,' she said, wishing she'd never spoken. 'I didn't mean …'

'No, dear, I know you didn't mean to upset me.' Alison heaved a sigh. 'Pour me another cup, will you, Phil.' She shook her head impatiently. 'I've been dreading this day, putting it off. Mr McFaddean said I must tell you how I felt – it wasn't fair to any of us, tip-toeing round the subject.'

'We heard you arguing.'

'*That man.*' Sparks flew from Alison's eyes. 'Always telling me what to do. He's not your father, even though he acts as if he is. All he can think about is taking you back to your village. To claim your rightful place were his exact words.'

'But we want to go, Mum.'

'It isn't that we don't love our home …'

'What happened a month ago, children, was unavoidable …' Ignoring the interruption, Alison continued speaking. 'And it was great fun. And so exciting,' she smiled over the top of her spectacles. 'I haven't had such a marvellous time for years – not since you two were little. For you, Phil, to prove yourself a swordsman, without having to practise every day for donkeys' years – why I can't imagine how that must feel.' She reached across the table, taking her daughter's hand. 'You too, Liz. Acrobatics are your forte, balancing on a bar an inch wide – why, that gives you no trouble at all. Throwing your thoughts when danger appears – child's play. It's only normal to want that sort of life. And the idea of travelling to India and Burma is all part of that – possibly discovering you have relatives. But ...'

There was a long pause. Alison stretched out her other arm taking Phil's hand in hers, her manner as grave and studied as when they heard her speak at the conference. Whatever their mother came out with now, Liz decided, she'd obviously thought about very seriously.

'I saw your mother die, her head ripped open by the Xhantu.' Liz shuddered at the picture flashing through her mind. 'Your father died too – killed by those terrible monsters. So were most of the villagers. Mr McFaddean was practically the only survivor and even he was badly injured.'

'But that was the dynamite, Mum.'

'*Shush*, Phil! What Mother is trying to say, if we go back we may be killed, too.'

'Exactly.' Alison smiled lovingly. 'What mother can expose her children to that sort of risk. Whatever Mr McFaddean says to the contrary – if you go back, you put yourselves in the gravest of danger.

'If Zheng-Li ...' Phil's mouth opened. Alison held her hand up to stop him interrupting. 'All right, Phil, I accept he exists. It's not logical but your argument made sense. What was that you said? *Only if he exists, do all the pieces fit together.* But that's all the more reason to fear the future. Or is it over? Was the fight in our garden the last of it? If we stay here quietly, can we live the rest of our lives without anything more ever happening? I'm not the only one to want that, you want it too, don't you, dear?' She stared into her daughter's face.

Liz bit her lip, trying to work out her answer. After a moment, she nodded.

'Liz!' Phil exclaimed angrily.

'I do, Phil. *I really do.* I hate battling all these noises, and feeling under fire from people's emotions whenever I'm walking down the street or at school. It wears me out. I long to be rid of them.'

'Oh, Liz, dear, why didn't you say.' Alison held onto her daughter's hand.

'And you're quite right, Mother, it's very possible we could be killed…'

'Liz! *You traitor!*' Phil shouted. 'I thought you agreed with me.'

Liz ignored him. 'But Mr McFaddean's right too. We don't have a choice,' she finished sadly.

There was a deathly hush. Alison, her eyes fixed on the wall, took off her glasses twisting them round and round. 'Can't you at least wait? If nothing else strange occurs then we won't need to do anything,' she pleaded.

'I don't think that's going to happen,' Liz said sadly. 'In a little over a year, fourteen months to be precise, I'll be fourteen too.'

'But what about the missing jade pieces?' Alison continued to protest. 'Someone's got them, why aren't they in danger?'

Liz closed her eyes, her mind flailing about trying to make sense of the bewildering assortment of words and feelings that besieged her dreams at night. All at once she felt them drop into place, as if for the past few weeks she'd been futilely trying to hammer square pegs into round holes.

She said carefully, 'The jade only comes to life to protect us, the Javean. To anyone else, it's an ornament. That's why Zheng-Li,' she shuddered at the name, 'can only get to it through us.' She stopped, almost thinking aloud. 'Before … when we found the piece in the market, it was almost as if the jade called out to him.' She shook her head frowning. 'That's the bit I don't understand. It's on our side … yet, at the same time, if we find a piece he instantly knows where to find us.' Liz whispered the words.

'But surely, you can stay out of it. Mr McFaddean, he

knows the village. He can take the three medallions back. There's no need for you children to become involved.'

'We have to go with Mac, Mother. If anything happened to him, we'd never forgive ourselves. Besides we're Javean, the only ones that can stand up to Zheng-Li's power. When soldiers stole the jade, the village was destroyed. We can't let that happen again.'

Silence fell.

Alison bent her head, concentrating on cleaning the lenses of her glasses on a corner of her apron. Sighing, she put them back on and got to her feet, leaving her tea untouched. 'In that case, we'd better go up to London next Friday and buy you some suitable clothes to wear.'

SEVENTEEN

The hotel was busy, new guests arriving even as they waited to check in. They were greeted by a young girl, smartly dressed in a grey pleated skirt and green blouse.

'Mrs Howard is a bit busy right now, but Mr McFaddean is expecting you,' she greeted the family. She passed over room keys to some guests waiting by the reception desk. 'Numbers eight and nine,' she addressed the other party. 'On the second floor. I hope you enjoy your stay.'

Mrs Howard bustled out, dressed in a grey suit and wearing an identical colour blouse.

'It's our new uniform,' she confided. 'It does save on clothes but I'm still not convinced. 'Isn't it astonishing Mr McFaddean knowing your parents? What a co-incidence? I could hardly bring myself to believe it when he said you were coming to stay.'

'Aren't you their mother, then?' The girl stared in surprise at Alison and the two children.

Embarrassed, Mrs Howard elbowed her to keep quiet. 'This is my niece, Janice, she helps out at the weekend,' she volunteered as if to explain the girl's impertinent remark.

Liz and Phil exchanged grins. Of all the things – to be taken for Alison's children was something quite new.

'They're adopted.'

'Oh!' Janice appeared relieved. 'I thought they looked a bit different, but you could have married a foreigner.'

'*Janice!* Your manners! Remember, they're guests. *I'm so sorry, Dr Shaw.*' Mrs Howard shook her head in reproof. 'Young people today. It's so difficult to get good help especially at Christmas time; the post office takes all the decent ones to clear the backlog of mail.' She shuffled some papers on the desk, pulling out a key. 'We've put you in the guest flat. It's in the basement but it's very pleasant and you have a separate entrance into the street, if you want to use it. I'll get Janice to show you. Mr McFaddean's in his office,' she said, smiling warmly at Liz and Phil.

'May I go up, Mother?'

'Of course, dear. You coming with me, Phil?'

'I'm carrying the suitcase,' he muttered, smiling shyly at the blonde receptionist, her long hair worn in a French pleat like her aunt's.

Seeing the lift on the ground floor, Liz hauled back the heavy gates, pressing the button for the fourth floor. Protesting vociferously it jumped into life, clattering slowly up the lift shaft and shuddering to a stop. Liz knocked on the office door. Hearing a voice calling for her to come in, she pushed it open.

'You got here all right?' Tom McFaddean raised his head as Liz came up the stairs. 'Where are Phil and Dr Shaw?'

'Settling in.' She peeked out of the corner of her eye at the warrior figure of the samurai, standing guard over the staircase like an avenging angel. 'Why do I get the feeling they are about to come alive.'

Tom McFaddean watched the careful way she stepped between the exhibits. 'Probably because one of them did just that – remember.' He picked up his cup, taking a sip of tea. 'I'm thinking of getting rid of them. Will Rutherford has expressed an interest; says they're just the thing to keep small boys happy on a wet morning at the museum.'

'What will you do with the space? Do you need it for the hotel?' Liz gazed round the large room, stretching the entire width of the top floor. 'It's a long way up unless you use the lift – and that's horrid. It gives me the jitters.' She screwed up her face.

Tom McFaddean rubbed his chin ruefully. 'I agree. It needs replacing. I haven't dared mention my plans to your mother; she's already decided I'm trying to take over. But I was hoping she'd let you and Phil come and stay occasionally – once all this is out of the way. My flat's too small.' He patted a chair. 'Sit! To what do I owe the pleasure of this visit?'

The desk was covered with drawings. Glancing down, Liz recognised the blueprint of a short-barrelled gun.

'Is that a real gun?'

'No, I'm designing a flame gun. Might prove useful. And that's another thing you mustn't tell your mother. She's doing enough worrying for all of us put together.'

'I know. That's why I came to talk to you. She's so unhappy about all this.'

Tom McFaddean rocked back in his chair, toying with a pencil. 'You mark my words, once Dr Shaw makes up her mind they'll be no going back.' He leaned forward again. 'Now tell me about you. You've lost weight. Your mother said you had. She asked if I could discover what the matter was. So what is it? Your head still buzzing?'

Liz nodded awkwardly. 'Most of the time it feels like a melon – full of pips that belong to other people. I'm convinced it's going to explode one day. And it keeps me awake.'

'People's thoughts?'

'More what they feel. School's horrid. I'm waiting at the bus stop and all around I sense anger and outrage and impatience because the bus is late or full. It's like being on a merry-go-round that's out of control.' She pulled a face. 'I get off the bus, walk up the road to our house, only to have Mother's feelings galloping round my head, wondering if we're doing the right thing. She's angry with herself for taking us to London in the first place – then we wouldn't have met you and none of this would have happened. It makes me dizzy.'

Tom McFaddean burst into laughter. 'That sounds like your mother,' he grinned. 'And?'

'Phil's rapidly changing into a love-struck poodle.' Liz rolled her eyes. 'All he can think about is becoming a Javean warrior and fighting. It's so boring.'

'And Fred. How's he coping? I've been too busy to visit him recently.'

'Except for us and Mr Reid, he doesn't seem to miss anything.' Liz smiled. 'He's really nice though. Never thinks unkindly about anyone, not even Mrs Reid, and she was so nasty to him. I was going to ask Mother if we could invite him for Christmas dinner.' Her smile faded away replaced by a frown. 'Except, I don't expect we'll be here now.'

'If we're not left by then, why don't you all come here – I'll cook. As for Fred, I'm working hard to get the authorities to agree to Mr Reid's adopting him.' He shook his head. 'Unfortunately, these things take time, they don't happen overnight.'

'That would be wonderful. You know I've got this feeling about Fred.' Tom McFaddean raised his eyebrows. 'I had a dream,' Liz explained blushing. 'And he was with us.'

'And you?'

'I wanted to ask about Mei-Xui.' Liz pronounced it, May-Shu, the syllables awkward on her tongue. 'Did she ever say anything about noises in her head and how to deal with them?'

'Not really. If she did I don't remember.'

Liz's face fell. 'Mother thinks I want to go back to the village to become a proper Javean, but it isn't that at all. I was hoping to find someone who can sort out these noises. There's so much going on, I'm scared I won't understand the warnings if they happen.'

'You're very different from Mei-Xui …'

'Oh! But Mother said I was exactly like her,' Liz protested, her eyes instantly filling with tears.

'You are.' Tom McFaddean patted her hand, offering her a box of tissues. 'It's your character that's different – you worry too much. At age twelve, you can't take the whole world on your shoulders. All right now?'

Liz nodded and wiped her eyes.

'Perhaps Tung Wei will be able to help. He knows everything about the history of the village and its legend. I've sent dozens of telegrams to the embassies hoping to locate him.' Tom McFaddean grimaced. 'No luck so far. I know twelve years is a long time but I can't help feeling he is alive.' He got to his feet. 'I'll come down with you; warn your mother I'm taking you up to Oxford Street tomorrow to see the Christmas lights.'

'But we're going shopping,' Liz protested half-heartedly.

'That's in the morning. If we don't leave here till after four, that'll give you plenty of time to get kitted out. And it'll be fun.' He wrapped an arm round her shoulders, peering down at her. 'Put a smile back on your face.'

*

Whiteleys Department Store in Westbourne Grove was located not far from the cinema where they had watched the St Trinians' film. Anticipating that department stores would be busy with Christmas shoppers, Alison had got them out of bed early. Unfortunately, clothes suitable for the tropics had proved difficult to track down, especially on a bitterly cold December day, and Whiteleys was the third store they had tried. Obligingly, sales assistants raided stock rooms to unearth clothes left over from the summer sales and, by the time Alison had ticked off all the items on her list, the market nearby was already busy. Hoping to visit the gem stall again, Liz asked if they could spend a bit of time there.

'Let you do your shopping in peace, Mum,' Phil agreed with his sister. 'We'll take the bags with us.'

Gratefully Alison passed over the bulky carriers, their string handles leaving angry red weals on her wrists. At first, containing only light-weight trousers, easily washed and hung-up to dry overnight, they'd felt quite light. With the addition of several pairs of shorts in brightly coloured seersucker, guaranteed not to crease whatever the climate, vests, pants, short-sleeved shirts, and a pair of sandals each, they now weighed a ton. At the Chinese restaurant, where they'd had dinner the previous night, Tom McFaddean had warned that snakes were a problem only if you stepped on them and Alison had bought both Liz and Phil half-a-dozen pairs of knee-length socks, 'In case we have to walk through long grass.'

In the market crowds were thickest round the food stalls, and both the butcher and fishmonger were doing good business, slapping pieces of meat and fish onto greaseproof paper before wrapping them up. Regretting his generous impulse to carry the bags, Phil elbowed his way through the gossiping shoppers, the reinforced paper carriers dragging clumsily behind him. Spotting the tousled head of their friend at the vegetable stall, he headed in that direction. Today, Jimbo's father was very much in charge. A slightly older and more worn version of his son, he was skilfully serving several customers at once, calling out to passers-by that everything had come in fresh that morning, while keeping a tally of items in his head.

Jimbo came out from behind the stall, beaming his delight. 'I've bin 'opin' you'd come back, miss.'

'Oh, do call me Liz,' she smiled. 'We were just wondering if Mr Smith had any more jade in, do you know?'

'Nah, 'e's no longer runnin' the stall, neether.' The boy jerked his thumb over his shoulder indicating the little gem stall, empty for the moment of customers, with someone different behind the counter. 'Got sick 'e did – I 'spect it was the tea. Drank it non-stop, given 'alf a chance. His missus sold up.' He ducked his head speaking out of the corner of his mouth. 'You remember that bird – an eagle you said. Well, you'll never guess but ...'

Picking up on the excitement in his voice, Liz glanced meaningfully at her brother. *Could Jimbo have found one of the missing pieces?* How extraordinary if he had.

'Me dad bought me a book about birds – so I looks up the picture. An' you was right.' Jimbo nodded his head in confirmation. 'It was an eagle. Wish I could see a real one though. Did you know they catch rabbits?'

'Yes,' Liz replied, her excitement vanishing as quickly as rainwater down a drain. 'You find them in Scotland, I think.'

'That's right, miss, I mean, Liz. That's what the book said. But I can't see me ever gettin' up there.' Jimbo shifted from foot to foot. 'Well,' he paused dramatically, 'I've bin keepin' an eye out, see. And I only spotted a bird like it.'

'You did!' she gasped.

Jimbo nodded again. 'Rotherhithe market – last Tuesday. That's why I'm whisperin'.' 'Don't – want – 'im – to know.' He emphasised each word with his thumb, gesturing over his shoulder. 'If 'e gets wind of it, 'e'll jack up the price, miserable old geezer. That's why 'e ain't got any customers, even if it is Christmas in a few weeks. Too expensive.'

'You sure?' Phil broke in.

'Pretty much. Course it ain't exactly the same, but it's an eagle all right and it's starin' right at you. It's got them silver bits, too. Recognised them straight off.'

Over the moon, Liz threw her arms round him.

''Ere, miss!' Jimbo stepped back in a hurry. He caught sight of the smirk on his dad's face, his arm poised ready to thrust some pears into a paper bag. 'No call for that,' he muttered his face pinking up.

'Oh, but there is. You're quite wonderful, Jimbo. If it is the jade piece, our friends have been searching for it for years. Only we didn't know that when first we met you,' she babbled.

'And that Chinaman, you saw in the market ...' Phil stopped, suddenly aware that to a cockney anyone talking about an evil spirit would be considered a lunatic. 'Um ...' He glanced at his sister for help.

'The man in the long coat?' Liz hastily corrected. 'You were right. He did want to steal it.'

'Thought as much – definitely somethin' odd about 'im. So I did good.'

'Fantastic,' Phil held out his hand, shaking the other boy's warmly. 'Where did you say?'

'Rotherhithe – know it?' Phil shook his head. 'It's by the Surrey Docks. Can't miss it. 'E's there Tuesday and Saturday. They finish early on a Saturday though. 'Bout two, earlier if they're 'avin a bad mornin'.'

Phil glanced down at the time. 'We'd better scoot off if we're to get there before it closes.' He stepped away from the busy stall, an unceasing melee of people jostling about, anxious to get their marketing completed and get home to listen to the football. 'Thanks, Jimbo. Come on, Liz, let's find Mum.'

'Will you come and tell me if you find it?' Jimbo called after them.

Liz nodded, racing after Phil. 'We need to phone the hotel,' she gasped, trying to keep up with his fast pace, people meandering about forcing her to stop and let them pass. She pointed to the cinema, a bright red telephone box visible on the pavement nearby. 'There's a phone booth.'

'I'll look for Mum while you phone,' Phil called over his shoulder. 'Fingers-crossed Mac's in.'

The store was now really busy, crowds packing in over the lunchtime. Phil ran up and down the escalator, hoping to spot someone with blond hair and a camel coat. Confused, he stared round seeing dozens of women with blonde hair, all of them wearing camel coats and none of them his mother. Giving up, he trailed back down to the ground floor, noticing his sister waiting by the revolving doors.

'She's nowhere to be found.' He glanced down at his watch. 'It's after twelve now– we'll never make it.'

'Mac's not there either. Mrs Howard says he's gone to Birmingham.'

'*Bother!* What do we do now?' he said helplessly.

'I know, get the Lost and Found to page her.'

'Brilliant!' Phil made a dive for the back of the store. 'This way. Come on.'

The main section of the ground floor was given over to ladies' fashion accessories, the counters nearest the doors selling perfume, leather bags and nylon stockings, a dozen different shades and deniers draped over shiny metal display rods. Phil pushed his way through a crowd of ladies trying on the latest fashion in beaded snoods, leaving Liz to trail behind.

'Liz?'

Hearing her mother's voice over the noisy chattering, Liz swung round, spotting her by the scarf counter. Poking Phil in the back to attract his attention, she ran over.

'Why the serious faces?'

'We found one of the medallions,' she blurted out.

'You don't know that for certain,' Phil said joining them, 'after all he's never ever seen an eagle.'

'Neither have you,' Liz retorted fiercely.

'Who hasn't seen an eagle?'

'Jimbo,' said Phil. Realising the name meant nothing to his mother, he added, 'He's the boy we bought your birthday present from.'

'And he's only been searching for the other pieces,' Liz added.

'And he found one in Rotherhithe. Liz telephoned the hotel ...'

'From the call box outside the store.'

Alison's head flew backwards and forward like a ping-pong ball, in an effort to keep up with the speech and excitement of the words being flung at her.

'But Mac's out, gone to Birmingham,' Phil finished up.

'Typical male, *never about when you want them*. Rotherhithe? That's the other side of the Thames. I'll take the pink and the turquoise.' Alison said to the assistant who was hovering behind the counter, a bemused expression on her face. 'We better get a taxi, it'll be quicker. Have we got time to drop these off first?'

Liz shook her head. 'It'll cost a fortune,' she warned.

'Mr McFaddean can pay. Serve him right for not being there when we need him. 'Come along.' Alison closed her purse with a snap. 'Which way out?'

Tipping the commissionaire, Alison bundled everyone into the back of a black cab, stacking the bags carefully on the floor. 'Stop worrying you two. After all, that's what London taxis are for, to get you to places in a hurry. Driver,' she leaned forward, sliding the glass partition across so he could hear her. 'I need you to stop at a bank on the way to cash a cheque, so I can pay you. But, be a dear and hurry now.'

The black cab raced through the streets. Screeching to a halt outside a bank, about to close its doors for the weekend, he waited while Alison ran in. Then, cutting down Park Lane, he headed for the river. Liz stared out of the window hoping to recognise the places they'd visited, but once past Trafalgar Square she was lost.

'Such a nuisance,' their mother chatted, pushing some pound notes into her purse. 'I was planning to take in a museum this afternoon.'

Phil groaned loudly, pulling a face. Catching sight of the cabby staring at him through the rear view mirror, he exchanged it for a grin. 'Not museums, Mum, they're deadly dull.'

'Well, dear, if we're off to India, it would make sense for you to know something about the country.'

The taxi swung on to London Bridge, the river flowing contently beneath it, the south bank dominated by the stark concrete exterior of the newly built Festival Hall and the flamboyant building occupied by London County Council.

Nervously, Liz glanced down at her watch. 'How long now?' she called to the driver.

'Fifteen minutes tops, miss. Where do you want again?'

'The market at Surrey Docks.'

The area they were speeding through still showed signs of wartime bombing, some of the docks so badly damaged they had been filled in and the cranes left idle. Jamaica Road, running parallel to the river, was quiet, allowing the driver to speed up. Traffic had ceased at twelve, when the dockyard closed and the heavy mesh gates swung shut behind the last worker. Over the weekend, only a single guard remained on site, plainly visible through the window of a small hut by the gates, reading his newspaper. Behind a string of warehouses, dark funnels poked up into the sky, from ships waiting to unload their cargo.

The taxi rounded a corner and pulled to a stop. On a muddy stretch of ground a dozen or more stalls had been erected, their counters piled high with cheap towels and dusters, knitting wool, cut-price slippers, scarves and hats, and underwear. Flimsy plastic covers had been draped over the iron stanchions to form a temporary roof and backcloth, giving some protection from the winter weather. A stallholder called out, 'You won't get better value anywhere in London,' to the handful of customers wandering about. Behind them, the Thames flowed sluggishly, and elder and buddleia struggled for survival amongst banks of earth littered with tin cans and rubber tyres, a discarded pram lying on top. A council lorry was parked against the kerb waiting to dismantle the stalls and, nearby, children were playing hopscotch on the pavement.

Leaping out, Liz ran over to the lorry, three men leaning against it smoking. 'Excuse me. Is the man that sells jewellery still about?'

'You mean Harry?' One of the men flicked ash off his cigarette. 'Wasn't 'ere today, luv,' he said politely, 'on account of 'e went to a funeral.'

'Any luck,' Phil called, joining his sister.

Liz shook her head. 'We came all this way – for nothing,' she said bitterly.

Noting their disheartened expressions, the workman, the collar of his heavy naval jacket turned up against the cold and wearing a woollen hat perched on his head, asked, 'What's the problem with Harry?'

'Oh, we don't know him.' Phil gave a half-smile. 'It's just that somebody told us ...'

'He sells pieces of jade,' Liz finished the sentence. 'We collect them.'

'That yer mum?' The workman nodded his head at the taxi where Alison was waiting.

Automatically, Liz and Phil swung round and she waved.

'Yes.'

'Looks nice.'

'She is,' Phil agreed. 'Pretty strict though.'

'My mum was strict. Belted us about a bit.' The workman caught Phil's grimace and grinned. 'Didn't do us no 'arm, lad. Kids are treated too soft today.' He seemed to make up his mind. 'So, Harry. Petticoat Lane termorrow, eh chaps?'

His mates nodded. 'He'll be there. The King's Arms serves a mean pint. Harry won't want to miss out on that.'

'There you are then, miss.' He grinned as the worried frown on the Chinese girl's face vanished. 'No need to fret. Be there 'bout twelve, he's bound to be there by then. That's when the pubs open.'

'It's like a ...'

'Wild-goose chase, luv?'

Liz smiled shyly. 'More like a maze, with loads of dead ends.'

Waving goodbye, Liz and Phil ran back to the taxi.

'Any luck?' their mother called out.

Liz grimaced and climbed back in. 'They were ever so helpful though.'

'It still leaves us no closer.' Phil dumped himself down on the fold-up seat, facing his mother and sister. 'That man was right,' he repeated gloomily. 'It *is* like a wild-goose chase.'

EIGHTEEN

Waving goodbye to Dad Reid at the main gate, Fred ran back down the drive and ducked through the side door into the kitchen garden.

On his first night back, Fred had been given a sheet of rules and told to learn them. He was quite aware that inmates, with permission to leave the grounds with their visitor, were expected to sign a register, giving the time of departure and an expected time of return. A large black book, this was kept in the porter's cubby-hole overlooking the front porch, and constantly checked throughout the weekend. Returning inmates were instructed to go straight into the house and sign themselves in again. But the practice was fraught with danger. When Fred had been living there before, Slasher had developed a very nasty habit of lingering by the front door. Whenever it opened, he would pounce on the unwary like an enormous and very greedy spider, forcibly removing any tuck or money they'd been given – and Fred was not willing to test if the practice had been discontinued. The two bob and some chocolate, that Dad Reid had given him, was his and *his* it was going to stay.

He felt a bit sorry for the little kids though but not sorry enough to interfere and risk a black eye. Presumably, they either submitted peacefully or waited outside till there were enough of them to confuse Slasher, his favourite method of attack being a hefty slap about the ears. If a member of staff happened to be passing, all they would see was a concerned and caring Norman Harris helping a child back onto its feet – or, as one hapless victim described later: *twistin' yer collar till ye can't breathe*. Fortunately, like all dictators, Slasher's reign was fast coming to an end. Fred reckoned staff and inmates would hang a banner across the front of the building, to celebrate Norman's sixteenth birthday and the day he left the home forever.

He felt gloomy, which was his second reason for not going back inside. Whenever Mrs Reid was on the warpath, he and Dad Reid had always vanished into the shed at the bottom of the garden, keeping out of the way till it was safe to go back inside. In Fred's view, a shed was a magnificent institution and discovering one standing empty, literally waiting for him to take possession, had been a godsend.

Pulling out a copy of *Beano*, which he'd swapped for cigarette cards, Fred had already reached page three when the door creaked open and a head poked round the edge.

The previous Monday he had gained a monitor's badge, the first thing he'd ever won in his life, staff liking his cheerful attitude and obvious determination to make the best of a bad job. It didn't award him any special privileges except helping to get tea on a Saturday afternoon, but it still made him feel more grown-up and responsible. Remembering his new status, instead of growling out, *beat it, if you know what's good for you*, he said, 'Wotcha.' But it still had the same effect. The head, surrounded by a halo of dark hair, instantly disappeared.

'Come back, as long as your name isn't Slasher,' he bellowed.

The head reappeared attached to a grin. 'It's not Slasher. The kids in the dormitory said I had to avoid him.'

The boy was Fred's height but finely built and of Indian origin, with a long straight nose and long lashes over very dark eyes.

Fred patted an upturned flowerpot, a thick wodge of newspaper left on it from Phil and Liz's last visit. 'Sit down and take the weight off. Not seen you before. You new?'

'Came in last night. My mother was rushed into hospital.'

'Is she okay?'

'I think so.' The boy nodded, deep bruises ringing his eyes from lack of sleep. 'Matron phoned the hospital. Appendicitis – but she's still very poorly.' He was carrying a small case. He lifted it up, showing it to Fred. 'A police car brought my things, because I can't go back home till she's well. I was hoping to find somewhere to hide this.'

'I guess they warned you then.' Fred grinned, his freckles lighting up. 'You should have asked for a police escort up to the dorm. What's your name?'

'Nicholas. I've got an Indian name too but I don't use that much.'

'Is your dad dead?'

The boy shook his head furiously, his long straight hair flapping against his ears. 'No, he works away. There's only me and Mum. Dad's family live in India.'

'I lost both my parents – train crash, when I was a nipper. But I got fostered.'

'So why you still here then?' Nicholas asked politely.

'Long story – and it's only temporary.' Fred eyed the case. 'Got anythin' worth swappin'?'

Nicholas frowned, his chin set stubbornly. He gripped the handle of the case more tightly.

Fred pointed to his monitor's badge. 'I'm not goin' to steal it off you – right. Never stolen anythin' in my life,' he admitted proudly.

'Okay, then.' Putting the case down on the floor, Nicholas unlocked it and flipped open the lid.

Inside was a thick stack of photographs – all of famous people and each one neatly autographed. 'Can I touch them?' Fred asked eagerly. The boy gave a reluctant nod. Fred leafed through them whistling in astonishment, recognising the faces of footballers and cricketers as well as film stars like Errol Flynn and Gary Cooper, Lawrence Olivier and Vivien Leigh.

'These must be worth a fortune in swaps,' he exclaimed. 'Where'd they come from?'

'My dad's a steward on the boats.'

'Boats?'

'He works on the White Line, on the Australia run. That's where he is now. He used to work for Cunard – on the Queen Mary. He was only ever gone a couple of weeks then. Now it's twelve or more. That's where he got most of the pictures, on the way to New York. You won't tell anyone?' The boy's tone changed becoming anxious.

'Not a chance. Wish I owned somethin' like this. What's this?'

He pulled out an embroidered bag fastened with a drawstring.

'Dad gave it to me. His mother sewed it. It's got an elephant on, see?' Nicholas pointed to the design, picked out in brightly-coloured sequins sewn onto cloth. 'You get loads of elephants in India,' he boasted. 'Have a look if you want. I don't mind swapping that stuff.'

Fred tipped a little collection of carved figurines onto the lid of the pressed-cardboard case, recognising a tiger, a monkey and several elephants.

'Who's this meant to be?' He picked up a figure with eight arms.

'Mum says it's one of their gods. Interested?'

'Not much.' Fred screwed up his face. 'Kids never bother with stuff like that.'

Disappointed, he was about to put them back when he noticed a small object, made of dull green stone, lying among the wooden animals. He picked it up, his chest tight with anticipation, staring at the image of an eagle banded with strings of silver, tarnished black, the jade dull under a layer of grime. Trying not to draw attention to it, he said casually, 'I wouldn't mind swappin' this. It's not bad. A bit chipped.' He showed Nicholas a small crack in the bird's wing. 'Where d'ye get it?'

Nicholas shrugged. 'You can have it.' Sweeping the wooden

pieces back into the bag, he replaced it in the bottom of his suitcase. 'I don't like it much, gives me the heebie-jeebies. Mum's thinks green's unlucky.'

'No, you've got to have somethin'.' Fishing in his pocket, Fred pulled out the Mars Bar Dad Reid had left him. 'Deal!'

Nicholas' eyes brightened. He nodded. 'Deal. And can I come down here sometimes? I won't bother you none.'

'As long as Slasher doesn't spot you. Here,' Fred knocked against the boxes containing tubers with the toe of his shoe. 'Leave your case under that little lot. It'll be quite safe for a few weeks. No one comes here, bar me.' Rolling up his comic, he stuffed it in his pocket and got to his feet. 'You'd better scoot off back to the house, it's gettin' dark. There's somethin' I need to do first.'

Leaving his new friend at the back door, in a hurry now, Fred scooted off down the side of the house making for the front gate. Tea was at five and his job was to put out the plates and cups. Angling his run towards a corner of the wall where there was no broken glass, he pulled himself up, dropping down onto the pavement. He could have used the main gates. They weren't locked except at night but they creaked loudly and the porter, whose job it was to catch truants and stop strangers wandering in, would hear them. Visiting ended promptly at four and it was way past that. Dad Reid always left a bit early to catch the ten-to-four bus, since there was not another on a Saturday till six.

The village street was empty which was surprising, until Fred remembered the store closed at one on a Saturday afternoon. Even so, there was generally a queue for the telephone, a private phone still a rarity in the small village. Deciding that Saturday football must have gone into extra-time, Fred pulled open the heavy door of the kiosk. Receiving no reply from Dr Shaw's number, he pressed Button B to get his money back, and pulled out the card Tom McFaddean had given him. Dialling the number, he stared out through the glass at the encroaching twilight, rays of light from the telephone box creating a small circle of brightness. Darkness didn't bother him, except it might have been more friendly if there had been a queue of impatient people tapping on the glass, telling him to get a move on. Hearing a voice, he pressed Button A, his money rattling down into the coin box as the connection clicked in.

'He's not here,' the voice said in reply to Fred asking to speak with Mr McFaddean. 'He's out.'

'Is he back later?'

Scarcely able to believe his luck at finding one of the priceless pieces, he pulled the green stone from his pocket and rubbed at the grime with his thumb, the jade dull even in the light from the phone box. Mr McFaddean would surely get him out of the orphanage after this.

'I don't know,' was the bored response. 'I'm not his mother, I'm only the receptionist. Do you want me to take a message?'

'Yes, tell him Fred called and I'll phone again tomorrow.'

A car approached. Heading slowly down the village street, it stopped almost opposite the red phone box. Leaving its headlights on, the driver leaned over to let someone out. Fred heard the clatter of heels on the pavement and the sound of a key in a lock. Taking advantage of the bright beam of light, he slipped out of the kiosk running back down the road, the gloomy silhouette of the large house beckoning from a distance. He heard the car move off. Then its headlights picked up a pair of eyes shining in the hedgerow and something moved. The car swept past, vanishing into the night.

Fred walked slowly back up the drive and round the side, keeping his hand firmly clenched around the little medallion in his pocket. In the wood, patches of solid darkness moved and changed shape. He wasn't mistaken. Something was going on out there. But how could that happen, when he'd only just found the jade piece himself?

Automatically, his hand strayed to the breast pocket of his blazer where he always kept his catapult, forgetting it was no longer there. He stared out into the dark, wondering if he should run and get it.

He shook his head firmly. 'Don't you go thinkin' I'm stupid enough to try,' he called defiantly into the trees, ''cause I'm not.'

Deep in thought he paused, his hand on the door knob. All at once his entire face lit up. Flinging the door open he screamed out, in a passable imitation of the cook's voice, '*Help! Help!* There's a masked man in the garden,' and stood back waiting.

Pandemonium broke out, light flooding the windows both upstairs and down. The back door opened and boys rushed into the garden at top speed. Yells of excitement were quickly overtaken by shrieks of pain as they stumbled about and fell into rose bushes, their long thorns scraping skin off shins and faces. Taking advantage of the chaos, Fred broke into a run heading for the line of bushes concealing the gardener's hut. Inside, the darkness was intense but that didn't bother him now, the little wood flooded with noise and movement as the searchers trampled through the wilderness. A sensible few carried torches and beams of light, like wartime searchlights seeking enemy aircraft, flashed skywards. A game of tag started – the participants making enough noise to scare anything away.

The bell rang out, jangling furiously, calling the boys to order.

Grinning, Fred felt for his catapult under the dahlia tubers, brushing away the loose sand. He'd already gathered up enough stones for a full-scale war. Grabbing a handful from the flower pot where he'd left them, he fitted one into the small leather strip at the back of the elastic, immediately feeling more comfortable with it in his hand.

Dad Reid had made his first catapult out of an old piece of leather cut from a pair of cast-off shoes. Boring holes in both edges to make the cup, he had cut short pieces of elastic attaching them to a Y-shaped length of wood. The one Fred carried now was the fifth version, and shop bought. Given to him by Mr Reid on his last birthday, it had proved its worth, outlasting all of the homemade ones. Now, if anyone tried to attack him, they'd better watch out.

Stuffing it up the front of his jersey, he walked calmly into the house and headed upstairs to the dormitory, listening as the ruckus outside gradually faded away.

*

When he woke next morning, Fred knew exactly what he was going to do – take the jade to London.

He glanced out of the window noticing the fog outside. In one way, that might help his plan. In another, it might hinder it. There were no Sunday buses into Salisbury and a seven-mile walk lay in front of him. Amesbury was only three miles away but it didn't have a railway station. At least, with it being foggy he could leave before church started and, hopefully, not be missed till lunch-time. Fred didn't bother worrying about his likely punishment – that could wait until it happened, especially since he was no longer a monitor. Regretfully, he fingered the lapel on his blazer, where the badge had sat.

Returning from his afternoon out, the director had been informed of the incident. Questioning a number of boys, all of whom swore it had been Fred's voice alerting them to the intruder, he had summoned the boy to his office.

'I am most displeased,' he lectured, removing the monitor's badge personally. 'You have misplaced my trust.' When Fred didn't reply, he went on, 'We thought you were going somewhere, young man. Provoking a riot …'

'But there *was* something in the garden,' Fred volunteered, knowing he wouldn't be believed.

'Do not lie.'

Fred shrugged his shoulders in protest. He never lied – well, not often. Then, remembering what Dad Reid had said about soldiers never arguing with an officer, he stuck out his chest, his shoulders back, and looked the director unwaveringly in the eye.

'Yes, sir.'

'You will also lose visiting rights for two weeks.'

'Yes, sir.'

Now, with his pockets stuffed with a notebook and pen, money, his catapult and the precious medallion, Fred lined up with the rest of the inmates for the walk to church. Close to the house the fog drifted lazily, but once outside the gates a thick curtain descended, cutting off the head of the crocodile of boys from its tail. As they neared the church, the five-minute bell began to toll and the member of staff, on duty that weekend, told the boys to hurry. Fred edged to the side of the little queue waiting to pass through the gate. Then, checking no one was watching, he ducked behind a gravestone. Two minutes later, he had vanished into the mist and was heading for Salisbury.

The village wasn't large but strung out and, for a time, there were houses on both sides, gradually becoming more and more infrequent. Up to this point, Fred hadn't given any more thought to the creatures in the garden and, it was only after passing the last house that he began to sense he wasn't alone. The hairs on the back of his neck stood up as tendrils of wet mist brushed against his bare skin. He listened intently but kept walking.

'No point grumbling about the weather, Fred, old-chap,' he muttered, hoping talking out loud might banish the feeling of disquiet keeping him company. 'Fog you wanted and fog you've got. So make the best of it.' Whistling cheerfully, he hurried on, aware now that he was being stalked. 'Just like my dad in the jungle, with those Japs about.' He spoke the words defiantly, determined not to look round. Anyway, what was the point, the fog was too dense to see anything.

Close by twigs snapped, and he caught the faint scratch of claws on the road. Hastily pulling out his catapult, he fitted a stone into the cup. Drawing it back ready, he twisted round, aware his weapon would prove useless in the mist. He couldn't fire at things that were invisible. Out here he was a sitting duck. So why didn't they attack?

He broke into a run, expecting to feel claws on his neck at any moment.

A moment later houses loomed out of the mist, a friendly gleam of light from their front rooms showing that people were at home. Gratefully, Fred slowed to a walk.

He couldn't do this for seven miles. No way. For a moment he paused, wondering if it would be sensible to knock on one of the doors. 'Come on, Fred, old chap,' he muttered. 'You've got a job to do.'

Around the little cluster of houses, the fog had thinned slightly, making it possible to see across the road where there was a wide ditch half-full of water. Stunted trees loomed from the scrubland behind, their branches reaching down into the water with long bony fingers, their distorted shapes eerie in the dense fog.

Keeping his catapult at the ready, Fred began searching the ditch for a likely weapon, still puzzled how the Xhantu had found him so quickly. After all, that little kid, Nicholas, had been carrying the jade in his suitcase for yonks, and they hadn't bothered him none. Okay, his mum had said green was unlucky but still … Fred gave a loud sniff. *Just his luck!* Good thing he'd told Dad Reid he wanted to be a soldier. He might as well get practising.

A layer of greasy scum had formed on the surface of the ditch, broken up by a slimy tangle of twigs and branches torn off in the autumn storms. He fished out a couple of the longest but they felt rotten to the touch, instantly breaking when he struck them against the hard surface of the tarmac road. The strands of fog shifted around him, as if something was edging closer and wanting to remain invisible. He swung on his heel and raised his catapult. Nothing moved, a dense silence filling the air.

All at once, he caught sight of a broom handle half-submerged in the ditch. Quickly checking behind him, he knelt down and dragged it out. The handle had split near the top but the rest was okay. Fred smiled. Actually – better than okay. The head with its long bristles would prove a formidable weapon. Grinning to himself, he swished the heavy wood through the air. It made him feel like one of those hammer-throwers. The teacher at his new school had told them all about her friend, who was so good at throwing the hammer, he had been chosen to represent Great Britain in the Olympic Games.

Confident that anything planning a surprise attack would be in for a very nasty shock, Fred tucked his catapult back into his pocket and continued walking almost cheerfully along the road. He set a fast pace, trying to make up the time he'd lost searching for a weapon. He wasn't particularly bothered about the distance, reckoning it would take him about three hours. He had money and could buy food at the station. With luck, he'd be in London by mid-afternoon.

The hairs on the back of his neck still prickled. Listening intently, he picked up a vague movement. Gripping his weapon he spun round, making out the dark silhouette of a huge bird – *except he already knew it wasn't a bird.*

Next moment, he felt a rush of wind and spotted the hairy snout, its jaws drooling, its teeth bared and reaching for his neck. Stepping back, he swung his make-shift weapon and felt it connect. The vibration from the hefty blow ran through the shaft and into his hands making them sting, and tumbling the furry figure head over heels into the ditch. Immediately, from above, he caught a faint hiss. Quickly side-stepping, he leaned back on his heels driving the head of his broom upwards and spinning his attacker back into the mist – like a cricketer hitting a six.

He heard the growl of an engine and a dark-coloured Morris saloon crawled slowly out of the fog. It stopped and a friendly voice called out of the window.

'Bad day to be out. Do you need a lift?'

'I don't suppose you're going into Salisbury.' Fred beamed his thanks. 'Only my ma's sick and I want to visit.'

'Of course, dear.' The lady-driver leaned over to open the door. 'I'm going right by the hospital. Jump in.'

Dropping his weapon on the ground, he climbed in, his freckles lighting up with gratitude. 'Thanks, that's smashin'. I'll get there ever so early now and Ma and me, we'll be able to have a good chat.'

NINETEEN

Liz undressed quickly and, leaving her window slightly ajar, climbed into bed. 'Goodnight,' she called, hearing her mother's bedroom door click open.

Alison stuck her head round the door, her hand poised on the light switch. 'Don't make a noise. Phil's already asleep.' She glanced over her shoulder at the put-u-up in the sitting room, Phil's dark head on the pillow. 'Nice time?'

'Lovely. I'm so glad we went. They had angels with gold trumpets in Oxford Street, and a Christmas tree in Trafalgar Square. It was so beautiful – like fairyland. Mac said it came from Norway. You should have come with us.'

Alison smiled. 'Too much work. Did he tell you the Norwegian people send a tree every year as a *thank you* for Britain's help in the war?'

Liz nodded. 'Yes. But I didn't believe him. The war was such a long time ago. I wasn't even born then.'

Alison smiled at her young daughter. 'For you, perhaps. But not for people like Mr Reid – old soldiers. They'll never forget. Are you happy about going to India? I know Phil is – he can't wait.'

'It will be nice to have some sun. But I really hate the idea of leaving Fred all on his own. I feel ...' she hesitated.

The expression on Alison's face changed, a shadow of uncertainty crossing it. 'Responsible? I know I do.'

'It was our fault,' Liz agreed.

'I'm not sure Fred would go along with that. He had such a great time. Told me, he hadn't been so happy for ages.'

'I know. He's as brave as anything. Even the yuppy didn't bother him. I wish I had that sort of courage,' Liz confided enviously. 'I suppose I wouldn't worry so much if he was back with Mr Reid.'

'I'm sure he will be – Fred's a survivor. And it's only a question of time. Mr McFaddean's pulling strings like crazy. Says Fred reminds him of him when he was a boy, and he deserves a chance. Goodnight, dear.'

Blowing her a kiss, Alison switched off the light and closed the door.

Liz stared sleepily into the dark space, allowing her thoughts to revisit the events of the day; the collage of bright images gradually fading away into sleep. She felt her eyes start open watching the shadows darken and become thick and sticky like treacle. Mesmerized, she stretched out her hands. The gooey substance moved as if alive. It clawed at her fingers sucking them down into a quagmire, till all that remained were her forearms, her hands severed at the wrist, eaten up by the blackness. Terrified, she tore them out, leaving behind great hand prints. Transfixed, she watched them change into a bird's feet with sharply dragging claws, its nails tap-tap-tapping noisily.

Jumping up in fright, she reached out a trembling hand to the bedside lamp and flashed it on. The room hadn't changed, no different from a moment ago, except for her alarm clock. That had moved on fifteen minutes. She'd fallen asleep, that was all. Feeling hot and thirsty, she leaned over and took a sip of water from the mug on her bedside table, all the while casting nervous glances round the room, searching for the cause of the noise she'd heard.

At the window, the curtain swung slightly in the breeze, rapping the glass sharply. Liz sighed thankfully and, climbing out of bed, shut the window tightly, the bars on the outside obscured by the thick curtains. For days now it had been cold, the sun hidden behind a blanket of rain and low mist that cut the heads off tall buildings. Still, it was better to be stifled than kept awake all night listening to that noise. Blaming her nightmare on being too hot, she threw off a blanket and tried to settle down. But the thought of facing the darkness made her feel sick. Reaching over, she put the bedside lamp on the floor and covered it with her jumper.

Beginning to feel sleepy again, she let her eyes wander round the room, the light dim but somehow strangely comforting. The flat had been decorated in light colours, the pattern on her bedroom wallpaper pastel-coloured daisies, with canary-yellow centres that radiated sunshine. The dull light had bleached the petals into soft greys and browns, leaving a solid dark blob at its centre. The black circles began to flicker, growing steady larger, the dark shapes deepening becoming more intense. Next moment, like an army of tadpoles, the elongated stalks began wriggling about. She tried to run but couldn't move as if she'd been staked out with cords gripping her arms and legs. Mesmerized, she watched them multiply and fill the horizon, drawing ever closer to her bed. Flinching back, she shut her eyes tightly holding her breath. Next moment, she was in a London street, except it wasn't a street. She recognised Ladbroke Square with its parade of tall white-washed buildings, spiked black railing guarding each of the properties. Then she saw Fred, a crowd of people chasing him. At first they appeared to be ordinary people going about their business. As she watched, their long fingers pulled him back away from her. Then the faces dissolved into the smiling image of the yuppy.

Gasping aloud in panic, she woke to find it was morning, her lamp still burning. With trembling fingers she switched it off, replacing it on the little bedside table. From the ground floor above, she caught the sound of voices accompanied by a crash of saucepans from the kitchen. She stared fearfully at the wallpaper. In the daylight, only delicately shaped flowers met her gaze.

Her head still felt muzzy and dark gashes, the remnants of her nightmare, continually streaked across it compounding her sense of unease. Climbing quickly out of bed, she tip-toed into the living room. Phil was still peacefully asleep. Pulling the curtains half-open, she peered through the window, surprised to see the little basement courtyard, with its row of dustbins, unchanged from the day before – only the air was different. A solid grey mist swirled about. A clatter of footsteps approached. Liz made out the pale outline of a pair of shoes and the lower half of a dark coat as someone hurried past on the pavement above.

'Phil.' She shook him awake. 'Wake-up. Fred's in danger.'

'What?' His voice was groggy, still half asleep.

'Fred's in danger,' she repeated.

Phil jumped off the couch and, grabbing his clothes, dived for the bathroom. 'Get Mac,' he shouted, slamming the door behind him. 'He's bound to be up.'

Alison opened her bedroom door, groping for the tie belt on her dressing gown, and came out into the sitting room. 'Liz?'

'I had a most terrible dream about Fred.' Liz burst into tears of relief, washing away the overwhelming sensation of fear that she'd experienced on waking. 'I knew we shouldn't have left him in that horrible place,' she sobbed.

'Come here,' Alison comforted, putting an arm round her. 'But you thought everything was all right last night.'

'It was. But then I got this dream.'

'Go on.' Alison said, her eyes pinned on her daughter's face.

'Fred was in Ladbroke Square. He was running towards the hotel and there were people chasing him. Only they weren't people.' She spoke the words solemnly. 'It was the yuppy.'

Alison picked up the telephone receiver then replaced it. 'Bother, he'll be busy.'

'It'll wait till after breakfast,' Liz said, beginning to feel stupid now. Perhaps it was the weather, after all. She'd certainly felt hot and, after she'd shut the window, there wasn't a scrap of air in the room.

'No, it won't,' Phil said, emerging from the bathroom. 'You're the one that can see things – remember?' He glanced down at his watch. 'It's half-past eight. He's bound to be finished soon. I'll go get him.'

'Use the inside stairs, Phil,' Alison called, heading for the bathroom. 'I don't want you venturing out alone.'

'Why not?' Phil stopped, his hand on the door to the courtyard.

Alison pointed at the window. Even in a few minutes the fog had thickened up.

Unlocking the outside door, he opened it and stuck his head out. 'Wow! You're right. It isn't half thick out here. How odd – it was fine last night. Phew! And it's boiling. Horrid!'

He came back in and stripping off his sweater tossed it onto the couch, running upstairs to the ground floor.

Ten minutes later, they heard footsteps. 'Fred's not there, I left a message,' Tom McFaddean called from the doorway. 'Thank goodness, we don't get many guests this close to Christmas. I've promoted the waitress to chef. Fortunately, they only want boiled eggs, so she'll cope.' He peered down at the bowl of cereal Liz was making a half-hearted attempt to eat. 'Would you like me to cook you something? Cereal always tastes so unappetising, unless you disguise it with fruit.'

'No, thanks.' Liz laid down her spoon. 'I'm not really hungry. It's habit more than anything. Where *is* Fred?'

'Gone to church with the rest of the kids. We just missed him. I left a message with the porter. So, what's all this about, Liz?' He glanced at her worried face. 'He phoned last night, by the way, whilst we were out.'

Liz bit her lip. 'Then there is something wrong.'

'Not necessarily. In any case, Fred's far more capable than you give him credit for.'

'I know,' she shrugged, reluctant to admit exactly how

uneasy the dream still made her. 'But what does Fred know that makes him a target?'

No one answered her.

'If necessary, I'll risk the fog and drive down to the home. Switch the radio on, Phil.' Tom McFaddean headed into the little galley kitchen, a rack of cupboards separating it from the sitting room. 'I want to hear the weather forecast. I'm making coffee, Dr Shaw,' he called. 'Want some?'

'Will they still hold the market?'

'Might put a damper on it, Liz. Hopefully, it will clear by mid-morning. Hang on a mo. *Turn it up*, *Phil*.'

The newsreader's voice crackled over the radio waves. "Extensive fog has blanketed London and the south. Extending over Europe, it has resulted in severe disruption to channel ferries, as well as trains and planes. Inward bound flights to the UK have been diverted to Birmingham and Manchester which remain clear. Outward bound flights are operating a restricted service, and significant delays are expected. According to meteorologists, the dense fog has been ushered in by a belt of unseasonably warm air, creating a substantial rise in temperature."

'I thought it felt muggy,' Alison said. 'I'd better put on something lighter, you too, Liz. You won't be driving in this, Mr McFaddean.'

'You're right. We'll take a tube to Liverpool Street. We can walk from there. I only hope Fred manages to phone before we go – otherwise we'll be playing cox and box.' Spotting Phil's frown, he added. 'Don't worry, we won't be out long and if necessary I'll phone every five minutes till we do get him.'

Liz buried her face in her hands.

'*Come on, Liz*,' he patted her on the shoulder. 'Whatever is it? Anyone can tell you're keeping something back.' He handed Alison a cup of coffee. 'You're our barometer, remember. We are relying on you to get us safely through this.'

'You are?'

Tom McFaddean smiled down at her. 'Absolutely. We used

to tease Mei-Xui by calling her telescope, because she could see further than us.'

'There's a hundred reasons to explain it,' she began hesitantly. 'It could be sleeping down here or something I ate – I mean chips, Tizer, and toffee apples ...'

Phil grimaced warningly.

'*Mr McFaddean, how could you?*' Alison leapt into the silence. 'The children know perfectly well they're not allowed toffee apples. Sticky toffee – it's the worst possible thing for teeth. Positively guaranteed to cause cavities.'

'Rubbish! Having things once in a blue moon never hurt anyone. Besides, they promised to give their teeth an extra scrub before going to bed.' He smiled reassuringly at the anxious faces. 'Go on, Liz.'

'It's nothing much ... It's so childish to be afraid of the dark,' she explained reluctantly. 'It's never happened to me before. We all agree I don't have any imagination. But this dark was different. It was like quicksand only black and gooey.' She paused, trying to think of something she could compare it to. 'A bit like Liquorice Allsorts – those black rolls with soft white centres.'

Grabbing Alison's hands, she gripped them tightly, peering intently into her mother's face. 'Mother, I know you're going say it's the weather, and you were hot in bed too ...'

Alison stayed silent.

'But it wasn't! Because then the wallpaper came alive,' she said, her voice still shaky, relieved that it was morning and she didn't have to battle her nightmare alone any longer. 'An army of shapes, like in Phil's dreams, were surging across the room. I couldn't move.' She gave a startled gasp and leapt to her feet staring at the window. 'Mr McFad ... I mean Mac. It's the fog, isn't it,' she gasped, her face ashen.

Alison broke the long silence. 'So something's coming.'

'Can we take our swords?' Phil said eagerly

'Not on the tube, Phil, you'll be arrested,' his mother reminded him.

'You're almost as blood thirsty as Fred. Let me remind you, Phil, this isn't a game.' Tom McFaddean said seriously, the angry red line of his scar giving him a bitter expression in the harsh daylight. 'Zheng-Li is determined to destroy us – and he doesn't care how he does it.' He got to his feet and peered out of the window. 'Devil take this fog. We'd never know if anything was waiting for us.'

'Then we'd better get it over and done with, before something does come hunting for us,' Alison said. 'I'm only sorry now I didn't bring my hockey stick. I thought about it, but changed my mind at the last minute.'

TWENTY

After watching buses and taxis inch their way along the Bayswater Road, most people had opted to travel by underground and the tube station at Notting Hill was busier than usual. Surrounded by brightness, the little underground train rattled noisily through tunnels carved deep under the city. Passengers read newspapers or chatted, everything so ordinary Liz began to wonder if it had been her imagination all along. Nothing had happened on the way to the station. They had walked briskly, keeping together, frequently searching the fog for signs of danger. Very few people were out, and they had only met up with an occasional person heading in the direction of the nearby church. In the gloom householders had kept their lights on, in a vain attempt to feel more cheerful, only to find they made little difference, the light dissipated into nothingness by the grey mist.

Liz was riding the escalator at Liverpool Street Station, when she felt the change in the atmosphere and knew for certain her dream was about to come true. She hesitated on the steps to the street, watching people come and go, busy with their morning's activities, oblivious to the sensation of danger that beset them from all sides. The air in the street was so muggy and dank it felt sticky to the touch, exactly like her dream, and tendrils of grey vapour clung to her face like the web of a spider.

Anxiously, she slipped her hand into Mr McFaddean's for comfort.

The streets were narrow and winding, with small shops displaying men's suits and ladies' dresses on headless mannequins. Shuttered and silent, they felt dark and claustrophobic. No one spoke, overwhelmed by an eerie silence that accompanied their echoing footsteps, a silence broken only by the chink of a milk bottle rolling along the ground. Liz had put on a blouse under her raincoat and had felt plenty warm enough until now. She shivered, momentarily feeling an ice-cold breeze sweep across her face.

After several minutes, they heard voices. Figures loomed out of the mist, ghostly shapes moving against a background of grey fog.

'Watch your back, luv,' a man called out.

Two men passed them, pushing a rack of dresses. They manhandled it across the road and into the market. On the corner of the narrow street, visible even through the fog, stood a public house, its exterior walls showered with electric light. Outside, half-a-dozen men were smoking, while they waited for the doors to open at midday. A woman, her shopping done, pushed past them heading home. All of a sudden the fog seemed less bothersome, as if the concentration of light and goods for sale, packed into a tiny area, had left no room for its swirling tendrils. There was little room for pedestrians either, the stalls so squashed together people were forced to squeeze past one at a time, only Tom McFaddean tall enough to see over the heads of the crowd in front of them.

Holding hands, they worked their way down one side of the market. A scent of chestnuts mingled with roasting pork and cheerful cockney voices, making it all at once a friendly place to spend a Sunday. Despite the atrocious weather, the famous market was busy, with both tourists and Londoners, everyone wanting the experience of visiting Petticoat Lane, to haggle with the stall keepers and snap up a bargain.

'Over there.' Tom McFaddean pointed to a display of jewellery sitting on a black cloth, like fish swept up from the sea.

'This can't be the one,' Phil argued. 'The men said Harry.'

Behind the makeshift counter, a dark-haired girl sat reading a book. Overhearing, she looked up. 'If you're a customer, I can be Harry.' She rolled her eyes flirtatiously. 'I'll be anyone you want if you buy something.'

Phil blushed. 'Is there a Harry?'

'That's my dad.' She gestured with her head. 'You'll find him in the pub, if you want him. So?'

'We're hoping you might have some jade,' Alison helped out.

'Not much call for that,' the girl said. 'Green's …'

'Unlucky.' Phil chanted in time with her. 'I know.' He laughed. 'Except that doesn't apply to paint. Our front door's green.'

Alison exchanged an amused grin with Tom McFaddean.

The girl pointed her finger at the medallion round Phil's neck, plainly visible without his sweater on. 'Well, I'm blessed. How astonishing! We've got something exactly like that.' Bending down, she pulled a small jewellery box out of a holdall on the ground and opened it up. 'See.'

Without warning, the ground began to tremble as if a giant was shaking out a carpet. Pottery toppled off shelves and crashed to the floor, followed by a chorus of frightened shouts. Noticing the legs of the table about to buckle, the girl dropped the box and made a dive for the jewellery cascading off one end.

'It's an earthquake,' Tom McFaddean muttered. He wrapped his arms around Alison and Liz waiting for the shaking to subside. 'Stay still, it'll be over in a minute.'

They heard a loud hiss and a shape flew out of the mist. Before anyone had time to react, it grabbed the box. Phil, closest to the table, lurched forward but the animal was the quicker, instantly soaring upwards again.

'Oh, no, you don't,' he bellowed and raised his hand. A flash of green light momentarily sliced a hole in the fog. The box dropped to the ground, covered in particles of dust.

The whole incident was over in a moment and the girl, on her hands and knees, struggling to pick up the necklaces and bracelets strewn about, noticed nothing. She got to her feet, her arms full of boxes and bits of coloured stone. 'You telling me that was an earthquake? *A real earthquake?*'

'We do get them from time to time even in England,' Alison said, her voice low and calm, as if replying to a casual question that a rare bird had been sighted or something equally ordinary. 'It's most likely the weather. They're unpleasant but they rarely do any damage. See, the ground has already settled again.'

The girl shook her head, wildly stuffing the contents of her stall into a holdall. 'Don't care. I'm off. I don't do earthquakes not even for Dad. *Do you want the piece or not?*' Addressing Phil, she picked up the little box. He didn't reply for a moment busily scrutinising the fog, his head swivelling from side to side as if searching for something, his left hand resting casually on the edge of the table.

'Well, do you?' she repeated, holding it aloft.

Phil nodded. 'How much?'

All around stallholders had also decided to close up, hurrying their stock into suitcases, the earthquake killing all trace of Christmas spirit stone-dead. In the distance, engines revved anxious to leave.

'Ten bob, a pound, two pounds. I don't care. Give me what you think it's worth, so I can get going.' She picked up the holdall, casting a cursory glance behind her to make sure she hadn't left anything.

A rumbling sound like thunder sliced through the air and, once again, the ground swayed alarmingly. People screamed as stalls collided in the air and toppled heavily to the ground. Tom McFaddean pulled some notes from his wallet and thrust them into her hand. 'Don't thank me – I promise you, it's worth every penny.' Shoving the box in his pocket, he grabbed Liz's arm. 'Come on, we need to get out of here.'

Panic broke out as people barged and shoved, fleeing

headlong along the narrow passageways, struggling to escape the confines of the market. Mothers with small children scooped them up to avoid them being trampled on. Behind the fleeing crowd, vans and lorries hooted loudly, hoping to force a passage through the press of people. Overhead, lightning flashed and thunder rolled.

'I know why Fred's in danger,' Liz called out. She stopped suddenly and the man behind cannoned into her, treading on her heel. He muttered a hasty apology and hurried past. She took no notice. Swivelling round, she stared at the fast-emptying stalls, their fabric roofs in shreds where the earthquake had ripped them apart, her eyes wide and fearful.

'Liz,' Tom McFaddean tugged at her hand. 'Come on, we've got to keep moving.'

'*But my dream*! It makes sense now. Fred's found the last piece – that's why.'

Terrified screams curdled into the air as shafts of forked lightning split the skies overhead.

'Then, we'd better get to Fred before they do. Otherwise there won't be anything left of him,' Tom McFaddean responded grimly, trying to make himself heard over the shouts of the crowd. 'We must hurry now.'

The crush of people had reduced their pace to a slow impatient tip-toeing from side to side. Gradually, the pressure eased and they found themselves back in the narrow street, families peeling off into side roads where they had left their cars. Doors opened and anxious residents came out onto the front stoop, staring at the sky, shaking their heads in disbelief.

'We heard nothing,' a disembodied voice called. 'Sure you haven't had a drop too much?'

'I promise you, we didn't imagine it, mate. Them stalls, they didn't fly through the air for nowt,' someone shouted back.

'Wait till you read termorra's paper. They'll confirm it,' a third voice commented.

Tom McFaddean, with Liz still clinging to his hand, forced his way through the stragglers, the voices fading as they distanced themselves from the melee of frightened shoppers. Gradually, the street began to slope upwards, the shops on either side closing in as the roadway narrowed sharply, the fog in the confined space pressing on their heads like the solid lid of a box.

Liz peered into the silence of the thick fog. She had the weirdest feeling that everyone had stopped moving and was holding his breath.

'This isn't the way we came,' Phil called out.

He glanced round, staring back over his shoulder, looking for someone to ask. Behind them stood a crowd of people. Unlike those that had fled the market, these were unmoving, their arms folded across their chests patiently waiting for something or someone.

'Anyone know the way back to the tube?' he called, his voice tinny in the dense air.

An ominous silence greeted his words, the air still reverberating with intermittent claps of thunder. Alison grabbed his arm, the force spinning him round. Coming into view at the top of the slope was a replica throng. Equally silent, they began shuffling down the hill, their arms still wrapped across their chest, their eyes fixed in a glazed stare.

As if a signal had been given, the mob of people behind them also broke into movement, their footsteps tap-tapping against the rigid surface of the roadway. Liz gasped aloud, her head ringing with the memory of her dream. She shivered, her whole body flooded with cold, and glanced wildly. On either side the long line of shops remained unbroken, dark and deserted until Monday morning. No amount of banging on doors would help here. By her side Phil was waiting, his left arm poised like a runner at the start of a race – tense, expectant.

Nearby, in one of the side streets, a lorry started up, its engine revving noisily.

'*Come on!*' Tom McFaddean broke into a run, dragging Liz

with him, Alison and Phil close behind. Their feet barely touching the ground, they raced back down the hill, dodging round the encircling figures clutching at their clothes, trying to pull them back, searching the fog for a side street.

All at once the tail lights of a ramshackle old vehicle came into sight, a green tarpaulin stretched over its load. It spluttered into movement, its gears grinding harshly.

'Up!' he bellowed. Lifting Liz with one hand, he swung her bodily off the ground. She caught hold of the top of the tailboard. Pushing up on her arms, she swung her leg over the edge and climbed in.

'Dr Shaw – your hand – quick!' Looping his right arm over the wooden side, he dragged Alison up. Liz grabbed her mother by the shoulders. Just then the rickety-old vehicle lurched wildly, hitting a pothole. Overbalancing, Alison tumbled face down into the bed of the lorry. Tom McFaddean sprang over the side and quickly helped her up. Swinging round, he stretched out his arm to grab Phil, still running behind.

'Jump, jump,' Liz screamed, feeling the vehicle accelerate.

Ignoring their outstretched hands, Phil grabbed the wooden side of the lorry, keeping pace with it. Springing into the air like a jack-in-a box, he vaulted easily over the side.

'Phew,' he gasped out of breath. 'What on earth was that all about?'

Liz gazed round fearfully at the all-enveloping fog, wishing she had ex-ray vision. Almost immediately, she felt a tunnel of wind blowing a pathway for her. Screaming, she leapt back in fright at the sight of the slavering shape, its front paws reaching for her eyes. Claws ripped into the hood of her duffle coat, tearing it apart.

A beam of green light shot through the air, shredding the animal into fragments, particles of dust trickling down onto her shoulders.

Bewildered, she collapsed on some sacking next to her mother, her hand automatically reaching up to brush the debris from her coat.

'Mother,' she said in a stunned voice. 'What just happened?'

Alison, looking remarkably like a naughty schoolgirl, flushed scarlet. 'I promise you, I didn't know.' She stared defiantly at the three faces gazing at her in disbelief. '*But I had to use it* … Liz would have been killed otherwise.'

'It was you that saved me once before,' Liz said. 'But how?'

Alison didn't reply for a moment, shuffling about, smoothing out the surface of the tarpaulin trying to get comfortable.

'Mother, we're waiting.'

Alison flashed a guilty smile and took her daughter's hand. 'Remember, when everyone was in the hall staring at Phil's hand? I saw the mark on my own. That's when I remembered what she said.'

'Who?'

'Mei-Xui, when she gave me the bundle with you two in it.'

'What?' Tom McFaddean's voice was stern.

'*This is my gift; use it to protect your own.* I promise you, I didn't know what she meant at the time,' she said, her tone still defensive. 'When I saw the children, I thought she was asking me to care for them. Is it really possible for a Javean to transfer their power like that?' Alison's blue eyes beseeched him.

'To be honest, I don't know.' Tom McFaddean hesitated. 'But that's how it happened for me. Mei-Xui's brother was my best friend. We did everything together. Tragically, he was mauled by a tiger and died soon after. He passed his gift on to me – exactly as his sister did to you.'

'So sad.' Alison pulled out a hankie, her eyes filled with tears. 'I never thought. She must have known she was dying.'

'But, Mum,' Phil's said in an indignant tone. 'If you knew you were Javean, why did you make such a fuss over us?'

Alison appeared offended. 'How can you ask that? I don't want to be a magical warrior. A doctor, that goes around killing things? Whatever would my colleagues say? I'd be disbarred.'

Tom McFaddean burst into laughter. 'No, you wouldn't. Killing monsters – they'd give you a medal.'

'Oh, Mother,' Liz hugged her. 'I'm so glad. I don't feel quite so lonely now.'

The lorry slowed for a corner, changing gear. Across the road, the bright-blue neon letters of an underground station broke through the fog.

'Time to go.'

Almost in synchronisation, the four figures climbed over the side of the lorry as it swung round the corner. Hanging motionless for a split second, they dropped to the ground, the momentum of the vehicle's speed running them forwards a few paces. Grabbing Liz by the hand again, Tom McFaddean made a dive for the lighted doorway.

The glowing brightness of the underground station embraced them, welcoming them in, its atmosphere friendly and exuding a warm radiance – a far cry from the menacing silence of the fog.

'I'm exhausted and I've not done anything yet,' Alison groaned, heading down the escalator. 'If belonging to the Javean race means jumping in and out of moving vehicles – I'm resigning my commission.' She smiled at the anxious expression on the face of her two children. 'For people as old as me, being forced to use muscles you didn't know you had, is not a good idea. A hot bath would be nice right now.' There was a rush of air and a long red tube train hurtled out of the tunnel. She broke into a run, leaping down the remaining steps two at a time. 'Quick or we'll miss it,' she called over her shoulder.

As the door slid to behind them and the train lurched into motion, Liz and Phil grabbed one of the straps hanging down from the roof. Liz glanced sideways at her brother, astonished to find he was now quite a bit taller than her. He must have grown recently and she'd not noticed.

Alison collapsed down onto a seat. 'May I see the jade?'

Tom McFaddean sat down beside her, removing the box from his pocket.

As Jimbo had promised, the bird faced forwards, its piercing gaze directed straight at them. Fishing in the inner pocket of his jacket, Tom McFaddean pulled out the other two pieces.

'Phil?'

Perched on the seat opposite, Phil untied the medallion from round his neck. Removing the ribbon, he handed it over.

The four pieces now formed a clear pattern. Each bird encased in its silver frame had their gaze fastened on the one in the centre; two of them airborne and hovering lightly.

Tom McFaddean pointed to the stone found in the market. 'If I remember correctly, it's this one's twin that is still missing.' He heaved a sigh, his eyes clouding over, his thoughts travelling thousands of miles to a village enclosed by mountains. 'It's almost fifteen years – 1945 – since these were last together. I dread to think what has happened to Bantu in that time.'

Phil picked up the piece he'd rescued from the Xhantu, the bird's proud eyes regarding him sternly. He slotted the piece of ribbon through the hole in the jade surround. 'You told me once that I'd find a piece that belongs to me.' He held it up. 'This is it.'

Tom McFaddean nodded, not seeming at all surprised. He handed Liz the little piece that had been with her since childhood – the bird flying towards sunrise – towards her brother. 'And this is yours, Dr Shaw,' he said handing across the jade ornament that Liz and Phil had bought in the market, it's silver links sparkling under the bright fluorescent light.

She gazed at it askance and shook her head firmly. 'No thanks, I've rather gone off jewellery.'

'*You really are the most exasperating woman I've ever met!* For pity's sake, Dr Shaw, *wear it* – it might save your life one day,' Tom McFaddean snapped.

Glowering, she took the small piece tying it round her neck. 'And you, Mr McFaddean, are a bully.'

*

At Notting Hill, the fog was even thicker if that were possible. A cocoon of slimy grey tentacles wrapped themselves tightly around the five figures, enveloping them closer and closer with every step they took, the pavements reverberating with the sound of their footsteps. They saw no one. Voices floating in the fog-bound air called out, 'Whoops! Sorry! Can't see a hand in front of my face,' as unwary pedestrians cannoned into each other.

Using hedges and garden walls as a guide, they rounded the corner into the square. Here a dull silence prevailed, the cheery whistle of people carrying out their normal Sunday task of cleaning the car, or sweeping the front path, missing. From somewhere behind them, the discordant bell of a police car cut through the stillness.

All of a sudden, Tom McFaddean hesitated and slowed to a stop, his face as alert as a questing hound seeking its quarry. In the square the mist had begun to pulsate like the tide flowing up onto the seashore – forwards and back.

'Mr McFaddean?' Alison called. 'What is it? What's happening?'

'Not sure. It's this damned fog – it's moving. It may just be the wind. Hope so, it might blow the stuff away.'

But it wasn't. Liz stared round, looking for evidence of a wind picking up. She found none, everything silent and unmoving, apart from the thick fingers of mist. Then, as if they were canaries in a bird cage and someone had removed the cloth covering the top, the fog drew back, making it possible to identify the huddled shapes on the scaffolding – as silent as the fog had been. Unmoving, their beady eyes were focussed on a single point, the hotel on the far side of the square.

Scared, Liz tightened her grip on Mac's hand. He patted her hand comfortingly.

'We'll never get through that little lot in a month of Sundays,' he said. 'We'll have to go round. We can get in through the garden.'

'Why, it's Fred!' Alison called, noticing the small figure standing outside the hotel. 'What's he doing here? He's supposed to be at school.'

'I don't care. He's safe, that's all that matters,' Liz said joyfully and, ignoring Mac's shout of warning, ran towards the waiting figure,.

As if they had been waiting for this moment, the drooling snouts swung round, fixing their beady eyes on Liz.

All at once, the pavement under her racing feet felt soft and mushy, as if it had absorbed all the rain that had fallen in the past six months. She stumbled. Then, with a suddenness that gave her no time to react, it changed into quicksand, her feet leaden, sinking ankle deep. Making a huge effort, she leapt for the railings, only to feel her feet snared by the gluey concrete.

She tumbled forwards, her hands breaking her fall. Bubbles erupted on the surface lapping at her fingers. She tore them out, leaving behind indentations like birds' claws. Deep down under the ground, she sensed something alive dragging her legs down deeper and deeper, until only the top half remained in sight.

Seeing Fred run out from under the porch, she shouted out, 'Don't come any nearer, save yourself.'

Ignoring her, he ran forward. She tried to scream, to warn him, but she was back in her dream floundering about unable to move.

'No, Fred,' she got the words out. 'Stay back.'

He leaned forward, reaching out to help her, and their eyes met. A dark hole opened in her head and she tumbled headlong into it.

TWENTY-ONE

The train crawled into Waterloo, its passengers fuming. It was bad enough being late. With engines running on rails, a little thing like fog shouldn't have been a problem. *But not to have a buffet car*, because staff couldn't be bothered to show up for work – *that was outrageous.* And, most likely, Fred, staring eagerly round the smoke-filled bleakness of the vast station, was the only passenger not intending to write a formal letter of complaint to British Rail. He had considered the train service great, arriving in London ages before he thought. And it didn't much matter about being hungry – he was quite used to that.

With a bit of time to spare, he stopped off to grab a cheeseburger from the Wimpy Bar outside the station. When he reached Salisbury station, after running all the way from the hospital where the driver had kindly deposited him, a train for London had been standing at the platform. Hearing the ticket inspector say, as he leisurely clipped Fred's ticket, *'if you hurry, lad, you might just make it,'* once again Fred had taken to his heels, pelting at top speed through the underpass to the platform.

He had made it, but only because a helpful porter had held a door open. Collapsing into the first available seat, he was so out of breath it took him quite ten minutes to recover, at which point he realised he had a two hour journey ahead him with nothing to eat or drink.

According to the map of the London Underground, Notting Hill was located on the Circle Line. The fact that he'd never set foot in London before didn't particularly bother Fred, neither did the confusing arrangement of steps and subterranean passages, some leading to the mainline station, some to the Underground, others finishing in a dead end. By dint of asking everyone he passed, he eventually arrived on the correct platform and, counting the stations carefully, emerged at Notting Hill to find he could hardly put one foot in front of the other without losing it.

Tucked into the open doorway of the tube station, he noticed a boy about his own age manning a newspaper stand and he crossed over the road to ask directions.

'I'm lookin' for this place?' Fred gave him the card.

'No point askin' me, mate, I can't read.'

'And you sell newspapers?' he exclaimed.

'You don't have to read 'em to sell 'em. Where d'je want?'

'Ladbroke Square.'

The boy paused, deftly folding a newspaper in two before handing it to a passing customer. He tipped his cap. 'Thank you, sir.' He turned back to Fred. '*It's an ill wind*. Get it?'

'Don't know what you mean.' Fred glowered at the boy. 'There isn't a wind. If there was, it'd most likely blow this stuff away.'

'It means, with folks usin' the tube station rather than the bus, I get me papers sold quick and can go 'ome early. Go along 'ere,' he said, speaking out of the side of his mouth, 'till ye come to Ladbroke Terrace. Straight up – can't miss it on a good day.' He grinned, his smile lopsided. 'But you might today. Good luck, mate.'

Waving goodbye, Fred set off, hearing the boy call out after him, 'You'll be all right, mate, you don't need a torch with that hair.'

Fred glanced back over his shoulder seeing nothing but a blanket of white, the entrance to the station and the newspaper seller vanished as if they had been swallowed up. A few cars still crawled along the Bayswater Road, travelling at a snail's pace, their owners driving with their heads stuck out of the window to make sure they were going straight. At the side of the road, adjacent to the traffic lights, two cars had collided. One had crashed into the rear of other, their owners noisily arguing about whose fault it was. Apart from that, there were few people about. Fred caught the end of a conversation and realised he'd walked straight past a couple of people and not even noticed them.

Keeping to the inner side of the pavement, he trailed his fingers along the wall, feeling his way along the street and, almost immediately, came upon a side road. He stopped and searched for the road sign – a neat black and white strip, confirming the directions that the boy at the newsstand had given him.

Rounding the corner, he headed on down Ladbroke Terrace, almost bumping into a car parked straight across the road. A police car was blocking the entrance to the square, a couple of policemen keeping back a crowd of perhaps a dozen curious spectators, who were craning their heads in vain to see what was happening.

Alarmed, he spoke to one of the women. 'What's going on?'

'Some sort of ruckus in the square, dearie,' she replied cheerfully. 'The copper says they've sent for the bomb squad. Unexploded bomb, I expect,' she reassured him. 'We still get 'em regular. But they won't let us back in, not till it's dealt with – and I live there.'

Green flashes of light penetrated the thick fog. Squeals erupted from the watching crowd who hastily retreated to a safe distance. Angling into the sky the flashes continued, as if there had been a lightning strike without the thunder, and an ugly hissing noise broke into the muttering of the crowd.

'That's not a bomb.' Fred counted the individual beams – three.

Ducking under the outstretched arms of the policeman, he

made for the thick wall of fog stretched across the road, ignoring the warning shouts, '*Come back 'ere, it's not safe!*'

For a moment Fred lost all sense of direction, the dirty grey layers spinning him round and pushing him back, as if he was trying to swim a river against a strong current. He beat at them with his fists, forcing his way through, following the distant sounds of the fight.

The square stood in an oasis of calm, blocks of tall white houses ringing it on all four sides. In its centre was a large area of garden protected by spiked railings, its trees as tall as the buildings on either side. Fred paused not sure where Number 10 was located, the scaffolding planks covering up the numbers.

Surprisingly, the fog was less dense here, as if London had been gripped by a hurricane and Ladbroke Square was in the eye of the storm. He caught a flurry of light from the far side of the gardens, thick branches of conifer and chestnut blocking his view of the street behind. Sprinting towards it, he spotted Tom McFaddean, with Dr Shaw and Phil, and saw the flashes of green light erupting from their hands. Not registering Dr Shaw's new-found ability, he looked beyond them. Stretched out motionless on the pavement was Liz, with someone, the spitting image of him, bending over her.

''*Ere, what do you think you're playin' at?*' he yelled indignantly.

Stopping only long enough to fit a stone into his catapult, he raced towards the figure. The stone struck it squarely in the middle of its chest. Startled, it jumped back.

Swinging round on her heel, Alison stared, unable to believe her eyes. She turned, and turned again, examining the two figures from top to toe.

'*Why you little weasel,*' she shouted with rage and directed a powerful stream of light at the figure, once again bending over her daughter. It disappeared in a sheet of flame.

Fred threw her a startled glance, wondering how all of a sudden she could zap monsters like Phil and Mr Mac. Perhaps it was the jade. He felt for the stone in his pocket, rubbing it against his left palm and glanced at his hand, disappointed not to find a mark. He shrugged. He had his catapult. He could still help.

All around him, an unending stream of light powered into the attacking animals. He'd not really seen them in action before, too busy with his catapult to notice much. Dad Reid had told him about the hordes of locusts he'd encountered in India, the air solid with flying bodies. This was the same; the furry shapes endlessly dive-bombing while others crawled in convoy across the ground.

Hoping the magical beams of light weren't like cars, which often ran out of petrol, he shouted, 'I can help but I need ammunition.'

'Over there, Fred.' Mac pointed to a bin of gravel which stood by the railings at the corner, used in winter to keep the entrance to the square open, whenever the streets became icy.

'Okay, thanks.' He pelted back down the road. Opening the lid of the bin, he stuffed handfuls of the sharp grit into his pockets.

'Fred, watch your back?' Phil bellowed. Raising his hand to the sky, he directed a narrow beam of light into a chestnut tree, a dozen or more forms perched ready to drop on to Fred as he passed underneath.

Fred gave a startled glance upwards. Swerving round the tree, he scuttled into the middle of the street unleashing his catapult at the lower branches, high-pitched squeaks of pain accompanying his strikes.

'Where is everyone?' he bellowed.

It was a good question considering the amount of noise in the square. Whenever the green light blasted a hole in the attacking Xhantu it emitted a zinging sound, which faded slowly like fingers rippling over the strings of a harp.

'Why aren't they helpin' us, Mr Mac?'

'It's the fog,' Mac replied grimly. He aimed a kick at the animal edging along the kerb, tumbling it back into the railings. 'One of Xheng-Li's many tricks. The people in their houses …' He waved an arm round the tightly knit houses peering down on them, the mist distorting their white fronts and black railings into army of giant penguins. 'Unless they happen to be walking the dog, they won't suspect a thing. When we get through this little lot, you can ask them.'

'*If* we get through, Mr McFaddean, I'm beginning to have serious doubts.'

'Then we push harder, Dr Shaw,' he roared. 'Keep your back to the railings and try to edge towards Liz. We can take refuge in the hotel.'

As if the conversation had been overheard by some extra-terrestrial intelligence, a torrent of creatures encircled the three figures, the sheer weight of numbers keeping them marooned in one spot. Next moment, a dozen or more people began moving through the trees quickly overtaking Fred, still standing in the middle of the road. Astonished, he recognised figures from the crowd, who'd been waiting for the bomb squad to arrive. Among them, the woman who had spoken to him. She'd been standing directly behind the policeman. How had they managed to get into the gardens without his noticing? There was no gate on that side. Besides, when he was fetching ammunition he'd have spotted them.

Puzzled, Fred watched the curious way the woman moved, sinuous as if on springs, abruptly stopping whenever a tree got in her way. Then, in a blink of an eye, the tree was behind her and no longer an obstacle, as if she had opened a door in the bark and passed through it. Her fluid way of walking reminded him of something. But what? All at once, Fred recalled the figure in the garden, its feet never moving, its body like rubber, bending and stretching, swaying round in a circle, the missiles from his catapult useless. But how could they be the yuppy – they had destroyed it?

He scratched his head, trying to recall what Mr Mac said about them: "Anything they see, they can imitate. And so well, it's often impossible to tell which is the genuine article." Instinctively, he reached down into his pocket for a stone. He could tell all right. The people at the barrier were the real thing – flesh and blood. And when they walked, they didn't swim through the air.

'Stop them, Fred!' Alison shrieked, ducking as she was attacked from the air. 'They mustn't get Liz.'

As if he was taking part in an obstacle race, Fred broke into a leaping run. Taking a deep breath, he swerved at top speed past the animals on the ground, firing shot after shot at the line of people slinking through the narrow railings into the street opposite the hotel. The stones slowed their progress but that was all. In the end, it would make little difference. He needed one of the pulverising beams to destroy them completely. He peered round, alarmed to discover his friends were backed-up against the garage doors, a thick layer of ash on the pavement surrounding them. It was hopeless. The trees were thick with the brooding figures, their faces fixed in a snarl exposing their gleaming canines. For every Xhantu they killed, another hopped down from the trees to take its place, and yet another; the branches almost cracking under their weight.

By now, the figures had reached Liz. Lifting her by the arms, they began dragging her away – impeded at every step by flashes of light.

'What can we do?' he shouted, watching his target crash to the ground stunned, as a tiny stone struck it forcefully in the head.

'*Leave it and get these doors open*,' Mac shouted. 'Here! He tossed some keys in Fred's direction. '*Oh no, you don't!*' he snarled, letting loose a stream of the green light, punching a neat hole through a little line of three animals intent on ambushing Fred. Instantly, ten more rose into the air, their front claws extended, their teeth bared. Mac gazed in despair and brushed his sleeve across his face, wiping away the sweat.

'There must be something in there we can use ...'

'I wish I'd got an umbrella?' Alison screeched, angling her beam upwards, half-a dozen of the furry-covered menaces dive-bombing her. 'It would come in very useful right about now.'

With fingers as awkward as thumbs, Fred fumbled about fitting key after key into the lock, searching for the right one, concerned that any delay could cost someone their life. He wasn't scared. It didn't occur to him that *the someone* might be him. But it might be his friends.

Mac flashed a glance in his direction. 'It's the old-fashioned one. Hurry!'

'I am hurryin',' Fred retorted indignantly. Quickly identifying the chunky black key, he rammed it into the lock.

The well-oiled cogs clicked back smoothly. Hauling the bottom bolt from its bed in the concrete, Fred reached up on tip-toe, wriggling the heavy metal rod out of its socket. He swung the doors open. He'd not seen the garage before and a fleeting glance showed him a place that Dad Reid would feel right at home in. Making a promise to come back when they were less busy, he began searching, noticing a hose coiled neatly on a hook. Grabbing it, he ran outside.

'Have you got a tap?' he bellowed above the racket.

'Behind the door,' Mac shouted back.

Hastily connecting the hose, he turned the tap full-on. A powerful jet of water spurted out across the concrete. Ignoring the crawling shapes, he directed it at the crowd of people, blasting them away from Liz.

Instantly regrouping, the cloned figures picked themselves up off the ground. Leaving Liz lying on the road, they drifted back towards the group by the garage, their arms stretched out in front of them.

'I'm going to get Liz,' Phil shouted. 'You keep them busy.'

Leaping into the air, he lunged for the top of the open garage door, grabbing it with his right hand. He reached up with his left, his body swinging like a pendulum and, bracing his feet against the wooden panels, pulled himself up. Balancing precariously on top of the open door, he reached over and grabbed the guttering, climbing up on to the roof.

'No!' Alison screamed out in agony. 'You'll be killed.'

'No, I won't,' he shouted back. 'Not if you give me some cover.'

'*Hell and damnation!* Get back here, Phil. You're a sitting duck up there.'

'Mr McFaddean, please. Your language.'

'Dr Shaw, if you weren't within earshot, it would be far worse I can promise you.'

Flocking together, their wings fully extended and their talons braced like a bird of prey, the Xhantu encircled the figure on the roof, the green ray from his hand almost useless at such close quarters. Phil screamed out. A torrent of light struck the slavering menace and, momentarily, he was free. Before they had time to regroup, he sprang to his feet and, clutching his blood-soaked arm, scrabbled fast on all fours across the sloping tiles.

'Phil, you're injured.'

'I'm okay, don't worry.'

Reaching the end of the garage roof, he lowered himself down the wall, searching with his toes for a foothold on the wrought-iron gateway, rarely used except as a back way into the hotel garden. Steadying himself on the wall, he shinned across it and, dropping into a crouch, flung himself over the gap, his arms outstretched ready to grab the top of the spiked railings. Pausing only long enough to wave, he vaulted over vanishing into the basement courtyard out of sight.

'Thank goodness,' Alison exclaimed, her usually neat figure streaked with dirt, her handbag lying forgotten on the ground.

'How come you can zap 'em now, Doctor?' Fred called out, thoroughly enjoying himself. Pity Dad Reid didn't own a hose. He aimed the fierce jet of water at the lines of animals squirming across the ground. They moved clumsily, their retracted front paws awkward to walk on, hobbling from side to side, their gait unsteady, their claws clicking against the surface of the road. Only in the air were they truly at home.

Fred laughed gleefully, watching them spin out of control, shaking their fur like a dog and hissing angrily in retaliation for the soaking.

'No time for idle chat, Fred dear. You keep that water going,' Alison called back.

From the courtyard of the hotel, something heavy landed on top of a metal dustbin. Next moment, Phil burst out from the courtyard steps. Holding a dustbin lid over his head, he sprinted over to the unconscious figure of his sister. Grabbing her by the shoulders, he slowly backed away. Immediately, a dozen of the creatures took off from the nearest tree, their long raking claws extended and aimed at his exposed neck. Beset on all sides, Phil tried to shield his sister as best he could, the space between him and the hotel solid with crawling and flying figures. He saw their beady eyes fixed on him, their drooling mouths with their long pointed canines glistening in anticipation of tearing their prey to pieces. Then Fred aimed the fierce jet, hurling them head over heels into the railings.

With a brief smile of thanks, Phil half-dragged and half-carried his sister into the shelter of the hotel porch.

'Right, come on.' Tom McFaddean hoisted Alison up so she could climb onto the garage roof. 'Now you, Fred.'

'But, Mr Mac …'

'*No arguing*! We haven't a cat in hell's chance of surviving that little lot.' He pointed at the massing hoards – Fred's water cannon the only thing keeping them back. As if it knew they had reached the end of the line, the water spluttered several times and the powerful stream dwindled to a mere trickle.

'*Move*!' He tossed the small boy up onto the roof and leapt for the top of the open doorway.

Fred, busily concentrating on keeping his balance on the sloping roof top, heard Dr Shaw scream. He glanced up. She was half-way across the slippery tiles, her one hand resting on the roof behind her for balance. She pointed, her face a mask of terror. The yuppy figures had reached the garage forecourt and were clawing at Tom McFaddean's legs preventing him climbing onto the roof. She flung a stream of green light at them but the angle was wrong and the beam hit the guttering, snapping it in half.

Forgetting about the danger, Fred leaned down over the edge of the roof aiming the sharp-edged stones straight at their heads aware, at so short a distance, if the figures had been living, the stones would prove fatal. Stunned, the figures keeled over onto the ground and lay still.

Kicking himself free, Tom McFaddean pulled himself up onto the garage roof – a trail of blood pursuing him.

'*Fred ... You're a life saver,*' he gasped, rocking back on his heels with exhaustion. 'And I really mean that. Phew! That was close. Come on.'

Slithering about, they made their way across the exposed roof, the Xhantu swooping down on them like scavenging birds, a sandstorm of dust swirling about as the light pulverised them into harmless particles. With Phil covering them, they climbed down the gate, zigzagging their way round the shapes blocking their path to the hotel.

Ducking under the shelter of the columned portico, Alison grabbed her son, hugging him fiercely.

'Phil, I'm so proud of you.' She ran to her daughter's side. 'Liz ... Liz ... for goodness sake, say something.' She bent down stroking the white face.

Liz groaned. Her eyes flickered and she sat up, her mother's arm supporting her. 'Why, am I soaked to the skin?' she mumbled. 'Have I been swimming?'

'No, dear, that was Fred. A bit too efficient with the garden hose – thank heaven.'

'Oh, Fred. You're all right,' Liz smiled weakly. 'I was so happy to see you waiting for us.'

'Except, that wasn't me,' Fred replied, his voice hoarse with shouting. 'It doesn't matter though 'cause Dr Shaw took care of it. How did you know? Thought I was seein' double.'

'It was the freckles, Fred, dear. They hadn't got them quite straight.' Alison stretched wearily. 'Thank goodness, at last we can breathe.'

Mrs Howard poked her head round the door. 'Oh, Mr McFaddean, you're there. *Thank goodness.* One of the guests has complained about the noise in the square. I must confess I didn't hear a thing. But …' She took in the dishevelled state of her employer and his friends, their clothes filthy from the garage roof. '*Whatever's going on?*' she exclaimed, her normally pleasant voice bewildered.

Fred piped up. 'The police say it's an unexploded bomb. They're warnin' people to stay inside and keep away from the windows.'

'I'll tell them.' Mrs Howard gasped, her head retreating at speed round the door.

Tom McFaddean raised an eyebrow at Fred.

'They did, honest,' he protested. 'That's what the copper said, anyhow.'

Across the square, a chorus of yelps broke into the air. Someone had unwisely opened a window. They heard it slammed shut again, as the resident came face to face with the hissing shape perched on the scaffolding outside.

'So what now, Mr McFaddean? Liz can't fight on. Neither can you, your leg …' Alison peered at it closely.

Impatiently, he brushed her hand away. 'I'm not dead yet.'

'And I'll be all right in a minute.' Liz sat up, clasping her head. 'But what happened to me? Will somebody tell me? I remember the pavement all soggy …'

'And, Phil, *your arm*? It'll need stitching …'

'I don't care. I'm not giving up, I could do with my sword though.'

'Me neither,' Fred chirped up.

'We'd better take shelter in the hotel,' Alison said, ignoring them. 'We'll be safe there.'

'I'm not so sure about that. Look!'

Picking themselves up off the ground, where Fred's missiles had blasted them, the cloned figures were once more gravitating towards their prey, their arms stretched out, uttering a weird moaning noise.

'You got the jade, Fred?'

'Yes, Mr Mac, that's why I came. Want it?'

'No, you keep it. It's our last chance,' he shouted over the hullabaloo. 'Let's find out if it will do what's it's meant to. Hold the medallion in your hands and link up.'

He helped Liz to her feet. 'Come on – into the street.'

The air was filled with the rasp of claws kneading the branches in preparation for an attack.

Alison stopped dead and tried to push the children behind her. 'Mr McFaddean, the children? *They'll be killed,*' she shouted.

The herd of animals rose into the air, hissing and screaming.

'*Now!*'

Five pairs of hands touched, the little green medallions bearing the imprint of an eagle gripped between their palms.

An explosion of light hurled them to the ground. All round the square electric wires crackled, rivers of flame running through them. Breaking away from their moorings, they showered the trees with sparks, setting their topmost branches alight, the flames spiralling greedily upwards. Cables feeding into the telephone poles exploded, drenching the front of the hotel in a fireworks display.

The attic windows flew open.

Figures crawled through them onto the parapet. Figures clothed in armour, wearing robes belonging to a different century. Grasping the broken cables, they abseiled down. From the gardens something heavy burst through the bushes and they caught a glimpse of a two-legged creature, twelve feet high, with horns on its head. Overhead, five eagles soared. Calling out, they hurtled down onto the flocking Xhantu tearing them apart.

Reaching the ground, the armoured figures, swords and pistols in hand, headed for the besieging hoard.

Liz, clutching her mother's arm for support, watched the demonic figure of the samurai, unable to take her eyes from him. A sword in each hand, one at arm's stretch the other almost level with his eyes, he pranced up close to the menacing figures. Once within range, he began to spin. Faster and faster as if taking part in a ritual dance. Then, like a whirlwind, his skirts flying out and grunting wildly, he sliced through heads and limbs with a single blow. Behind him, the chain-mail figures of the Burmese fighters waded into the animals on the ground, their teeth and claws making little impression on their armour. Then the leather-clad Mongolians loosed arrow after arrow into the trees, hurling the injured creatures to the ground, where armoured figures were waiting to despatch them.

Slowly, the noises faded away and a deep silence spread over the square. Scattered along the roadway in front of the hotel, as if protecting the five friends from harm, were the warriors, their limbs frozen in a final act of aggression – the sky above empty and unmoving.

A solid layer of ash lay strewn thickly across the ground, mingling with wings and broken claws, the yuppy figures disembowelled, their heads severed from their bodies.

Feeling sick, Liz closed her eyes on the gruesome sight.

A keen wind started up and the temperature dropped like a stone. Under her light jacket, Liz shivered, feeling goose bumps on her arms.

Still sounding out of breath from the fight, Phil put his arm round her. 'It's okay, you can open your eyes now.'

Timidly, Liz stared round, watching the carnage fade into fluttering ash that was blown harmlessly away. Not a vestige of fog remained. Overhead, an early-evening dusk approached under a sky that felt clear and icy-cold, and clouds thick with snow filled the sky. Thick flakes began to tumble, dousing the few remaining spirals of smoke from the blazing trees. Now, only the warriors remained, quite incongruous in an ordinary London street.

Tom McFaddean climbed wearily to his feet. 'That piece of jade you found, Fred, it sure saved our bacon today. Pass it over, there's a good lad, it's the one my friend gave me.'

'It's got a chip in it.' Disappointed at not being allowed to keep it, Fred passed over the silver and jade medallion. 'I sort of wondered if I might wear it, like Phil and Liz.'

'Sorry, Fred, can't do that. This one belongs to me.'

'Mr McFaddean, *really*!'

The tall man gave an exhausted smile and affectionately ruffled the small boy's hair. 'I can't do that, Fred, because, one day soon, this will belong to you.' He held up his hand, a piece of jade showing a green bird flying towards the sunset grasped in it.

Liz smiled happily, remembering Fred's face at the dinner table and his reluctance to give the little medallion back.

'Oh, Mr McFaddean. Having Fred with us, it's like having Christmas and my birthday rolled into one.'

Fred gulped. Then a huge smile radiated through his freckles. 'I tell you what. I wish it was, then I could eat two dinners. I'm starvin'.'

EPILOGUE

As the sun drifted over the mountain tops, seven figures gathered besides the waterfall, a thunderous roar accompanying its descent into the valley below. As far as the eye could see, peaks and escarpments, belonging to the great plateau, dominated the skyline, a boisterous wind making it an inhospitable place to live. Steps in the rock led down into a nearby valley thick with trees, the scarlet petals of the Gulmohar catching the last rays of the evening sun. Here, there was evidence of a new village taking shape. Shielded from the savage winds, houses were springing up using freshly hewn wood from age-old trees and curved tiles brought in from India and Burma. Carried through the mountains on the back of a mule, they had lain forgotten for more than twelve years. The few houses already completed gleamed in the warmth of lamp light.

Of the figures waiting for the sun to set, three were young. Dressed like the villagers of the region, in black cotton tunics and trousers, they wore heavy jackets of woven black cotton, bearing the scarlet symbol of an eagle on the back. A tall man, his red hair worn long and caught back in a pony-tail, wearing an identical jacket fastened with a fine black belt, stood with them. Next to him, neatly dressed in a shirt and slacks, a scarf on her head, was a young woman.

Of the two figures standing slightly behind them, one was an older man, upright and strong, his hair still showing no sign of grey. He smiled joyfully at the three children, who smiled back. The final figure wore European clothes and carried a stick, his right trouser leg flapping loosely in the evening breeze.

From the village below came a burst of happy laughter and, in the far distance, carried on the breeze, the roar of a tiger.

The boy standing in the centre of the group stirred and took a step forward. In his hand, he held a small jade medallion. He held it high in the air; the four figures standing with him imitating his action.

In the distance thunder rumbled and the sun vanished over the horizon in a blaze of green light.

THE LEGEND

A thousand years ago, with magic and sorcery dominating the Mongolian Empire, Zheng-Li, a powerful sorcerer, attempts to overthrow the emperor with a vast army of monsters. Five Javean, from a race of magical warriors, offer to rid the empire of his evil presence but a hundred years passes before the last monster is wiped-out and Zheng-Li captured. Recognising the sorcerer's awesome power cannot be destroyed, the Emperor orders him sealed in a vast ravine deep in the heart of the interior, to be guarded for all eternity by the warriors. To help them in their task, imperial sorcerers create five pieces of jade powerful enough to stop Zheng-Li ever escaping. Centuries later, with the story passed into legend; tales still exist that wherever great evil raises its head, so the five warriors will appear.